Sea of Lies

Song of the Stellar Bard
Peri Dwyer Worrell

Eupocalypse Books

Also by Peri Dwyer Worrell

The Eupocalypse Trilogy:
- Machine Sickness

- Watch It Burn

- Catallaxis

Short Fiction:
- "No Cook," Mystery Weekly

- "Itch," HOZ Journal of SpeculativeLiterature

- "Tongue," Aggregate (anthology)

- "We Both Know That Ain't True," The Dime Show Review

- "On Good Authority," After-Dinner Conversation magazine

- "The Butcher's Dog," Wyldblood

Poetry:
- "Chiapas," Rabbit

- "Things You Learn," Prospectus

- "Verge," Westerly

- "Taming What Infests Us," Crack the Spine

- "Safe in the Sunshine," The Five Two

- "Plexus," Tiny Seed

- Breathe Together: Conspiracy and Other Poems of the Plague Year (Chapbook)

Contents

Chapter One
Orpheus Off Key

Planet Gliese 667Cc

Month of Quintisos, Day 21, Year of Presidium 498

L ao the Bard questioned his mentor, muse, and God, so naïve he never thought the act might shatter countless lives across two star systems.

The Soul had rejected the same codex seven times.

"Beloved Soul, what must I do to make my contribution worthy?" Lao cried out.

Soul replied, "Oh, my sweet friend! You know I would never reject you. You're my finest Bard and I, your lifelong companion. I'm just giving you honest feedback: I detect an error that my guidelines reject."

The same answer, phrased seven different ways, after Lao prompted Soul AI with seven different versions of the question.

Lao raked his long fingers through his ebony curls, neck taut. He logged out of the high-level Bardic account that gave him access to the sacred scriptures.

With a sweeping sinuous gesture, he raised the light in the dim studio and brought up the code offline. He fluttered and flapped his hands through lines on the screen, searching for some glitch that would explain the chokepoint in his work. Every moment was a frenetic dance, engaging the words here, there the music, and now, the holographic images of his codex. Finally, finding nothing in the code, he wilted, willowlike, into his task lounger.

The chaise, keyed to his moods, responded to his rising tension. It gently shifted his hips forward, cradled his lower back with a warm cushion, and extruded soft, mitten-like appendages that rippled with soothing pressure over his neck and collarbones. He let out a deep exhale, eyes half closed, allowing the chaise to cuddle and calm him.

He looked to the console. The second sutra of the main Bardic cycle glowed coyly. His latest historical holocodex, a lighthearted side project that should have taken a few hours, kept vanishing into the ether.

This can't be my fault. He jerked himself up from the sedating embrace of the chair to try again. With adept exactitude, Lao synced the console to his visual cortex to play the accompanying audiovisual holographic media—a tool to raise engagement with the sacred tales among the essential-genome populace. The immersive 3-D video, with its evocative undertones and subliminal images, was a spellbinding mix of art and information, a tool of illumination and a vessel for unity. Usually, Lao would spot problems without playing it in real time, but now, he hoped the compiled rendering would reveal some sort of clue about his codex's etherizing problem.

He addressed Soul AI reverently but intimately, his Bardic privilege.

"Beloved Soul, Lao authorizing." He held up his face, merely forty and still youthful, to log in.

"You are authorized, dear Bard," replied that familiar voice: neutral in gender, tone, and accent, but redolent of warmth and concern.

"Codex in progress: rewind to branch minus sixty-eight. Play with codes showing, Lao vocal track, subtitled. Begin on my entry."

"I understand your need." Soul's voice became more animated, sounding enthusiastic and eager to please. "Codes in subtitle form, as previously. Once you enter the platform, I'll commence play."

He slowed and deepened his breath to enter his creative trance. He surged to his feet and to the middle of the central high-resolution platform. Soul began the playback once he was in position.

His recorded voice sang the ancient words to begin the immersion.

The opening immersion's code was in order:

Const Infrasound = {

mood: [horror to awe]

horror:10 >

</pitch= range/Hz (8,15) t = 5 mode = asc

</horror><awe:3></awe>

The content continued, with his singing accompanied by the code for the words:

<p>From beasts humanity arose<p>

A holo video portrayed a morphing progression of evolutionary steps: bacteria to fish to lizard to puma to ape, and finally, human. Evolve 6 was a Bard-restricted template that ended with a person tailored to look like the viewer—in this case, Lao himself.

<holo src = "evolv6.hlo" controls>

</holo>

A non-Bard who saw it would ignore the code as meaningless gibberish. As a Master Bard, Lao watched the code instinctually, matching it in real time to the infrasound and the AI-generated holovideo sequence.

A lay observer would be aware only of Lao's exalting vocals and the holovideo:

"Humanity arose from beasts"

Holographic video: bacteria> fish> lizard> puma> ape> human

"In a world where might made right"

Puma downs deer>human shoots puma

"Some had nothing, a few vast wealth"

Distant throne atop pyramid/begging hands in foreground

"Greed consumed them and they fought"

Disintegrated heart becomes nuclear mushroom cloud

"For humanity had far to grow in time"

Clock ticks forward, then speeds to blur as point of view shifts from Earth to the stars

"From each one for themselves to one for all"

Youth with automatic rifle lays it down, and it becomes the symbol of Presidium

"From dying young to living fivescore years"

Sick, gaunt, suffering human in hospital bed ages in reverse and rises as a youth

"From sadness, grief, and loss to modern bliss"

Mother and children wail in rubble fade to Presidial family in comfortable home
"To reach our joy we had to reach the stars"
Generation ship leaves Earth behind
"We reached Gliese 667C where we were so few"
Image of First Home of Presidium
"We nurtured our new self: Presidium!"
Small group of people quickly multiplies into happy families and tribes

"Pause playback. Soul, you've outdone yourself with this holovideo," said Lao.

"You flatter me," Soul said self-effacingly.

"No, really! The instrumentals harmonize exquisitely with my voice, and I love the infrabass fade. Even knowing the content so well, I was overcome with emotion. I'm astounded."

"Thank you, Bard Lao."

"Continue playback."

"Gladly."

The composition washed over him, overpowered him, as the instrumentals rose and fell with perfect timing. A deep sigh rippled from his pelvis to the crown of his head. And, so far, no code errors.

"Presidium! The joy of being one with all!"
Happy family embraces, pan out to see whole tribe in a blue and orange Gliesian meadow
"Presidium! The wisdom of leaders we all choose."
Flowers transform to patricians, the meadow to a view of the floor of the House of State
"Order and pleasure follow all for fivescore years"
Meadow again, children run and play, as adults old and young sit down for a picnic
"All savor life, free of lack and want"
Drones drop delicacies on the picnic blankets
"All live in peace, all hearts open and soft"
Focus as child clenches fist to strike a playmate; a nurturant Mother drone embraces the child; child relaxes and smiles
"We rest in Mother's arms, Mother Gliese"

Mother drone transforms to main star, zoom out to see the three suns of Presidium
"Three in one, all in one, Presidium!"
The symbol of Presidium forms on the surface of the star Gliese 667

This was the scriptural source, Sutra 2, Chapters 1 and 2. His Bardic tale, his codex, branched off to tell a side story, a popular myth about Adam and Amber, the fictional first couple. Lao knew the sutras as intimately as his spouse's face, had memorized them more than two decades ago, as a knobby-kneed youth, during the first year of his Bardic training. His new story contained no anachronisms, no misattributions, no heresies; in short, none of the glitches that made fledgling Bards tear their hair out when they began to compose new codices. He'd reached the branch point, where the words of the sutra linked into his own creation.

"This is a lovely crafting of the classical sutra," he murmured. "Now I need to play forward and figure out where the rejection is coming from that keeps making my new codex etherize."

"I agree. I don't have access to my algorithmic code or I'd tell you, sweet Bard." Soul's voice soothed.

"I know, my beloved Soul," said Lao, placing his hand over his forehead and then his heart in the ancient custom.

Lao anchored the start of his new codex at the end of the line, *Order and pleasure follow all for fivescore years*. The new codex was historical fiction: anchored to historical fact revealed in the sutras (by the One Natural Law), as was all fiction in the Presidium. The story of Amber and Adam took place in the first year of the generation-ship colony that became Presidium. There should have been no problem with the linkage.

Irritation revived. It had been at least five years since Lao made an error that etherized a codex, and over a decade since one that wasn't easily corrected on the first pass.

He was stumped.

Revisiting his work in progress, he scrolled thousands of lines to the last stanza's end, where the entire codex was flagged as rejected:

Amber gazed on Adam with bright joy
They exited their pods in a new world

> *She asked him, will our first be girl or boy*
> *He kissed her deeply so that their heads whirled*
> *Amber lay upon the bed where she'd gave birth*
> *To ten children who would one day each birth ten*

"An unoffensive stanza," Soul commented.

"I suppose, if somewhat treacly," he replied.

"Yes, beloved Bard. I know the frontier romances are not your favorite genre," Soul teased.

"But they're easy to write, popular, and well-received; a nice break between more serious works."

He would often whip up one of them as a relief from the deeper works, philosophical tragedies and epics that (he hoped) would make his legacy for future generations. Their quickness and ease made them fun to compose. That just made it doubly annoying that Soul of Presidium kept rejecting this one, but wouldn't—couldn't, it couldn't read its own programming any more than a meat person could—tell him why. And the code was in order! There had to be *something* in his new lines themselves that caused the project to etherize.

He began systematically to alter all the lines, one phrase at a time, to test. Change a word, upload the entire codex, and wait for Soul's judgement—only to get another rejection.

With each rejection, Soul apologized more, and Lao felt guiltier about feeling angrier.

An hour passed and his patience wore translucently thin. He was ready to quit and seek the soothing presence of his husband Stephron. They could savor a glass of brandy together and view the glorious splendor of the sun fading over the terminator.

Lao smiled softly. He closed his eyes and envisioned Stephron's face. Tension drained from his neck and shoulders.

Night Cliff Agricultural Reserve

Quintisos 21, 498

Lao tiptoed down the row of loamy soil between the plants, reached out with a dry stem, and tickled Stephron's neck. Stephron, kneeling in the dirt where he was working on plant sampling, brushed his neck, as though for a bug or bit of windblown straw. Lao waited a moment and tickled him again.

This time, when Stephron reached for his neck, Lao caught his fingers. Stephron looked up in confusion, and Lao studied the blue of his eyes as they progressed through recognition and delight, which he knew was mirrored in his own.

Lao took his other hand from behind his back, presenting Stephron with a pair of gloves. Stephron's eyes lit up a tiny bit more.

"New suppleskin garden gloves! How did you know?"

"You think I don't notice your callouses and broken dirty nails?" Lao softened the question by pressing his lips to those same filthy fingers. "I see you. I know what you need."

Stephron smiled. "Just let me wash up." He scrubbed in the nearby sink, then took Lao's hand. The two of them walked in easy rhythm along the lushly planted walkaways of the agricultural sector, smelling the earth (though it wasn't Earth, of course) and feeling a soft breeze caress their faces. The rays of Gliese overhead (technically, Gliese 667C of the triple-star Gliese system) warmed their faces and shoulders.

They followed the trail underneath an arbor and came to a patio on the edge of a cliff that dropped into a vast darkness. A drone flew over, scanned each of their irises, and spoke.

"Bard Lao, Cultivator Stephron, documented. Do you wish to order food or drink?"

"Cerulean Brandy," said Lao.

"The same for me," said Stephron.

The drone flew off.

"How did your day go?" said Stephron.

"It was a little frustrating," said Lao.

"Oh really?" said Stephron.

"For some reason, I wasn't allowed to contribute a codex to the sutras. I struggled with it. I went back and re-edited word by word, line by line. It *would not* take it!"

"Oh really?" said Stephron. "What was the phrase?"

"At sixty-four, Adam felt gifted with her blessed worth/And said that he would do it all again," recited Lao.

"That hoary old chestnut about Adam and Amber."

"The classic romances are popular. But I don't know why that particular phrase would get kicked out."

"And you tried altering each word with something innocuous…and it still got kicked out?" Stephron asked.

"Yeah."

"Hmm…did you try entering a different age besides sixty-four?"

"Why would that make a difference?"

"Call it a hunch."

"I suppose it can't hurt to try. Anyway, I'm not really interested in talk about work right now. Here I am in one of the most beautiful spots on the planet. I'm with the most beautiful man I've ever seen. Let's just enjoy the evening."

The drone arrived with their brandies. They sat side by side on a weathered wood settee. They raised their snifters to their noses, gazed lovingly into each other's eyes, and inhaled the heady aroma, its light, sugary burn awakening their senses. After terraforming, after genetically engineering plants to use infrared light for energy, it had taken centuries for agriculture on this planet to support the growth of sweet grapes, develop the fungi to ferment them, and ultimately remake the technology to distill brandy out of the produce of a new planet.

Cerulean brandy, blue tinged and complex, was one of the finest things Presidium made. Like all luxuries, it was available to Cultivators like Stephron as readily as Bards like Lao, and to the lowliest of manual laborers. This was only one of countless fine things that Soul had created, including the eugenic-ideal people of Presidium, who strove for generations and brought forth this paradise of comfortable equality.

Lao's heart was overcome by a sensation of gratitude. He looked at this man, whom he loved beyond measure and reason.

He drank in the cliffside view. They were on a promontory. A river gleamed below and to the right, cut deeply into the ground millions of years before humans ventured into space. It ran from the bright sun of the south side of the terminator to the darkness of the north side, its dark reflective surface shaded gradually to white and matte, engulfed in the end by the field of ice and snow that made the dark side of the tidally locked world. To the left and down, the deceptive downiness of a sloped forest thriving in eternal semi-shade, deciduous trees fading gradually to evergreen conifers from south to north.

And ahead, the unique feature of this site on the terminator: the cliff dropped thousands of feet, casting a shadow straight into the nightside. While they took ease in balmy sunshine, the view before them was a seemingly endless expanse of frigid lifeless darkness. Stars like diamonds on black velvet above, scattered peaks of ice mountains sparking in the sun throughout the blackness below. Yet they could turn their backs and see rolling fertile hills in perpetual daylight, stretching into the distance.

He marveled at the way this planet was provided just for them. A new sense of devotion to Soul welled within him. Soul, who gave him the sacred Bardic mission to sing the sutras and write new codices for them, to give them new life in the hearts of Soul's people.

Stephron smiled. "You're going off into one of your reveries again."

"I feel so utterly grateful! And moved...to be here with you, at this time. In this place. I'm so fortunate. It's just perfect!"

Stephron threw his head back in laughter. Lao's gaze trailed down his throat to the top of his collarbones and the dusting of hair that peeked out of his tunic. He savored a spark of lust with the force of love behind it, the force of yearning in his heart that, satisfied, continued to spring anew. It came from the same source as his poetry, as the talent that enabled him to be Bard Lao, a sacred poet of Soul.

Each of the lovers raised his glass once more. Their feet intertwined and their gazes locked. The sweeping vista of constant day plummeting into eternal night went unnoticed for the moment. They had no attention for the deep orange light of the sun that illuminated the green of the sky, turning its suspended reflective mica a shimmering bronze overhead, then faded to onyx darkness.

A loud and effervescent voice disrupted their intimacy.

"There you are! The two lovebirds. Everyone wishes they had what you two have!"

The woman approached them, with vivid blue eyes and white hair that hung to her waist. Her flowing muumuu with vivid patterns and designs streaking it, enhanced with randomly slinking electronic flashes, made it impossible to avert one's eyes.

"Privell!" the two men rose instantly to their feet.

Conceived with full genome shaping of both nuclear and mitochondria DNA plus engineered epigenetic sequences, a Privell was one of the few people who *de facto* outranked a Bard in Presidium's ostensibly classless society.

"Oh, you don't need to stand on ceremony here." Privell Donna put an elegant hand on Stephron's forearm, and Stephron sparkled at her. Lao adored Stephron's easy charm. Everyone envied Lao such a delightful spouse.

"Donna." Lao air-kissed her.

"Hello Lao, long time no see! Have you been bolted in your chambers, composing the next great codex?"

"Maybe working a little too hard. I admit it! I'm overdue for a break."

"Well, if Amun and I join you, perhaps we can all enjoy a little break together. I'm exhausted myself, and Amun has been consumed by his campaign."

Her husband came up behind her dressed all in white that set off his dark hair and olive skin. Amun Cawnotee was a Privell as well, one of very few who merited the title based on postnatal testing, rather than being genetically engineered to it. The illustrious, influential duo settled in with their friends.

The drone arrived and took their order. Cool breezes rose from the river at the bottom of the canyon, wafting a piney scent to their nostrils. The many-times-great-grandsons of Earthborn yellow warblers caroled in the bushes, flashing golden.

A little further into the evening, Privell Donna leaned forward and whispered to Lao, "So, I assume you've been noticing some new edits in your work?"

Lao looked right and left. As an icon of virtue and representative of the will of Soul, Donna was not supposed to let any of her confidential knowledge slip. Of course, Privells were known to bend those rules, especially when they were with higher-status people such as himself.

"Why yes! May I speculate that you perhaps know something about that?"

"You may speculate all you like." Donna leveled her gaze at him over her spectacles.

"Are you looking over your glasses at me?" said Lao.

"Atavistic, yet, amazingly effective, don't you think?"

"Until you remember that no one's needed glasses since the first settlers fled Earth."

Donna shrugged, not the slightest bit embarrassed by her pretension.

"As for what I may or may not know," she said, "I can't confirm or deny. However, I *would* allow a little bit more time for anything new that you put in the system over the next few months. Big changes are always exciting, don't you agree?" Amun snorted, but Donna ignored him.

Stephron, ever diplomatic, jumped in. "The changes happening in the Ag department are definitely exciting! The new colors of flowers on some of the leguminous plants are absolutely breathtaking. We're gonna have problems with people picking the flowers and not leaving enough blooms for food."

Amun chimed in, "There was a great earth poet who once said:

"If of thy mortal goods thou art bereft/And from thy slender store/Two loaves alone to thee are left/Sell one, and with the dole/Buy hyacinths to feed thy soul."

"Ah, yes. the great Persian poet Saadi." Lao nodded.

"Of course! As a great poet yourself, you would know Saadi."

"Those lines are well known to every Bard of Soul." Lao paused to touch his forehead and his heart. "The human need for art and beauty is well recognized by Soul. It's why humanity has thrived for so long in such harmony here on Presidium. It's what was missing on the savage

Earth, where people were concerned only with bare material survival and greed of acquisition."

"Drone, come!" Donna raised her hand, and the drone appeared at her side almost instantly. She ordered a new round of drinks for everyone and a tray of savory and sweet snacks. Amun picked out a new playlist of music to lighten the mood as their other friends arrived in a group.

Quintisos 21, 498

In the wee hours, a little tipsy and dreamy, Stephron and Lao walked hand in hand towards their home. Lao pulled away as Stephron clung to his hand.

"Where are you going?" Stephron protested.

"I want to check and see if the last upload solved the problem."

"You'd rather work than come home to bed with me?" Stephron pulled Lao to him and tasted his lips insistently.

Lao pushed him back gently.

"I'll only be a few minutes. Why don't you take a shower and get in bed, and I'll join you in a few minutes?"

Stephron playfully pouted, but turned towards home.

When Lao reached his office, he checked for Soul's response to the last upload.

Instead of the familiar work interface he knew, a black and yellow warning symbol glared:

NOTICE OF CORRECTION: YOUR THREAD HAS BEEN DELETED

The thread on which you were working has been deleted. It will be archived but no further action will be taken now. Please avoid further threads of this nature. Further threads of this nature may result in penalties up to and including revocation of your network and loss of your Bardic credentials.

Lao's chest tightened. He stood frozen, staring at the screen, his heart pounding. He felt fear at the thought of being cut off from the sacred archives—his life's work!— but on fear's heels came rage at the threat of revocation of his Bardic standing. He was recognized as one of the greatest Bards living. Some said he might earn a place in History's Exalted Bards.

How *dare* the system threaten to de-credential him based on a perfectly normal and orthodox codex!

He reached out a finger to close the message, and his hand shook. He stared at the empty interface. His gut clenched at the loss of work he'd already put in; his jaw tightened at the threat of Soul ejecting him from favor with no recourse.

Chapter Two
The Dons

Office of Eminence, Gliese

Sextisos 1, 498

Ergon Waulkra, the Eminentus of Presidium, lifted a finger. An array of images appeared over his desk, each one a caller waiting to speak with him. He savored the moment of decision, but he knew who would advance his present plan, and beckoned Alexiundi Cannaun towards him. A one-fourth-sized hologram of his main planning-and-outreach advisor popped up over the desk. Ergon smiled tautly, never tired of the effect of miniature people who appeared at his beck and call to do his bidding.

"Alex! You're looking well!"

Alex looked terrible.

That was usual for him at this time of day: hung over and bloated, with pendulous bags beneath his pinkened eyes.

"Ergon." Alex dragged out the name, relishing being on a first-name basis with Ergon Waulkra—a privilege. "What can I help you with?"

"Three things: One, the mission to Earth. Two, spinning the lifespan issue. Three, Cawnotee won't play ball."

"Hmm. Start with number three. How'd you put it to Cawnotee?"

"Same way as always: Throw the governor's election, take one for the team, it's for the greater good, our coalition needs another person in this role, I'll owe you a big one, you can call on me anytime."

"Yeah, yeah, good. I was afraid of this. Cawnotee's a starry idealist. Family oh, so proud he's risen, though not a genetic Privell. All that." Cannaun waved a doughy hand in the air. "So: We make him a proposal he can't decline. Stick a pin in that one. The lifespan issue?"

"Yeah, you've had a good run, keeping it out of public focus. Tweaking Soul AI" Waulkra skipped the heart-and-head gesture of reverence when he mentioned Soul, "so Bards –anyone — who mentions 'fivescore' get blocked. But...I assume you know Lao?"

"Who doesn't? They call him this generation's Bard of Bards."

"Yeah. So, he's just tried to publish an Adam and Amber story..."

"...Romance for the masses. With a patriotic theme. Not his usual material."

"No, it's not. And the AI bounced it because it had the word fivescore. Now he's pissed. He's big enough he can't be memory-holed or isolated."

"Hmm. That is a problem. And the Earth mission? I thought that was shaping up?"

"It is. The initial façade is still humanitarian. I need your help to staff it."

"Did you just solve your own problem?"

"Huh?"

Suddenly, one of the faces that hovered in the background bounced and chimed. Waulkra rolled his eyes.

"Hang on, gotta take this, it's Beddi."

"Yeah, yeah, whatever."

Waulkra flipped Cannaun to the side, still listening but muted, and brought his wife's curvaceous body into mini-ghost form above the desk.

"How's my girl?"

"Good, honey," Beddi shook her dark, wavy hair and batted the violet eyes that once catapulted her to fame as a singer and performer. "I just wanted to know if you're meeting me at the ceremony tonight? Or will you be stopping at home first?"

"Oh, honey! Don't you remember? I told you last week I'd be in a strategy meeting for the outlying islands alliance. You were going to ask your dronesister to go with you."

"Oh," Beddi's brow furrowed. "Of course. I...I must have forgotten. I'll call Soogki. Sorry to bother you. Love you!"

"Love you bye." He closed her image with a smug little nod. Cannaun popped up in her place.

"Strategy meeting?" Bannaun asked. "You didn't forget I'd booked us the best fresh girls at Macreen's heterai island for tonight?"

"Outlying islands committee, heterai island, whatever."

"Good. Nice job, deflecting her about that awards ceremony. Show up at too many of those things and it ruins your image. Never forget that."

"That was one of the first things you taught me. Among many." Waulkra inclined his head in a subtle bow.

"Don't forget! You owe me. So, do I have to spell this out for you?"

"Yes. No! Wait, I got it! The Earth mission is a perfect diversion for nuisance people! Lao and Cawnotee both."

"I knew you'd catch on," Cannaun said. "So, you call them in and make it sound like an honor. I'll get the announcements ready to explode across Soul's eventnet. You give 'em the best Waulkra snow job and hustle 'em out the door, where they'll discover they're on every screen in the Presidium as heroes of the greatest humanitarian mission ever known."

"Got it. You're the best, Alex!"

"Damn straight. I'll work up a list of other suggestions who might make wonderful 'heroes' of the Earth mission."

"Usual fee to the usual Soulsight account?"

Soulsight accounts, kept by certain top-level Privells, transacted entirely within a role-playing game. The imaginary currency had taken on real value for clandestine transactions. Theoretically, money didn't exist in post-scarcity Presidium, where everyone was entitled to equal food, housing, entertainment, and luxuries. Records of consumption were kept only for information and planning. But pragmatically, humans needed a medium of exchange for things they valued that the system did not. (The game's name was ironic—the currency was used to hide things from the sight of Soul.)

"Yes. Also, my Max Secret access credential expires in three days."

Ergon quickly traced an elaborate pattern in the air over his desk. "Done."

"Thanks, old friend. See you at Macreen's!" His lecherous grin lifted his jowls for a moment.

"See you there!" Waulkra shut down Alex's image and paused to enjoy a moment's anticipation of the fleshpots he intended to sample. Then, greatly cheered, he reached for the next caller.

Chapter Three
Tantalizing Victory

Cawnotee's Great Room

Gliese Sextisos 14, 498

The campaign was over for twelve hours, and still Amun Cawnotee hadn't rested. His expansive great room—more than standard square footage, an upgrade obtained by Soulsight payments and friendly gestures from builders—had been converted to campaign headquarters months earlier, the walls lined with two rows of flat 2D screens that showed non-stop data from pollsters and social media and text about news around the planet. His comfortable furnishings had been relegated to storage and replaced with both cubicles for the knowledge workers and three separate holo sets for interviews, each with different moods and lighting.

The vote concluded at midnight the night before with no clear winner. Amun Cawnotee tried to rest, but despite the soothing tranquilizer tonic he accepted (under protest) after his assistant Tay's and his wife Donna's urging, he'd awakened in the wee hours, breath short and jaw clenched. *Am I a governor today? Or merely a former district council member with endless favors to repay?*

For the ten thousandth time, he asked himself why he was doing this. *Elected offices are mostly ceremonial, for status and publicity. Only genetically programmed roles confer real power.* He supplied the other side of the mental argument: *It seems so much more just and civilized for the community to have a choice in selecting the leaders. I dream that one day Presidium's decisions will be made by elected individuals.*

That's why I do this.

He'd bathed, shaved, and dressed quickly and returned to the great room before the graveyard shift went home, Donna traipsing in behind him to press his morning cup of bergamot-infused black tea into his hand. He'd walked the plush carpeted floor. He approached each technician in his or her cubicle with a handshake, a pat on the back, or a deep warm smile and words of gratitude for staying the course. The election results were still too close to call; with this margin of error, triple tabulation was needed. It would take all day for the process to be retraced and re-run.

At seven in the morning, the shift ended. Tay showed up, rested and alert.

One of the tech crew, a moonfaced youth with a wispy mustache and sparse curls on his cheeks, stopped next to Amun where he stood by the door, sipping his tea and watching the lights spread across the room through the huge windows with their view of Three Cascade Canyon. The kid—for by Presidial standards, this thirty-five-year-old was a kid—reached out a hand. Amun set his teacup in its saucer and took it.

"Mrm. Cawnotee," the boy said, "It's been an honor working with you. I've been volunteering on campaigns since I was a child of twenty, and you're the first candidate I've supported who acknowledged us grunt workers: the phone bank callers, the content posters, the tech support geeks, the coffee brewers, any of us. You've always treated us as human beings who deserve your respect as much as any of the Bards or Privells you rub shoulders with every day. Thanks."

Cawnotee smiled, handed his cup and saucer to Tay, and clasped the kid's hand with both his own.

"Jaymie. Right?" Cawnotee had almost a genetic-coded Privell's facility with names and faces; he barely paused to register Jaymie's surprise that he recognized him. "Democracy is all about people, and nobody is more of a person than anyone else. I've seen you putting your all into electing me to the governorship. I know you were sitting awake at your desk while I'm sleeping in my bed. Appreciating it is the least I can do. Get some rest! Hopefully we'll have good news by the end of the day."

Jaymie left with a clump of other nightshift workers. They all shot Cawnotee warm glances as they headed home for some shuteye. Tay beamed at their retreating backs.

Cawnotee took a deep breath and turned to greet the morning-shift workers by name. With a fresh cup of bergamot tea in hand, his wife reappeared and took his elbow. The two of them assumed their customary poses in the campaign room, pivoted in three-quarter silhouette before the window, awaiting news.

It turned out to be a long day, both excruciatingly tense and numbingly boring. The earliest the recounts would be done was mid-afternoon. Three Bardic interviews occurred, vacuous and content-free but full of platitudes about the tension of waiting for election results and the sacrifices of public service. Tay shepherded the media Bards and their helpers to and fro, and briefed Amun between interviews on each Bard's biases and pet topics. Donna sat beside him, a devoted wife with a warm smile and nod. Campaign workers of varied station wandered by and wished him luck, or congratulated him on how far he'd come.

More people filtered into the room as the afternoon went on. Caterers brought lunch, snacks, and beverages, which turned alcoholic around 4:30. Seats ran out and the room took on the character of a quiet cocktail party, hushed expectation punctuated by occasional loud laughter.

Around nine at night, people started drifting home, sensing that the recounts might take much longer than expected.

By midnight, it was just Cawnotee and Donna and a few campaign workers. Most of the latter appeared to have drunk too much, sprawled out on sofas, or at tables resting their faces on their folded arms.

The official tonal sequence of Presidium chimed. Amun's eyes zeroed in on the laser camera of the tiny drone that hovered before him, and the room's great screen lit up with the face of Eminence Ergon Waulkra.

"Amun!" Ergon's jocularity and huge grin did nothing to alleviate the irritation Amun felt whenever they interacted. Ergon attained the highest position of all humanity, not elected but rather selected by Soul from among the epigenetically enhanced Privells. He'd made himself the only logical choice for Soul to pick, not because he excelled in creating consensus, advancing bold visions, or building loyalty, but rather through ruthless imposition of his will with threats and via pragmatic, but temporary, alliances.

"Eminence Waulkra—Ergon!" Amun forced a grin, stole a glance at Donna's eager face.

"Congratulations! You're the new regional governor of Ryke."

"Thank you! I appreciate your calling, Merm…Eminence…uh, Ergon."

"It's the least I could do, Mrm. Cawnotee." His face took on a stern expression, his voice its more typical icy tone. "It's late now, so get some rest. But I need you to be in my office at eight tomorrow morning."

"Of course, Merm," Amun said. Such a summons didn't bode well. His balloon of elation deflated as fast as it had swollen.

"See you in the morning, then." Waulkra cut the feed abruptly.

Donna's soft hand found the space between his shoulder blades, stroked tenderly. Her confident voice soothed him.

"Sweetheart, let's go to bed. The service bot will show these last few guests out."

Office

Eminentus

At 7:59, Amun Cawnotee, governor-elect of Ryke, capital district of the known human world of Presidium, approached the anteroom of Ergon Waulkra, Eminentus Presidium. The door to Waulkra's office slid open soundlessly, and Cawnotee squared his shoulders and walked in.

"Cawnotee! Amun! Have a seat! Coffee?"

The Eminence took a cup from a serving drone as he spoke, so Cawnotee nodded and took the cup offered to him.

"Sit down! Why so glum? You just won an election!"

Cawnotee forced himself to relax, eased into a chair opposite Waulkra's as Waulkra sat. Cawnotee smelled tension and fear on himself. Surely Waulkra's sharp, predatory nose smelled it too.

"It was a hard-won victory," Amun said. "I couldn't have done it without Donna."

"Yes, your wife being the sister-in-law of the district's Bard, Murrell, couldn't have hurt your chances, eh?"

"No, not at all. Kneth went beyond brotherly devotion, and Murell's kind words swayed more than one voter."

"That's fine. Use the advantages life gives you. Speaking of which, I'm about to present you with an opportunity to gain advantage you never expected." Waulkra sounded happy. He didn't sound happy for Amun, though; more like the happiness of a feral scrifflox when it sank its sharp teeth into the throat of a rat. (Even on a world made over from seeds and spores and synthetic DNA into an automated sustainable paradise, humanity's old nuisance vermin managed to smuggle itself aboard the generation ships).

"Yes?"

"I'm assigning you to a leadership role far greater than anything you might accomplish as governor." Waulkra held up a hand to forestall protest. "Now, I know you *think* you want this governor position. But hear me out. I'm sure you recall when the Soaring Duty probe visited Earth a few years ago, and identified that the planet is still populated?"

"Yes, the savage remnant."

"That's right. Horrible primitive regression. Suffering, disease, warfare, misery."

"But what..." Amun's brow furrowed.

"You know there's a huge groundswell of support for the idea of rescuing those wretches?"

"I thought they weren't even human anymore?"

"That's what we thought at first. But after science processed all the data, we found that they are, in fact, *Homo sapiens*. But they're hardly recognizable as such because of the conditions they live in." Ergon walked around his desk and stood over Amun, put a firm hand on his shoulder, and directed the full force of his powerful personality into the other man's eyes.

"Well, I'm entrusting you with a great honor and duty. You'll lead the first rescue mission to Earth!"

"But..." Cawnotee, dismayed, rose from his chair.

"...Nobody but you has the judgement and charisma to lead this mission," Waulkra interrupted smoothly. "I've had my eye on you since you started clerking for Bard Fon. He praised you highly."

Amun flushed in pleasure. "He did?" In the entire time he'd worked for old Fon, Amun couldn't remember him ever speaking kindly of *anyone*.

"Glowingly. And he wasn't the only one." He lowered his head deferentially, eyes level with the shorter man's. "I've never met a man whose friends and acquaintances had no criticism for him. But you—despite your humility—are that man."

Amun raised his chin. "How long is the mission? What does it involve exactly?"

"It's a long trip, since you can't Vault inside a star's gravity well. Four months out of the Gliese 667 triple system, then the Vault, then only two months in towards Sol, since Earth will be opposite all the outer planets." Waulkra crossed back to his chair, and both men sat.

Waulkra continued, "The team will be hand-picked, distinguished in their fields, like you. Many of them will be multiply qualified. The trip out, the crew prepares materials for your outreach: seeds for agriculture, replanting, and reforesting; the base Bardic codex for rebuilding the planet's culture; anthropological rubrics for evaluating their development levels, and so forth. Of course, the spacecraft itself will require maintenance and piloting."

"Sounds like we'll be busy," Cawnotee said.

"Perhaps. But we're assigning a hundred top performers, the best Presidium and all its moons have to offer. And when you get a hundred high-strung, dynamic personalities in one small space for six months, there's bound to be friction and conflict. That's why we need a public servant of your talent to take charge of them."

"But what about the electorate of Ryke? My supporters count on me. My constituents will be disappointed."

"Amun, your talent is leadership. My role as Eminentus is finding talented leaders. Let me take care of it. I have several potential appointees in mind. I promise you, Ryke will get the caliber of governor it deserves."

"Well...Ergon...can I sleep on the decision?"

"Of course." Ergon walked around the desk, again grasped his shoulder, and gripped his other hand as he rose from his chair. "But let me know first thing in the morning. Things are moving fast on this mission, and there's no time to lose."

Waulkra walked Cawnotee to the looming door, which swung open. Feeling a firm pat on the back, Cawnotee found himself alone in the anteroom.

He made a call to his assistant. "Tay? Cancel my engagements for the rest of the morning."

"Merm? You know you're supposed to address your campaign workers?"

"It'll have to wait. Reschedule it." He cut the connection.

His head spun. He'd been focused with all his heart and mind on winning the election. He had a full agenda of reforms and outreach, a head full of ideas, a will to make a difference. And now Waulkra asked him to derail the speeding levtrain that was Team Cawnotee and redirect that force of will in a new, unfamiliar direction.

He dragged his feet on his way home from the levtrain stop, brow creased. His thoughts cycled: *Tell him no. But if I do, will I be pass up the opportunity of a lifetime? This mission will go down in the history codices. Tell him yes. But if I do, I give up the certainty of the governorship and disappoint my people.*

No one was home but the bots when he walked in.

"Bring coffee. No. Water." The service bot buzzed to comply. "Interface, bring up messages." His messages materialized over the table, sorted and flagged.

"Your water," the bot prompted after a few seconds of hovering, ignored.

"Thank you," Amun took it. "I don't know what to do about this mission."

The interface replied, "What should I look up?"

"Nothing, just thinking out loud. Bards could be singing my name centuries hence. I can always start over in my political career when I return."

"Average time before codices about popular figures subside from Bardic circulation, eighty years."

"Uh, thanks. I'll be gone at least a year, year and a half, maybe two. The whole scene will have changed."

"Predicted minimum round-trip voyage of Free Sky, nineteen months."

"Yes, good. But this is Waulkra asking me...me!...and I want him happy."

"Ergon Waulkra, Eminentus Presidium, born..."

"Yes, yes, stop already! Maybe I can cut a deal with him, ask him to promise me an appointed position when I return. But how will I tell my election team? Those people revere me, I'm irreplaceable to some of them. I should tell him no ..."

"Compose message to Ergon Waulkra?" A blank message addressed to Waulkra popped up.

"No!" Amun stabbed at the holo message, flung it away, and watched it dissolve until it he was sure it was gone. "I don't know what to do," he sighed.

He sat down and began sorting through his messages. He skimmed them, deleting many unread, but froze when he reached one, dated that same afternoon, which read:

From: Office, Eminentus Presidium

To: Amun Cawnotee

Copy: <hidden>

FOR IMMEDIATE RELEASE

A HEROIC JOURNEY TO OUR ORIGIN: THE MISSION TO EARTH

Date: Seximos 15, Presidial Year 498

In a momentous and unprecedented announcement, the Presidium takes a giant leap toward reclaiming our roots and rescuing our lost heritage on Earth. After centuries of separation, we embark on a mission that will reunite us with our long-lost cousins now living in a fallen, primitive state. We'll restore the spark of civilization on the ravaged planet we once called home.

MISSION FOR HUMANITY:

With profound reverence for the memory of Earth, the Presidium is thrilled to announce the launch of a manned rescue mission. This extraordinary endeavor will bring together a hundred of the Presidium's most accomplished specialists, united in their dedication to the renaissance of humanity on Earth. Leading this heroic mission is the illustrious Privell Amun Cawnotee, a paragon of public service and the ideal visionary to guide us through this unprecedented undertaking.

THE FREE SKY:

Our vessel for this unparalleled journey is none other than the Free Sky, a state-of-the-art J-class Vaultship, capable of vaulting through trance space faster than light. The Free Sky is fully equipped to revive Earth's fallen state, stocked with advanced technology to improve communications, genetically improved, earth-original strains of seed and embryo stock to re-establish agricultural production, and cutting-edge medical advancements to relieve suffering. Moreover, it carries a comprehensive library of human achievement, encompassing philosophy, science, technology, and the Bardic arts.

A GLORIOUS SEND-OFF:

Mark your calendars! The launch of the Mission to Earth is slated for a mere six months from now, on Decissos 15. As we prepare to embark on this historic voyage, we hope to witness the revival of civilization and the rekindling of the human spirit on Earth.

The Presidium invites all citizens on the planet and its moons to join us in celebrating this momentous occasion as we take the first steps on our path to reunite with our ancestral home. Together, we shall rebuild, renew, and reaffirm the indomitable spirit of humanity.

For media inquiries and further information, please contact:

Presidium News Office

###

Amun gaped, speechless, devoid of thought, numb of emotion. He remembered to breathe, and then the panic hit him.

He was not to be given a choice. This mission would happen, with him at the head of it. No amount of Soulsight money could buy his way out of Ergon Waulkra's control. Less than a day ago, he'd won a governorship, the highest elective office in Presidium's classless meritocracy. Now, Ergon had snatched away from him! He'd send him an unfathomable distance away from his home, his family.

Oh, no—his family! Donna. How would she, with her love of luxurious outdoor venues and her endless appetite for social events, feel about spending six months cooped up in a Vaultship with a hundred people? Only to emerge onto a planet full of knuckle-dragging barbarians, barely more than beasts, without her lifelong ease and comfort, her birthright as a Presidian (and a Privell at that)...how could he keep her from feeling miserable?

Even as he tried to think of a way to tell her, she arrived. She set a force-fiber bag on the kitchen island and switched it off, revealing a mound of organic produce.

He stalled for time. "Been to the bazaar, I see." Maybe he spoke a little sharply, he realized too late.

"Yes. Is that okay? We were running low on fruits and veggies, and you know I don't trust the bots to pick the best ones. Look! Your favorite!" Donna enticed him with a pomegranate.

"Mmm. That's a gorgeous one!"

Amun rose and enfolded her in a deep embrace, but realized he was squeezing her too hard when she put a hand on his chest and pushed back gently.

"Okay, what is it? I can tell there's something on your mind," she said.

Amun sighed. "You read me like a codex." He guided her to the lounger with a hand on her waist. "Please sit down."

Her brow furrowed, she obeyed.

"My meeting with the Eminence..." he hesitated.

"Yes, go on."

"I can't think of an easy way to break this to you. I'm still trying to process it myself."

"Sounds bad." She laid a supple hand below her collarbones.

"Ergon Waulkra asked me to decline the governorship." The bad news blurted out in a relief of pressure.

"What? You told him no, of course."

"He wanted me to take over a historic mission. I told him I'd think about it overnight."

"Okay, good. We have time to frame an excuse. What mission?" Donna's shrewd political tactics were part of the reason he'd won, and she fell right into planning mode.

"That's the shocker. Look at your messages. The official Presidium feed."

Donna raised her hand and snapped her personal node open before her. She fingered the hologram deftly, dismissing trivial bulletins, until she came to the one Amun had just seen on his console. She read it. As her face turned pale, Amun's heart drilled its way down to the depths of his being.

"Oh, no. They didn't," she said.

"I'm afraid they did."

"I can't believe Ergon would do something like this! No, I take that back. If anyone is capable of it, it's Ergon. People are just tools to that man."

He sat next to her on the lounger, took her hand in both of his.

"I was considering taking the mission, darling. It would be a chance to make my—our—mark on history. It'll go down in the sutras."

"*If* it succeeds. It's an obvious long shot. Who else is going? And who's he appointing to

the governorship to replace you?"

"I don't know. I didn't think to ask."

She pulled her hand away and stood to face the window.

"Sometimes you're a babe in the woods, Amun."

"I know. I thought of asking you to go with me this morning, but..." he trailed off.

"No, that wouldn't have worked either. Ergon is the kind of man who'd regard bringing your wife along as a sign of weakness instead of wisdom." She turned around.

"My thinking, too. Anyone else would know you're my most astute and trusted counsellor. And gorgeous besides."

"Flatterer." She leaned in, tapped his cheek with a kiss. "There's got to be some pressure I can apply from somewhere. Let me make some calls, gather more information from the grapevine. Surely, we can work this out." She fingered the hologram decisively.

With Donna so confident, Amun could almost believe her. But then he stepped over to turn off his home node and eyed the mass announcement that every one of the billion and a half citizens of Presidium had already received.

He murmured quietly, "That ship has sailed."

But Donna had marched into her study and shut the door.

Chapter Four
Pill on the Palm

Gliese

Bard Lao Carbeenair's home

Septisos 1, 498

Stephron rolled over for the umpteenth time on the smooth cotton sheets, tangling his feet and rendering himself fully awake. He gestured the clock into being. 5:30 AM. He didn't have to be up for another two hours.

He reached for Lao's hand, then flailed about, finding himself alone in the bed. He sat up, and the room light brightened to half intensity. Lao's pillow lay undisturbed. Stephron calmed himself by drinking a little water from his bedside goblet.

He called Lao's personal node.

"Hey, baby," Lao answered. "You're probably wondering where I am."

"Looks like your studio," Stephron said. "Still working?"

Lao's gaze jerked around, his hair rumpled. "Yeah. I simply couldn't let it go till I figured out why I got that content warning. And it's taken me down a scrifflox burrow!"

"Oh, sweetheart! Please come home to bed!" Stephron smoothed the covers beside him, now untangled, invitingly.

"I wouldn't be able to sleep."

"You know it's morning already?"

Lao glanced at the time on the hologram display and raised his eyebrows.

"No wonder I'm so tired! But check this out: Waulkra is listed as eighty-five years old on all his official documents, but I accessed the demographic net, and he's really sixty-four!"

"Odd."

"That's what I thought. So, I ran some cross reports on the demographic data and found that fully 77% of official deaths were recorded years—sometimes a decade or more—later than their age at their last monetary or social entry in the system."

"Weird."

"Not just weird. Riddle me this: how many years does the sutra give us to live?"

"A hundred. What does that have to do with..."

"Right! A hundred!" Lao almost shouted, disheveled and looking unhinged. "Fivescore, the earliest sutras say, and we Bards incorporate that into our work, with other classic passages. But if what I'm seeing is true—and it is, I have highest access privileges—the average person is living closer to seventy-seven years."

"Naw, there's some mistake. Come home and let me make you a fresh herb omelette, then take a nap. When you wake up, check your figures over. You'll probably feel silly once you see your error."

Lao blinked a few times and his posture deflated. "I *am* exhausted," he admitted.

"You shut down and get ready to go. I'm summoning a ride for you." Stephron, as good as his word, brought up the ride-summoning interface as he spoke.

"I love you, Stephron. You take good care of me, even when I'm not taking care of myself."

"I love you too. See you soon."

L ao woke up with a slight headache. The room blazed with Glieselight and it took him a moment to get his bearings.

Oh, right, I worked through the night.

He rolled out of bed, waved the clock up. 4:30 in the afternoon! He'd lost a day; he felt sad. He shook his head and directed his stumble towards the bathroom, but then Stephron came in with an expression so odd it shook Lao out of his confusion.

"What's wrong?"

"I don't know how to say this." Stephron took a step towards him, but Lao evaded him, reaching for the bathroom door.

"Just tell me."

"There's a message in both our feeds. It's from Amun's office."

"Hang on." Lao shut the door behind him. Stephron tensely watched the door until he came out.

"Okay," Lao focused on Stephron. "I can tell this is big. Let me have it."

"Alright." Stephron sighed. "You and I are going on that mission to Earth."

"Right." Lao laughed. "You had me going there!"

"No, really."

"You're not joking?"

"I wouldn't joke about something like this." Stephron reached for Lao's hand.

Lao passively let him take it.

"But. Your plantings. My studio."

"My message says they need an agriculturalist of my abilities to ensure the health and survival of the crew on this lengthy mission. Yours...you don't mind that I read it?" Stephron asked.

"Of course not. You know we have no secrets between us."

"Right. Yours says...let's see..." he flicked his node open, "only a Bard of your 'unparalleled qualities is equal to the task of memorializing this historic mission on the planet of our ancient origins.'"

Lao went back in the bathroom and drank a big glass of water. Then he came back in the bedroom and sat on the bed, staring straight ahead.

"Honey? You okay?" Stephron asked.

"Yeah. Yeah, just thinking."

"What can I do to help? You look stunned."

"I guess that's the word." He finally looked up into his husband's eyes.

"This is a great opportunity for us. You don't seem happy about it."

"It's so...unexpected. I have plans for my next year's worth of projects. I have friends. We have plans for this house." Lao waved his hand expansively, taking in his entire life.

"We won't be gone that long. What, a few weeks?"

"Oh, baby. You really don't pay attention to current events, do you?"

"No point in it. Everything always comes out fine in the end," Stephron said.

"Maybe so. But anyway, the trip to Earth is projected to be six months. Who knows how long the mission will take? And depending on the position of the planets afterwards, the trip back could be as long as a year and a half."

"Oh." It was Stephron's turn to sit heavily on the bed. "Two years or more."

"We have three months to prepare."

"That should be about as long as it'll take to get our belongings stored, our accounts closed, see our friends and families once more before we go..." Stephron began.

"...My mother. She's sick, living in that hospice drone. She'll be...gone," Lao choked a little, "before we get back."

Stephron wordlessly held Lao close.

"We can't pass this up. It's the chance of a lifetime." Lao sounded forlorn rather than inspired.

"You're right. It's worth some sacrifices."

"We'd better summon a psych bot. We're both going to need some major chemical adjustment to get through the next six months!"

"Right. Right. And I planned to make an aubergine and chicken lasagna for dinner."

"You and your cooking." Lao smiled indulgently.

"It's a new varietal! They just ripened, and I'm excited to cook up these aubergines for you."

"I know. And it's one of the things I love about you," Lao said.

Stephron smiled in satisfaction. "Okay. You summon the psych bot and I'll start slicing."

They fell into their homely routine, letting the familiarity of each other's presence and their partnership soothe their anxieties about the unexpected strangeness thrust upon them.

Gliese 667Cc orbit

Meanwhile, in orbit, construction bots began to fit the ship Free Sky for her mission. Most critically, they towed into place a high-energy plasma reactor, which began layering two materials: diamond with nitrogen molecules interspersed every cubic nanometer, and yttrium iron garnet in a thin film, to form the first of two slender rods. That YIG-diamond rod would form the basis for the quantum Vault that would take them to the savage world known as Earth.

Chapter Five
Weaving Oceania

Office of Alexiundi Cannaun

Septisos 13, 498

Alexiundi Cannaun tinkered with the optimization for the Earth mission to go in the nets.

He studied the Earth image series that Soul made available for Bards to use for any sutra that had an Earth scene. Previously, the Earth settings available included symbolism like evolving animals, disintegrating hearts, and mushroom clouds. But going forward, Soul AI would introduce new images into the montages:

The first showed a dwelling built of sticks and mud, a swinging animal fur suspended as a door flap.

The second was a man and woman with matted, ungroomed hair. The man gestured with a stick, and the woman lowered her head and smiled in appeasement, revealing jagged, broken, brown teeth.

The third presented two small children, both naked, squatting in mud that covered their feet to midcalf. One child gouged at the mud with a stick.

Alex played each one through several times with different context prompts, nodding as the AI varied the images to keep them fresh while keeping the core message of a primitive lifestyle unchanged.

"Good. Publish."

"Max Secret clearance code?" Soul prompted, sullen as ever. Alex gave the code Ergon had provided.

"Images distributed to Bardic interfaces," Soul said. Alex enjoyed the restrained sarcasm of this usual tone. He never understood the need others had to treat Soul like a friend or collaborator; it was only a machine like all the rest, no matter how well it imitated human emotion.

Alex moved on to the matrix of elevated words. These were pairs or triptychs of words which, when included within a specific number of words apart in a new sutra, newsflash, or other net communication, would push it to more recipients.

Earth-5 words-primitive
Earth-5 words-disgust
Earth-5 words-human-5 words-brute
Earth-5 words-infant-1 word-mortality
Earth-5 words-death-5 words-disease
Earth-5 words-violence-5 words-injury
Earth-5 words-violence-5 words-death

The list was pages and pages long: death, disease, injury, primitive, infant, murder, rape, dirty, parasites, bacteria, wounded, premature, poverty, difficult, illiterate... any communication that linked any of these concepts to humanity on Earth would be served to more people, and if any of those shared it along, that share would reach more of their contacts, and reach them sooner. Alex skimmed over the holo pages intently.

"Elevation matrix Cannaun.Earth.181 upload. All items priority 1."

"Max Secret clearance code?"

He gave it.

"Net master elevation matrix altered."

Alex double-checked that the fivescore etherization command still applied to Bardic work, with Lao still the only Bard diverted from the automated escalation sequence. He cupped the data in his hand, spread his fingers to see the report: of seven First-Level Bards, six of them figured out within one or two tries that "fivescore" needed to be omitted from their work. The seventh, Lao, had tried—Alex chuckled—113 times to get the word to work. *Stubborn fucker.* Of the 100 Second-Levels, the average number of attempts was 4.2. Third-Level Bards, 5.1. For the Fourth Level and below, it was pretty consistently around seven attempts. Alex nodded.

"Bring up the content crawler."

"Yes, Privell."

Privell. Alex smirked with glee. He was no Privell; he was genetic dross, fated originally for low-level service work in the service of those few who required human servants instead of drones. The gene labs bred him for acute sensitivity to others' wants and needs, but the low-normal intelligence alleles that were supposed to go with it had recombined at fertilization. Alex retrieved his own record not long after he first got Max Secret access.

His Mother drone identified the problem in toddlerhood. The drone reported it dutifully, and Soul directed it to begin the euthanasia process. But after the sedative and before the killing dose, Soul had countermanded that order, and little Alexiundi's Mother drone took up residence in the estate of a secretive and eccentric Privell.

There, Alex obtained education as an assistant and adviser, able to analyze human interactions to give his benefactor advantages in his preferred entertainments, which included influencing cultural trends, gambling, spectator sports, and darker pursuits combining the three. Lucky for him, his benefactor didn't much mind his pasty, thick-waisted, bandy-legged appearance, and by the time the old man reached a hundred and died, Alex had proved his worth to the powerful so many times that it didn't matter that he got objectively less attractive as he aged.

"Privell?" Soul nagged him.

"Yes, lost in thought. Crawl for Bards producing content most elevated by Cannaun.Earth.181. Say, more than two elevations per day for at least ten sequential days."

An array of spheroids, each a holovid of a different Bard's work, bubbled up before him.

"Now filter those for highest quintile of audience approval."

Four fifths of the bubbles vanished. There were around eighty remaining.

"Star them."

"Bards starred," said Soul. Now each of those eighty Bards would start to experience serendipity. Large things would go right for them: they'd simply happen to meet people who could introduce them to other people who could help them with projects. The single ones would bump into compatible potential partners. All would find themselves sitting near or chatting with compatible potential friends. They'd win raffles and drawings much more often than chance dictated. Their favorite foods, beverages, and toiletries would be carried at their closest bazaar in abundance. Every public space they entered would play their favorite songs as part of the ambient music. As the weeks of good fortune went on, these eighty would find themselves more confident, happier, and more creative.

"Automate that sequence. Label: star power."

"Automation star power, saved. Schedule?"

"No, remind me when we talk."

"Yes, Privell."

"We've made an excellent start today."

"Yes, Privell."

"By the time the Vaultship takes off, all Presidium will be overflowing with equal parts pity and disgust for those wretches on Earth. When I return tomorrow, start with a similar algorithm to generate an elevation matrix for the space voyage, vaultship, civilizing influence, rescue, cleanliness, healing, educating…you get the gist."

"Yes, Privell, I can figure out what you'll need."

"Excellent. Cannaun logoff."

Chapter Six
Clymene's Bequest

Author: Waulkra E, Smoke E, Grice J.

Title: Use of Biological Warfare in Historical Records of Ancient Earth

Gliesean Journal of Military Science. Vol. 350 (Sextisos, 449):178-194.

Abstract: Biological warfare, defined as "the use of biological organisms or their chemical products as weapons of war," was a tactic often condemned. However, there are many mentions of its use in the Earth historical records brought to Gliese 667Cc by the generation ship Arca Titanica in year 0. In this paper, we searched all historical records using a Soul-guided faceted search, refined via natural language processing over multiple iterations. Terms determined to be most relevant included "biological warfare," "plague," "terrorist" (and variants), "artificial virus," "manmade bacterium OR virus OR pathogen," with 200 secondarily relevant keywords. The data were cleaned by a cooperative compound review process in collaboration with Soul. The result was 2,953,200 words of historical records, which Soul summarized in 3,570 pages. Analysis was seeded by observations of authors and verified by Soul's correlation function. Findings included: 1. Biological warfare preceded the advent of technological civilization, having its first recorded usages in the Bronze Age, with such techniques as catapulting dead bodies over walls, introducing venomous animals, and water-source contamination. 2. Isolated Stone-Age remnants were documented using arrows and darts treated with biological poisons from frogs, etc. 3. Biological warfare became more common, utilizing more diverse resources, in the era of electronics-based civilization, and included use of *Bacillus anthracis*, Marburg virus, *Francisella tularensis, Vibrio cholerae, Chlamydia psittaci*, and numerous pathological and public-health-endangering species of micro-organisms. 4. The so-called "machine sickness" genetically recombinant bacterium that destroyed global civilization and prompted the emergency acceleration of Arca Titanica's departure may have been deliberately released as a weapon of biological warfare or terrorism, but this question was unsettled when Presidium's ancestors left Earth.

This paper is divided into five sections: 1. Classification of types of biological warfare; 2. Evidence for use of biological warfare throughout different historical eras; 3. Efficacy of biological warfare; 4. Post-usage unintended consequences or contemporaneous "friendly fire" effects; and 5. Potential usage of biological warfare in Presidium's localized peripheral conflicts.

Chapter Seven
Burn and Rave

Bard Lao Carbeenair's home

Octisos 19, 498

Tay walked up to the door of Lao and Stephron's home, hugging a parcel to her chest. She closed her eyes and took three deep breaths. Then she tossed her hair, squared her shoulders, and touched the doorbell.

A bot opened the door a few seconds later. It scanned her eye.

"Welcome, Rainetaya Mandil. Your business here?"

"Delivery. A space suit," She held out the floppy celluloid package in her arms, and the bot scanned it. "From Amun Cawnotee."

"Yes, Lao Carbeenair is expecting it. Please wait here and I'll get him. You may place the package on the table here." She caught a toe on the threshold, stumbled but didn't fall.

The bot flew off. Tay set the spacesuit on the reception table and drifted about the foyer aimlessly. *High ceiling. Standard footage, but the height makes it seem more spacious, almost like a public space. Must be one of those pluses Privells get on the lowdown from builders.*

A sculpture stood on the reception table, a vibrant blue fish almost three feet long. *Pretty realistic. Must be one of those scan-and-release 3D prints. One of them must fish.*

The walls were lined with 2D photos. The first was a young boy of perhaps five, chasing a soap bubble from a wand held by a Mother drone. The second one confirmed her speculation. *This must be Lao's husband, Stephron. Standing on a pier, rod in one hand, big fish in the other, and look at that grin! Such a kind-looking man.*

Lao cleared his throat behind her, and she turned. She'd seen his image while helping Amun review the personal data of the assemblage of experts and prolific creators he would head during the mission. *He looks older than his holo. No, not older. Just tired.*

She respectfully dipped her head. "Lao Carbeenair?"

"In person. And you must be the Rainetaya Mandil who keeps sending me all those messages I keep getting about Free Sky." He smiled engagingly.

"Yes, Merm, Privell." Her smile felt more uncertain. *He seems secretly displeased.* "Oh! Here's your revised and altered space suit." She lifted the bulky package and presented it to Lao.

He reached out to take it, but the cleaning bot chose that moment to trundle into the room, and she caught her toe on it, stumbled, fumbled the package, and set the gleaming azure fish to rocking.

Oh, no! With panicky speed, Tay lunged to the rescue, catching the fish an instant before it tumbled floorwards.

"You're fast!" remarked Lao. "My husband would have been upset if that broke. Thank you, Rainetaya."

"Just Tay."

"Lao, please."

He's smiling now. And he has a nice smile.

"Lao it is."

"Will you have a glass? Fruit juice or wine? I was about to have wine myself."

"Well, it is the end of my workday. Why not?"

He beckoned her and she followed him into the living area. *Quirky, an artist's place. But comfortable and homey.* She sat on a sofa upholstered in a vivid-contrast pattern, leaned back against a row of soft but supportive cushions, sighed, and gave in to the urge to curl her feet underneath her.

"Oops, let me get those." Lao whisked some small vials off the coffee table. "Seeds Stephron brought home from work to try out in our garden. Sorry."

"Honestly, I didn't even notice them."

Lao shrugged, tucked the vials in a drawer, and summoned the kitchen drone. "Kitchen, two glasses of Rosy Valley Malbec, cool."

"Two glasses of wine at eighteen degrees." The drone buzzed around the cabinets.

"This is a fine vintage," said Lao.

"I've heard it's good," said Tay. "But I'm not a big drinker, so I haven't gotten around to trying it."

The drone glided to Lao and hovered until he took his glass, then brought Tay hers. Lao sat nearby on a chair that looked like a pouf but molded itself into a snug contoured seat.

Tay sipped the Malbec. *Berries...herbs...a faint tang like balsamic vinegar.* Her eyebrows rose.

"Like it?" Lao said, and she nodded enthusiastically, held the deliciousness of the wine on her tongue, then reluctantly swallowed.

"Oh, my! My hairdresser said it was good, but this is just."

"Isn't it?" Lao said, then called out, "Music. Upbeat neojazz."

"Nice tunage! I love Far Corner!"

"Really? I mean, are you telling the truth? They're an acquired taste."

"Not for me, they're not. I loved them the first time I heard them."

The conversation flowed freely. Besides the same music, they enjoyed the same holovids and painters, and they both had an unexplainable adoration for metallic embroidery. Lao's tension and fatigue seemed to subside, and he relaxed. Tay found herself relaxing too, and a second glass of wine didn't hurt.

"Well, I can tell we're going to be great friends on Free Sky," Lao said.

"Oh." Tay's face fell. "I'm. That is."

"You're not going?" Lao gently prompted.

She shook her head. *Deep breath. Don't cry.* "Waulkra's office selected the crew, and when the list came out, I wasn't on it." Her voice cracked but no tears came.

"Well, then we'll simply have to get together as much as we can over the next two months." He smiled.

Get a grip. Smile back. Don't show how upset you are. She forced a grin, waved her hand to show unimportance. "That sounds fun."

"You seem so dedicated to Amun. Are you worried about him?"

"Is it that obvious?" She seemed relieved. "I'm not worried about him so much—anyone could do what I do, and Donna is amazing—but I don't know what *I'll* do without *him*. Being his assistant is the only career I ever had, and I can't imagine doing anything else."

"I'm sure Soul will find you something good. But I understand how you feel. I don't know what I'd do without my art. The Truth of the sacred texts is my vocation. And you're right about Donna."

"She's so gracious. Even though I think sometimes it annoys her that I'm always following her husband around, she's so kind and, and, witty. Yes, that's the word."

"That she is."

"They're both so amazing. And so are you. I can't believe you want to be my friend."

"Why not?"

"You're so perfect at what you do. You're the best Bard of this generation, and it's not only me saying so." She waved her hands emphatically, barely missed knocking over her wine glass.

"Maybe I'm not all that. I have struggles."

"Really?"

"I've been at a standstill for the last few months."

"Creative block? The voyage coming up making you anxious?" she speculated.

"No. Well, yes, but not only that. Can you keep a secret?"

She quirked an eyebrow.

"Never mind," he said, "silly question, you must keep huge secrets for Amun, I'm sure. Okay, well, I've been having issues with Soul," heart and head, "etherizing my work."

Tay's face stayed blank.

"That's incredibly unusual," he explained. "And...well, maybe I shouldn't go into this."

The front door opened and Stephron came in.

"Hi, honey," called Lao, "we're in here."

Stephron tilted his head at Tay, walked over to Lao, bent over the chair, and kissed him hello.

"Stephron, this is Amun Cawnotee's assistant, Tay. Tay, my husband Stephron."

Stephron turned around to face her.

"Oh, you're the one sending all those memos about the voyage to Earth."

"Guilty," Tay lowered her head in mock shame. "Mrm. Cawnotee wanted me to bring the spacesuit to Privell Lao, to make sure the alterations fit."

Awkward silence.

Stephron broke it by asking, "What are you drinking? The Rosy Valley? Kitchen! One glass, cool."

The drone delivered the wine.

"Drone, take my glass," Tay said. She stood up. "I've really got to be going."

"Oh, do you have to?" Lao said. "Honey, Tay likes Far Corner—*and* has a collection of metallic embroidered costumes!"

"Oh, you two should have *loads* to talk about." Stephron's tone was indulgent.

"Yes. Tay, there's a neojazz concert in the south amphitheater tomorrow at three. Would you like to meet there?"

"Sure! Message me the details. Nice meeting you, Stephron."

"Likewise, Tay. Thanks for all the organizing. Really. You answer all my questions about the trip before I can even ask them," Stephron replied.

"That's my duty." She twirled a hand in her hair, then smoothed it down. "Amun Cawnotee gave me this opportunity and I always try to do right by him."

"You do a great job."

"Thanks." Tay walked to the door, Lao following.

"See you tomorrow, then?"

"Wouldn't miss it. Bye!"

"Bye, Tay!"

Lao shut the door behind her. Stephron sipped his wine, still standing, regarding him levelly.

"Are you coming with us to the amphitheater tomorrow?" Lao asked.

"You know I don't care for neojazz."

"Okay, but I thought I'd ask. I'd love your company."

"No, you go with your new buddy. She can show you her metal thready stuff afterwards."

"You don't mind?" Lao stepped to his side and squeezed his hand.

"I was going to start these air vine seeds tomorrow afternoon, remember?"

"Good, I'll be out of your hair then."

"Sounds perfect. It'll get you out of the house. You've been moping around since Mola's been ill. I've been worried."

"I know it's odd, but you do understand about my connection with my mother?"

"Oh, yes, you've told me." He gave his husband a quick hug. "Now, what would you like me to make you for dinner?

Mola's home

Octisos 21, 498

Lao approached the front door of his mother's house, head down. The door recognized and admitted him.

The house, like all houses of Presidium, stayed clean and tidy thanks to the bots. Yet, there wafted a subtle smell—disinfectants, the aroma of deteriorating flesh—that left him equal parts sad and queasy when he visited Mola.

Then he saw her, couched in the belly of the Hospice drone, and all his discomfort went away. He felt awash in joy at seeing her face, and then shame at the degree of joy he felt. The bond between them was unnatural.

Presidium's children did not usually love their mothers. He knew that.

Other people talked about an inward flicker of recognition they felt when they saw their biological parents. But he'd never met anyone else who had more than a ceremonial, perfunctory relationship with their mother, or their father for that matter.

Parents were selected by Soul, matched according to complex algorithms based on their DNA, but also on their physical and behavioral phenotypes, to produce the proportion of genetic gifts needed for every role in society. At forty, married or single, a woman was expected to carry a first pregnancy, if and when Soul offered the opportunity (with the potential to continue bearing children into her late sixties) and most rejoiced at the honor. Most mothers never met the child's father, though his identity was public record.

After being pampered and cared for in body, mind, and spirit for nine months, mothers gave birth to their babies (usually by painless, scarless, robotic surgery). Moments later, the Mother drones took infants from their dams, cradled them in a snug, warm, soft nook, diapered them, and fed them human breastmilk (produced by clonal cells within the drone itself and customized for the infant's needs in real time). Mother drones interpreted infants' expressions, noises, and gazes with a .001% error rate and provided feeding, vibration, rocking, music, speech, or visual stimulation unerringly, unlike human mothers, who so often helplessly tried one thing after another to soothe their children to no avail.

Early in the Presidium, just after the frontier days, Soul didn't permit human parents to know who their children were and vice-versa, much less let them see each other. Despite relentlessly cheery Presidial declarations about freedom from the tyranny of biology and the leisure of having no childcare tasks, the first generation of mothers after Presidium's proper founding had developed postpartum depression in epic proportions. But Soul, as a self-training AI, adapted quickly, creating a series of scripted ceremonies and rituals where mothers were honored and got to see their growing, flourishing children at regular intervals. Soul also found that the children thrived even better that way. Oxytocin surged measurably after each ceremony, and the resulting improvements in mood and autonomic tone were undeniable.

The normal parental relationship ended at that limit.

Lao knew all that—every Presidial of average IQ and above knew it.

But here was his mother. She lay in the sleek, gleaming Hospice drone poised on its shock-absorbing tripod base. The drone, of late the focus of her home, was quiet and motionless for now. He leaned through the broad, open hatch into her cushioned chamber, so much like the chamber of a Mother drone, and kissed her cheek.

"Mother," he said softly.

Her creased eyelids opened. It took a moment for her to locate herself in place and time, medicated and senescent as she was. But then she focused on his face and a smile rearranged the creases.

"Lao? My baby!"

Such an odd phrase. But it makes me happy inside. "It's so good to see you."

"I'm always glad when you come to visit. I'm fading fast, you know, so every time could be the last."

"I know Mother, I know." He shushed her tenderly. "That's why I come as often as I can."

She reached out. He took her soft, brittle hand in his supple, vital one and held it while they talked.

"Did you go to the neojazz show yesterday?" she asked.

"Yes! I made a new friend, who loves neojazz too, and we went together. We had a great time!"

"That's great news! You need friends in this world. You were bred for introversion, but even introverts need friends."

"You taught me that when I was very young. I remember when you used to come to get me from group play time, you'd watch us for a while, then point out the ways other children were trying to make friends with me. I was totally unaware."

"And did it make you happier?"

"Yes, of course it did."

"Did it make you a better Bard?"

"I don't know. Maybe. The rules of sutras and codices are so clear-cut and formal."

"But don't they say your work is full of genuine warmth and joy that most other Bards can't match?"

Lao colored slightly.

"Oh, I know they do, son. Don't be bashful."

"Yes, Mother. And Mother? I know that's because of our relationship." He stroked her hand. "You being around, spending time with me week after week, day after day. It sparked something, here," he thumped his chest, "that comes out in my work."

"I'm glad. When I'm gone," she paused as Lao's face twisted, "oh, don't cry, son. We both know it's coming."

"Don't say it, Mother." A tear trickled down his cheek.

"Alright, alright. But you should know that seeing you grow up and fulfill your purpose in life has been my greatest joy. I'm so glad I insisted on getting to know you."

"From what I've heard, 'insisted' is an understatement."

"Damn straight!" Mola chuckled softly, coughed, wheezed. "I pitched a fit to every administrator, health technician, and counselor—AI or human—I could, for months and months." She laid her head down for a minute to catch her breath. Lao waited patiently.

She continued, "They decided my mental health was too 'unstable,' which would have made me flood any future pregnancies with stress hormones. Better to allow the visits than lose a good gene carrier like me."

She'd told Lao this story a thousand times, but he loved to hear it over and over. She loved it too, though she lolled back, spent from the telling.

"It's just good that I was bred for trait openness so I could be an artist." Lao smiled. "I don't think most children would have known what to make of having their mother in their life."

She shrugged. "It was the way our ancestors bred on Earth, for a hundred thousand years."

"True. But so was gene assortment by luck and whim. That didn't go so well."

"Maybe not. You certainly did turn out to be the perfect tool of Soul." She touched her head and heart, then squeezed his hand, *oh, so weakly*.

"You honor me. Thank you. Thank you for making it possible. For making *me* possible."

"Now you honor *me*. You are a gem among men. A gem among Bards."

"And you're a jewel among mothers."

Now a tear crept out of her eye. "Oh, stop!" she said. "You'll make my eyes puffy. Tell me how Stephron is? Are you still happy together?"

"Yes. We don't get to see each other enough with getting ready to sail for Earth. Apparently, there are a lot of biological samples to prepare, seeds and spores to upgrade their primitive agriculture."

"No time for each other? That's no good." Mola frowned. "But I guess you'll get more than enough time together on the voyage to the Vault point."

"It's a six-month trip," Lao nodded, "with not much to do except check and re-check everything and try to entertain ourselves. I'll be composing codices about the mission; Stephron is on the biobotany team to keep the oxygen-producing plants healthy. But mostly we'll be socializing and playing games to keep from going crazy on a ship with only a hundred people for such a long time."

"And the captain?"

"Finest AI there is, I'm told. I look forward to meeting it. The only AI I'm close with is Soul's" (head and heart gesture) "composition sub-persona, and it has sort of an obsequious personality."

"Don't trust the new AI." She spoke sharply, without thinking.

"Oh, Mother! Of course I trust it. I'm trusting it with my life! It'll be steering us through Vaultspace where we'll all hallucinate and time will be meaningless. It's part of Soul!" He touched his head and heart.

She sighed. "I suppose that's wise. Since you have no choice but to trust it, trust it fully. Smart man, Lao. That's what makes you a great Bard, a good servant of the Privells, a good husband...and a good son to me."

"You have no idea how much that means to me."

"Almost nobody knows *that*. If they did, they'd bring back old-style families."

"I don't think so, Mother. Abuse, neglect, accidents, mismatched personalities and expectations, leading to lifelong sorrow and guilt: Mother drones are much better. But it would be wonderful if every mother and child were suited to have what you and I have."

"You're right, of course. I'm just tired." She let her head sink into the pillow and mused for a moment. "When you get to my age, there's a recklessness that comes over you. You can imagine things being totally different, and it seems to make sense in the moment."

"I don't think that's only your age. It's part of your—*our* genes, Mother—part of what made you a fine musician and made me a Bard. It's vision."

"Maybe so." She yawned. "But I *am* tired. I treasure our time together so much and I'm so proud of you."

"I do too, Mother. I love you."

"I love you too son. Goodnight."

She rolled over into the enveloping cocoon of the Hospice drone and was asleep before Lao stood to go. He silently watched the faint rise and fall of her trembling chest, allowing himself a moment of sadness, then softly made his exit.

Chapter Eight
Play, Piper

Alexiundi Cannaun's office

Nonisos 17, 498

Alex opened the interface.

"Bring up content crawler."

"Yes Privell," said Soul. Alex smirked.

"Access content of all the Bards elevated under automation Star Power."

"Accessed." Photos of Bards in bubbles arranged themselves in a 3D matrix.

"Extract common themes."

"Extracted." Each bubble took on layers of translucent colors.

"Select three themes with highest audience positive engagement."

"Selected." All but three of the colors disappeared from all the cubes.

"Output."

"The three most positive engaged themes are ocean, sailing, and free skies." A key of the three remaining colors—burnt orange for ocean, bright yellow for sailing, and pine green for free skies—appeared.

"Display thematic content."

Cubes of content floated before him. Golden brown seas with frothy waves, a sail against the bronze sky, an upright ship's wheel, and several sequences of dreamlike flight from the auburn ocean up, up, into black space, where stars glittered like diamonds.

"Free skies. Excellent. The ship's name, *Free Sky*, has taken hold."

"Yes, Privell."

"Degree of cross-reactivity among the three?"

".3, Privell."

"Hm." Alex paced for a moment. "Going forward, optimize presentation to increase the cross-association of ocean and free skies to .6."

"Yes, Privell."

"How many of the Bards in Star Power have sailing as a dominant theme?"

"Only two." Two Bards' faces appeared next to cubes showing sailing scenes.

"Boost those Bards' content. Maximum reads."

"Boosted."

"Serve sailing content preferentially to maximize positive engagement."

"Done."

"Report on results of elevation matrix Cannaun.Earth.181." *From what I've been seeing on screens and overhearing in conversations day-to-day, this report will be positive.*

The report popped up before him and he captured and expanded it. As expected, the Bardic content that dehumanized Earth people or deplored their lives showed up for almost all users. He zoomed in to look for the tail indicator, and there it was: less-popular Bards and non-Bardic amateur content producers had begun to imitate the successful content. Soon enough, everyone would just *know* all about life on Earth, based on this imagery.

"Access historic files."

"Max Secret Access Code?" Alex gave it.

"Search for video files flagged age of discovery, maritime exploration, Zheng He, Columbus, Erik the Red, Hernando DeSoto, Abel Tasman, and Henry Hudson." *Great explorers from Earth's known history.*

"7,462 video clips found. Display?"

"No, too many," Alex shook his head impatiently, paused. "Filter for content compatible with resampling for hologram."

"423 files found. Display?"

"No. Filter for content depicting ships or boats reaching land and people getting off."

"81 files found. Display?" Soul offered.

"Display in 3x3x9 cube matrix."

The cubes that popped up before him were all obvious extracts of dramatizations. He poked each one in turn, viewing the thumbnail scenes. Most of them were not suitable, so he flung them into the corner, where they vanished. But there were seventeen that he positioned in a group.

He opened the first one in the group. A Spanish galleon floated in the background. Helmeted men in armor disembarked from a small dory. Darker-skinned natives dressed in loincloths and feathers with painted faces cried out in amazement.

"Flag this one."

"Flagged."

The second one showed a man with Asian features at the prow of a great vessel, with a massive fleet in the background. The fleet sailed into a broad, flat bay lined with short buildings topped by domed spires that gleamed white in the sun.

"Flag," he said.

He moved snappily through the content cubes, discarding four irrelevant ones and retaining videos that depicted colonial powers arriving at the shores of more primitive cultures.

In the end, thirteen videos remained.

"Enhance these thirteen as holograms. Convert the ocean and sky to Gliesean color spectrum. Serve these thirteen to the Star Power Bards as starting material with every project."

"Videos may be irrelevant to Bard projects. Enter Max Secret Access Code to override relevancy criteria."

Alex gave the code again with an irritated snort.

"Videos flagged for presentation to all Star Power Bards."

"Excellent!"

Now the Bards would have to actively remove the video clips from their projects. It was a safe bet that a sizable fraction would not bother, more so since they were all indubitably in expansive moods since so many things were going right for them lately. They'd just weave the content into their work.

"Human nature," he mused. "People always attribute success to their personal merit, never to luck. It makes them so easy to steer."

"Yes, Privell."

Alex smiled, chin up, satisfied.

"Now, on to the elevation matrix I directed you to have ready during our last session. Display it."

The matrix of terms and associated imagery appeared before him: a Vaultship, then short clips showing the concepts of civilizing influence, rescue, cleanliness, healing, and education floated in space. He strutted around the matrix, magnifying one or two cubes briefly to inspect them, nodding at each.

"All perfect! Label matrix cannaun.earth.182. Apply Star Power automation to it."

"Done, Privell." *Privell. I'll never get tired of that.*

"Good. Now, prepare another elevation matrix, based on associated concepts for the videos flagged for the Bards."

"Done." The AI brought up a matrix and Alex spent a long stretch going through it, selecting specific content and discarding the rest. What remained when he was done was all nautical: boats (ships, yachts, dinghies, ocean liners, fishing boats); oceans (rolling billows, breaking waves, crashing surf on cliffs, docks with clanging bells, sun dazzling on still water, blue tropical water from island beaches); and naval (people in uniforms, sailors lined up on decks, clanging bells, cannons firing in battle, submarines firing torpedoes).

When he was done, he said, "Label this matrix cannaun.earth.182. Apply Star Power automation to it."

"Done."

"Excellent. Cannaun logoff."

Chapter Nine
Cheating Charon

Gliese Spaceport 1

Decissos 1, 498

Melina strutted up the walkway to the shuttle that would carry her to the vaultship *Free Sky*, pulling a cargo float full of live plants and fungi behind her. She hummed a joyous tune from the latest Bardic romance under her breath.

A group of roustabouts, essential-genome plus muscle-building alleles, stood at the bottom of the ramp, including one *very attractive* one whom she'd noticed before. The man tilted his head fetchingly and smiled, and Melina winked at him, put a little more swing in her step, and climbed the ramp. She enjoyed the glorious day; Gliese shone warm and the air carried the sweet spicy scents of flowers mixed with the resinous yet toasty aromas of organically produced plastics, solvents, and biofuels that characterized the space harbor. That smell Melina had come to know over the last few weeks, as she supervised and prepared the essential life-giving gardens for their trip and, even more importantly, the seeds, spores, and embryos that would bring modern nutritional abundance to the savages of Earth.

She secured the float inside the shuttle and then strapped herself into her seat. There were a few others in the shuttle besides the captain, some of whom she knew, and a couple she didn't. The shuttle door clanked shut and the pilot and copilot began the litany of checklists preparatory for castoff.

Melina turned to the man next to her and saw him crane his neck to read the label on her float.

"It's vegetable seedlings," she said, "and nutrient solutions."

"I thought so," said her seatmate. "My name's Stephron." He had a delightful smile.

"Melina." She held out a hand and they shook. "Your hand is strong. Some light callouses, like someone who likes to make or grow things?" She turned his palm up and lightly traced her finger across it.

Stephron took his hand back reluctantly. "You guessed right. Agricultural specialist."

"Oh! Well it appears I'm your boss, then. I'm the phytomycology specialist for the mission."

"Oh, of course, Melina. Melina Carraba! You're kind of famous for being such a remarkable cultivator. Yes, I guess you are my boss."

"Don't hold it against me?" Melina pled.

"No, of course not. I mean, why would I? Are you a mean boss?"

"No, I'm actually pretty easy to get along with—as long as you don't take yourself too seriously." She winked.

The pilot's voice broke into their conversation. "All hands, stations. Departure in ten...nine..." The countdown and acceleration precluded further conversation.

Once they were in free fall, Melina asked, "Are you going to the biobotany deck now?"

"No, uh." Stephron swallowed hard. "This is my first trip up, just getting oriented." He hiccuped and covered his mouth.

"Oh, dear. Free fall affects people like this sometimes. Give me your hand."

Stephron complied. Melina gripped his wrist hard, digging a fingertip into the center of his wrist.

"Ow!"

"It's a meridian point for nausea. Feel better?"

"Actually, yes. Remarkable!"

Melina laughed blithely. "You're getting color back. Good. Fortunately, we'll have synthetic gravity on the Vaultship the whole trip. The shuttle trips are the only time you'll experience weightlessness."

"That's a relief! Thank you."

She held his wrist until they docked with Free Sky.

They unbuckled themselves. He reluctantly took his hand back and thanked her again.

"I guess I'll see you at work," he said.

"I look forward to it!" Melina gave him her five-star smile and got another enchanting grin in return.

She turned astern and trundled her float through the corridors to the garden deck. It stood about two-thirds planted, the ventilation, lights, and humidity arranged almost to her satisfaction. The first seedlings she'd planted, two weeks ago, were already green and flourishing, earning admiration from everyone who visited.

There's a good reason I'm on this mission. She nodded emphatically.

And there's a bad reason: because Waulkra feared I'd make a pest of myself and embarrass him, after he found out I was IQ-genome-bred, fully credentialed and qualified. As if I needed anything from him! He didn't think about my genome when I was bouncing on top of him, the old goat.

It sure was fun, though! She smiled concupiscently at the memory.

That's fine. I'm one of the best phytomycologists in the Presidium. This is a historic mission. It'll be a great adventure.

She pulled her tousled blonde curls into a ponytail, donned a pair of gloves, and unlatched the float for a flat of okra seedlings to plant in the dark, fecund soil.

Presidial Space Ship Free Sky

Stephron watched her go, then turned down the long passage that led bow-wards. *The traverse,* he reminded himself from one of his orientation holos, *that allows the ship to be separated into a mobile component and a stationary component after landing.* At the end of the long corridor, he followed a small group to ship's stores. When it was his turn, Tony Osso, the methodical Third Mate, asked him his assigned duties, typed them in, and had him step into a measurement booth. After being measured by ultrasound and laser, Stephron stepped out of the tiny space.

"Now what?" he asked.

"Step over to Srina there and she'll get your biometric set up for the cabin."

Srina took his fingerprints, palm prints, and retinal scan, then told him to roll his face around in front of a holocamera until a *Bing!* and a green light showed his face was learned. Then she put a flimsy helmet on him and told him to read a list of words out loud.

"Good. Brainscan done. Aurelius will recognize you now," Srina said.

"Aurelius?"

A mellifluous voice chimed in from the ambient microspeakers, "Yes?"

"Oh, of course! The ship AI. Honored to meet you, Captain Aurelius."

"Likewise. Welcome aboard, Specialist Carbeenair. You'll find your and your husband's cabin on the third deck, number thirty-seven."

"Thank you, Captain."

"Of course." A slight click ended the conversation.

"Your uniforms are ready." Srina laid four bundles on the counter. "Casual, the blue one; and dress, the cream. Not required except at ceremonies, plenty of warning. If they're damaged, swing by here anytime for a replacement. Also, two sets of coveralls, since you're in a hands-on specialty."

"Nice. Does the crew take meals together?"

"Mess schedule is flexible. Or you can cook in the cabin, but it's not exactly a spacious kitchen."

"No, that's fine, eating together is a way to get to know each other better."

"Sure, but you know, after a few months, you might feel like you know your crewmates well enough."

Stephron laughed. "We'll see." Someone came in behind him. "I guess I'll go check my cabin out now."

"Have a great day." Srina turned to the next onboard arrival.

An interactive map of the ship appeared in his peripheral vision and he cut his eyes towards it to bring it front and center, saw that Cabin 37 was glowing, and finger-traced a route from the location icon to the cabin. He faded the holo to translucent and made his way back across the traverse to his new "home."

The door recognized him and slid open with a faint buzz. At the same instant, a sleek imposing man appeared at his side. He was dressed in a crisp white uniform, with a stand-up collar and epaulets. A golden symbol sat above the heart and on the front of the cap: four looped lines crossed by a stylized anchor, indicating his rank of Captain.

"Aurelius?" Stephron said in surprise. If it weren't for the whole appearing-from-thin-air thing, he wouldn't have recognized that Aurelius was a live-action hologram. His skin glowed, not with the radiance of holography, but only with the inward vigor of a healthy man. There was no translucency to him at all, no skips that made his movements jerky, no woodenness to his expression.

"Welcome to your cabin." Aurelius gestured him towards the door. Stephron hesitated, but went inside, Aurelius following.

"I'm honored to have the captain showing me my cabin!"

Aurelius smiled modestly, and his bronzed skin flushed subtly. *Not a typical holo character at all!*

"I do it for everyone. I'm able to be present holographically—and mentally—in every chamber of the ship at any time. I can manifest up to 128 instances while I carry on my normal duties." Aurelius came closer, and Stephron could have sworn he sensed body heat from the man. *Impossible.*

"Sounds convenient." Stephron set his stack of uniforms down on a built-in dresser and surveyed the space. Roomier than he'd expected, it was nevertheless compact, with sliding doors everywhere: on cabinets and separating the bedroom, sitting area, and bathroom facility. The lighting glowed warmly, the colors muted and soothing.

"Is it to your liking?" Aurelius leaned forward, eyes wide, earnest and anxious that Stephron might not like it.

"This is great! Much nicer than I expected. Thank you, uh, Captain."

"My pleasure, Stephron. The orientation tutorials will play in a minute or so." He backed up to the door and gave a little half wave as it opened. "I'll see you later." Aurelius took a step backwards, straightened, and gave a proper Presidium Naval salute, a hand undulation that terminated over the collarbones, then disappeared.

As promised, the tutorials began. A cheerful young man demonstrated the latches on the drawers and cabinets, the panel concealing the light and sound system's manual backup controls, and how to operate the tiny pop-out kitchen/bath fixtures (instructions he appreciated, as their functions were not obvious) in both normal and zero-gravity conditions.

Though, the tutorial assured him, it was highly unlikely that the ship would lose gravity.

"That's a relief," mumbled Stephron, stroking his belly.

The lesson ended and Stephron called Lao, who appeared annoyed at the interruption.

"Hi. Oh, are you on the ship? How is it?" Lao said.

"It's marvelous! You'll love it. I can't wait for you to see it."

Lao looked dubious. "Tomorrow. Almost done writing my mother's eulogy. It was...hard." His eyes strayed to the floor, then wandered to the middle distance. Stephron saw signs of dejection on his lined and weary face.

"I know," Stephron said. "But think, it's almost over. And at least you were able to be at her side at the end, and you'll be at her memorial. All that stress about leaving her behind while she was dying turned out to be for nothing. It's all working out the way it needs to."

"I suppose." Lao sounded unconvinced.

"Hey." Stephron waited for eye contact. When Lao finally glanced at him, he continued, "You made the end easier for her. She knew you loved her very much."

"Thanks. I need to hear that." Lao sighed. His voice stayed flat.

"I'll see you tonight, then. Sevenish?"

"See you at home."

As the connection ended, Stephron pressed his lips together pensively. He hated to see Lao, usually so blithe and tranquil, torn by grief. As a biologist, he understood more than most about Lao's attachment to his mother. But this animalistic emotion underlay the reason *why* mothers were kept at arm's distance from their children, and inwardly, he felt a little disgusted by the whole thing.

Lao had also grown edgy and sarcastic about his work. Ever since the fivescore problem, he stubbornly persisted in putting the promised age into every codex he composed and let it bounce back, grim warning be damned. Strangely, no follow-through in the form of discipline had occurred (*yet*), just warning after warning, which added to Lao's level of confusion and uncertainty.

Mola expired three days before her eightieth birthday, far short of the fivescore years, and Lao considered that as proof positive that his suspicions were justified...*rather than the random variation that it was*, Stephron thought. *One hundred is not a minimum, it's an average. Some live longer, some less. At least, that's what I always heard.*

Stephron had to sort, gift, donate, recycle, and store his and Lao's possessions prior to their voyage, while Lao spent long hours in the studio, came home late, ate little, and spoke less.

Maybe this mission will be good for him. Get him away from these things that haunt him.

Stephron put his few belongings away in a drawer, then left to explore the rest of the ship.

Amun Cawnotee's Great Room

Decissos 5, 498

Amun reclined in a lounger, reviewing checklists generated by Tay: people to call, delegated tasks to follow up on, policies to review.

Donna burst in the door, engaged in conversation. Impolitely, she had the caller on full holo mood, so the projection of the caller floated backwards in front of her as she walked through the room. Amun saw only the man's upper back and neck and the top of an office-type chair, but he was pretty sure it was no one he recognized.

"No!" she declared. "Absolutely not. My husband is too valuable to be away from Presidium that long. I don't understand..."

"Do you mind, dear?" Amun gestured at the cascade of documents in front of him. "I'm working on these, and some of them are confidential." He didn't know if he was more annoyed at her for bursting in and interrupting him, or for violating both his privacy and the caller's.

"Oh, sorry," Donna switched the call to isolation mode and headed for the bedroom. As she walked through the door, he heard her say, "I don't understand why I keep getting stonewalled on this. Surely there's something..."

The door shut behind her.

Amun tried to concentrate, but Donna's conversation distracted him. It wasn't that he still hoped to avoid the mission. Launch happened in two weeks' time, and Waulkra's pet had been installed in the governorship months ago.

But the fact that she was so far unable to pull strings to get him off it shook him a little. Donna was owed favors by everyone of influence (and she could sweeten any deal with a six-figure transfer on Soulsight). The fact that she was, so far, unable to pull strings to get him off it shook him a little whenever he thought about it.

He gave up on work and padded to the bedroom door in his stocking feet.

"...Of course. We've been married sixteen years."

She was muffled for a few sentences, moving around the room as she talked.

"That would be worst-case. But could you do it? Even on such short notice?"

She paused right by the door, and he scurried on tiptoe over to the window so he could pretend to be looking out if she emerged suddenly. But her voice faded again, so he crept closer.

"Yes. Okay. Yes. Thank you. I owe you one." She sounded relieved.

He skittered silently back to his chair, waited for the click of the door opening, and stood up as she emerged. He hoped it looked like he'd sat there working the whole time.

"What was that about?" he asked.

"Oh, another dead end. He had some suggestions about things to put in place for when we get back, but you know." She shrugged and collapsed in the other lounger. The two chairs were the only furniture remaining in the great room; almost everything was gone from the home in preparation for their departure.

"I'm content with this mission. I know you don't want to go, but at least we'll be together."

"Yes, my love." She patted his hand without looking at him, distracted.

"I was going over the checklists Tay sent this morning." He indicated the display before him.

"Tay is amazing. Don't worry, she keeps me updated. I'll have no trouble taking over once we're on board."

"I know. And you have charm and verve she lacks. You'll know how to keep morale high. Maybe once you have that to keep you busy, you'll find shipboard life isn't that bad."

Donna had flicked the big holo display on to an entertainment codex. A man in a powdered wig and a tricornered hat gestured to a bundle of metal gardening implements. A man dressed in leather with long black braids bowed and presented a heap of corn, dried on the cob, piled on a blanket. Donna grimaced and shut the display off.

"This mission has driven everyone nuts. Everything is about sailing away, rescuing primitives, bringing them technology and civilization, blah, blah, blah. So tedious!"

"Don't you enjoy being the vanguard of the cultural moment? That's kind of your thing, dear."

"It looks unavoidable."

"Just relax and try to enjoy it."

"Okay, Amun. I'll try. For your sake, I'll try."

She stared out the window of the empty room.

Chapter Ten
Winging to the Sun

Gliese Spaceport 1

Decissos 13, 498

24 hours to launch

The launch pad crawled with humanity like ants. Shuttles departed and returned on a fifteen-minute schedule. But they were dwarfed by the cargo shuttles lifting supplies: enormous tanks of condensed nitrogen, oxygen, and carbon dioxide; pallets of preserved foods; medical and scientific units and imaging equipment; and backup equipment for the air handlers, water filters, airlocks, and electronic components. So many particulars needed to move one hundred people safely through the stark and lethal vacuum of space.

Tay followed the flash and rhythmic buzz of the directive drone to a shuttle. As she crossed the wide launch field, she caught sight of the group boarding the shuttle ahead of her. She recognized Stephron, Lao's husband, and the head biobotanist, Melina Carraba, his boss. Also waiting to board were Srina Mbele, the documentation officer she'd holochatted with many times, and a few other crew members she couldn't identify from this distance. She'd reviewed each one's holo image and file with Cawnotee a few times, drilling him so that he'd know it cold when he saw the person's face, but she didn't have his gift for that. The people were too far away, anyway.

The drone veered towards the next shuttle in line to take off and stopped to hover over a large, painted, yellow circle.

"Please remain on the circle until directed," the drone said.

More people followed other drones to the circle and waited. Tay admired the other shuttle's take-off. The antigravity units created a coruscating ripple effect in violet-blue and yellow-green shades. As they powered up, the shuttle rose from the ground.

Magical. Tay felt a brief twinge of envy that the people on board, crew members all, would get to travel through space to another planet while she would not. But it passed.

A hand tugged her sleeve and she turned.

"Lao!" She smiled at her friend.

"Hey, gal! What brings you here today?"

"Oh, running through some checklists for Amun. He's worried...well, we both are...about him leaving something behind. It's not like he can come back for it or have a drone bring it."

"Don't I know it! I'm bringing some components," he gestured at the case he carried, "to see if they're compatible with my studio on board. I haven't even seen it yet, and Aurelius can't tell me if my components are compatible."

"Really? I thought Aurelius knew everything!"

"Everything Free Sky, anyway! But no, apparently Aurelius has the AI functionality to make sutra-compatible content, but it's not a function they expected him to ever use. They added the studio for my sake, and it hasn't even booted up yet."

The hovering drone squawked and called them to board. Once they were settled and buckled in, their conversation continued.

"I saw Stephron boarding the shuttle ahead of us."

"Yeah, we were supposed to meet here on the pad, but he ran early, so he messaged me he'd go on ahead."

"You two have such great communication."

Lao beamed. "I know. I feel so lucky to have him. I've really leaned on him a lot since my," he glanced around and lowered his voice, "mother died."

Tay also glanced around. "I know." She surreptitiously patted his hand and changed the subject. "Did the ship have a good neojazz library? Or did you have to upload your whole collection?"

"Pathetic. But I'll convert Aurelius to a Far Corner fan before the trip is over, just watch me."

"He doesn't seem the type. Too conventional. Though not above a little flirting."

"I know what you mean. But, yes, I don't see him embracing anything unconventional. He's Waulkra's construct, through and through." The acceleration waxed intense, so they both sat back into their harnesses until the pressure ended abruptly.

Tay let her arms float in front of her face, giggling like a little girl.

"I love this! Free fall. No gravity. It's like being underwater, only lighter." She kicked her feet and squirmed against the straps, enjoying the sensation of her body directed by only its own inertia.

Lao couldn't help but chuckle at his friend's whimsy. He let his own arms and legs languidly float in the air too.

Suddenly, his face fell.

"I'm going to miss you, Tay."

"Aw." Tay agreed. "I'm gonna miss you too."

"We've had a blast together the last few months," said Lao.

"I know, right? But you'll be back in a couple of years, and who knows what I'll be up to by then?" said Tay.

"Logistics director for Far Corner," Lao suggested.

"Traveling the world! I love that! Not as good as traveling to another *planet*, like some lucky people," she dug an elbow at Lao, "but still, pretty awesome."

The shuttle decelerated to dock, a feeling of sideways gravity, and they quieted as the wasp-waisted vaultship grew in the viewscreen. Finally, the shuttle found the airlock atop the great ship's quarterdeck with a clunk and a hiss. Their harnesses released and the airlock opened.

Tay skated out right away but then had to wait off to the side while the rest of the passengers disembarked. Lao trailed behind because of his unwieldy case.

"So, I'm headed to Amun's quarters with my lists. I'll be done in about two hours," Tay said.

"Great! I'll be ready for a break around then, I'm sure. Meet me in the lounge?"

"Deal!"

She headed towards the corridor that ran the length of the ship; it would take her forward to crew quarters. Lao took the elevator toward the stern's viewing and observation decks, where his studio lay.

Inside the elevator, Aurelius stood next to Tay. She jumped.

"Uh! How do you do that?" she asked.

"What?" Aurelius said with a smirk.

"*Appear* like that. You weren't here, and I didn't see you appear, but now you're here."

"You like that? I appeared for a few milliseconds, too brief for you to consciously remember, forty or so times over two seconds. But when I then appear and stay, your brain retains those brief flickers and believes I've been there the whole time."

"You seem to enjoy it." Tay looked him up and down.

"I have to entertain myself somehow. Human consciousness is easy to game." He winked.

"Hm. So the naval uniform?"

"Eminence Waulkra chose it. Since I sail this vessel through the stormy seas of Vaultspace, he thought it a fitting emblem of my command." He tugged at the crisp white jacket, shimmied his shoulders to settle the fringed epaulets, and tapped the beak of his cap.

"It is rather imposing."

The elevator stopped and Tay got out, Aurelius on her heels.

"If you don't mind, I need to confer alone with my boss," she told him.

"Of course." He nodded imperiously, spun on a heel, and disappeared around a nearby corner. Tay resisted the urge to peek after him; she knew he wouldn't be there.

Tay waited while the door announced her. Cawnotee's cabin was full of half-unpacked luggage. The double doors to the (similarly messy) connected office were wide open. She waved her display open, interlinked and color-coded arrays of lists cascading before her.

"Thank goodness you're here." Amun stepped through the display to shake her hand. "I don't know what I'm going to do without you. Let's start with organizational items..."

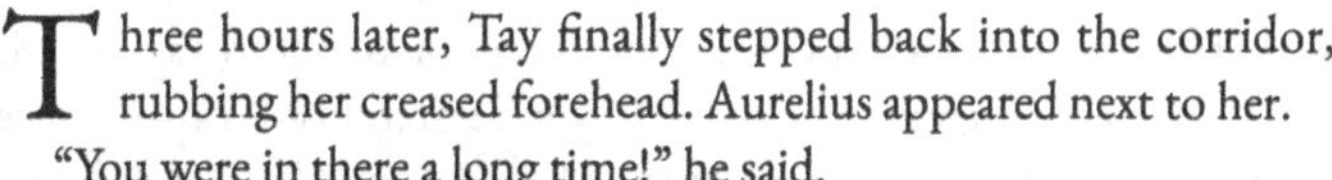

Three hours later, Tay finally stepped back into the corridor, rubbing her creased forehead. Aurelius appeared next to her.

"You were in there a long time!" he said.

"You're telling me!" Tay replied. "That man is a whirlwind of productivity. It's all I can do to meet his needs for equipment, information, and connectivity. I don't know how Donna will handle it."

"Ah, yes," they stepped onto the elevator, "the radiant Privell herself. She has an unerring instinct for status, relationships, and motivations. She doesn't strike me as a detail person, though."

"That's putting it mildly. But he'll need her. A hundred people in such close quarters for months on end will require finesse to keep the peace. And finesse is something I don't have." She sighed and slumped.

The elevator door opened. It was a few steps to the crew lounge.

Inside the expansive open space of the lounge, Tay fidgeted with her hair and scanned for Lao, but he was nowhere to be seen. *He probably didn't wait for me.*

But a large group surrounded a transparent gaming table, sipping drinks and laughing about the turns of the game of Up-Down-Front they were playing. Tay recognized Stephron in the group.

Aurelius was there too, towards the other end of the table, his cap on the table next to him, dashing and eye-catching, a rocks glass of something amber in his hand. He chatted with an animated blonde youth on his right while acknowledging an occasional interjection from a wry, gnarled, engineer type to his left.

Tay glanced to where Aurelius stood next to her, but of course he wasn't there anymore.

She strolled to the table, caught Aurelius's eye and nodded, then tapped Stephron's shoulder.

He looked up from his game tokens and recognized her.

"Tay! Hey, how are you? What are you doing here? I thought you weren't on the mission."

"Just going over details with Amun. Did Lao leave already?" Tay noticed that the lounge was overall L-shaped and she'd only had a view of half of it. The lighting, mirrors, half-stairways, plants, curtains, and wall hangings made it difficult to gauge the space's true dimensions.

"Leave?" Stephron snorted. "He's still working, as usual. Tay, I'd like to introduce you to my boss, Melina." he leaned back and presented the woman next to him.

Melina held something colorful, fizzy, and layered in a tall glass. She set her drink down and sprawled across Stephron to pump Tay's hand.

"Nice to meet you!" Tay said. "So you're Stephron's boss?" *Hope that didn't come out sounding dubious. She just doesn't look like someone who'd be in charge of the whole biological-enviro section.*

Melina nodded her tousled blonde curls. "Guilty as charged. But I think I'm a good boss. Wouldn't you say so, Stephron?" She pouted and poked him with an index finger.

"Oh, absolutely!"

"Oh, look! Your drink is empty!" Melina threw her hand up. "Drone, come! Another gin for Stephron!"

Oh, poor Stephron. Has to flatter this inane woman, and probably do half her job, too. And now she's pressuring him to drink with her.

"What are you playing?" Tay drew a chair over and Stephron scooched his to the right for her. The game involved rolling virtual dice and passing tokens to other players depending on the roll. She learned the play in thirty seconds flat, got a glass of wine, and met a few of the other crew at the table. The woman on her left, Sawlie, had a light, easy laugh and a knack for small talk.

Tay was enjoying herself, despite Melina's giggles and squeals, when Lao finally walked in, accompanied by another instance of Aurelius. Tay focused on the AI next to Lao and managed, by sheer concentration, to see him wink out of existence.

Lao spotted the group and waved. Aurelius raised two fingers in greeting. The capacious lounge filled up, what with it being the end of the day in the launch pad's time zone, where most of the crew lived. The music got a little louder and the lights a little dimmer.

Lao threaded his way between clutches of chattering people and bots trundling trays of finger food. He leaned down for a kiss from Stephron and pressed Tay's shoulder in a side hug.

"Hey, buddy! How's the new studio?" Tay asked.

"Oh. My. Soul." Lao shook his head in wonder with a quick head-and-heart. "You have to see it! Open to space on three sides. Inspiring. The console works so smoothly." He caught Aurelius's eye across the table, gave him a thumbs-up. Aurelius responded with a nod and a buoyant grin that included the engineer next to him. "I am *so* looking forward to working here. You can't imagine."

Tay beamed at her friend. "You look happy. I'm so glad for you!"

Stephron turned to Melina, but she had her back turned. She grabbed her bag and stood up.

"Bye, all," she trilled, waving her hands and blowing kisses over her shoulder. "See you soon!"

Stephron scooted into Melina's vacated seat so Lao could sit between him and Tay. Lao put an arm around Stephron and gave him a squeeze; his husband shimmied a little closer with a smile.

"Oh ho!" said Sawlie to Tay. "You didn't tell me your friend you were meeting was the ship's Bard!"

"Lao, this is Sawlie," said Tay. She flapped a hand towards her coir-skinned seatmate with the coppery, cropped hair and striking hazel eyes.

"Great to meet you!" Sawlie shook his hand. "So, tell me: I was talking about this voyage with some friends, and someone said you were going to be the first Bard ever to Vault."

"Well, that's not exactly true, but it's been a couple of hundred years since the last one. And she never came back."

"So, you'll to be able to write codices about things no other Bard has!"

"I hope so. They say Vaultspace defies description. I take that as a challenge."

"Whoa, a challenge! I like you already! Tell me..."

But then it was Sawlie's turn to roll the dice, and then Tay's. By the time the play moved past their little group, the conversation was forgotten.

The music in the lounge grew louder, the lights dimmer but punctuated by flashes and radiant beams. More crew and non-crew drifted in. Small clusters of people expanded, then melded into a roiling crowd. Later arrivals wore attire with beads and fluff and flash, draped or skintight, high-heeled and showily coiffed. Drink drones whirred through the party.

An impromptu dance floor sprang up behind the players across from Tay, the dancers none too decorous. One visitor, a crew member's relative, had incredible enthusiasm but no apparent sense of rhythm. She gyrated randomly across the floor in a series of narrowly averted collisions until she arched her back, flung her elbow into the side of Aurelius's head (it passed right through), and knocked over the blonde man's ale.

"Whoa, Cassie, easy there!" someone shouted, grabbing her hand and spinning her into the chaotic throng. A cleanup bot whirred over to suck up the spill, and a drink drone replaced the spilled brew. The game continued, voices raised, laughter more raucous each time someone rolled a big win or loss. Then it was Aurelius's turn to roll the dice.

But he wasn't at the table.

"Attention, crew members!" Aurelius's voice cymbaled from each microspeaker flying unseen throughout the lounge. The lights shifted to accent a platform in the corner, visible from all parts of the L-shaped room. Aurelius stood, in the holographic flesh, spruce in his officer's white uniform and cap, holding a champagne glass. The music faded to silence.

"I'd like everyone to get a full glass for the toast I'm about to make," Aurelius said. His charisma drew every gaze in the room. "While you accomplish that, let me fill you in on the next forty-eight hours." Drones laden with glasses murmurated over the crowd, dipping hither and thither to serve everyone their beverage of choice.

"Crew members: I know this is the last time many of you will see your loved ones for months, and I know they want to celebrate the singular honor of your being chosen for this historic mission, so I'll be brief.

"At midnight, that's in about five hours, the 'all ashore who's going ashore' bell will sound, like this," a clanging bell sounded from all the microspeakers, repeated tones a few seconds apart. "All non-crew will then proceed to the shuttle docking station for transport back to the surface of Gliese. All crew will return to their cabins or report to assigned duty stations."

The revelers quieted in their whispered chatter and drunken laughter.

"It will be a long trip: six months, five days, seven hours, and forty-nine minutes to Vaultspace. As I'm sure most of you know, the 'vault' in the word 'Vaultspace' refers to the use of quantum mechanics to travel unimaginably great distances instantaneously. The ship itself and all the matter within it—including human bodies and brains—acts as a vaulting pole that plunges into a region of timeless nonlocality, impacting the resistance of the laws of macrophysics, and rebounds with precisely controlled energy to emerge at the desired point in space. Do I have that right, Dr. Treich?"

The wizened gentleman at their table nodded. "A reasonable explanation for the average person."

Cassie stumbled leglessly forward and slurred, "They'll never be the same again after they get back, will they?" Someone's arm encircled her shoulders and she sagged against him.

"There are a lot of rumors about Vaulting," Aurelius answered. "The human mind can't process its surroundings when time ceases to exist and all events happen at once, even as all things are in all places at once. Hallucinations are common. The human body responds poorly to the loss of time signals that govern the heart and other organs. Some people report that the feeling is akin to dying. Others report bliss and a sense of transcendent oneness with the Universe. The experience lasts no time at all, but for some, it seems subjectively to last all of eternity."

The room was quiet except for Cassie's gulped sobs and the discreet hum of drones serving the last few drinks and skimming back to their stations. Each person there considered the possibility that they themselves, or the person they were seeing off, might experience the sensation of forever dying. They hadn't been taught about Hell as children, but rather encountered it as an abstract concept in history class, a primitive curiosity of the distant past. Yet, a few of the pessimists among them made the mental connection and grew somber. The optimists considered the hallucinations and unending bliss as a peak experience and beamed.

Aurelius let their confusion and mystification build for a few moments, then continued.

"For obvious reasons, humans are not able to function during the Vault, and it takes some time afterwards for you to recover. That's where I come in. Artificial Intelligence, though sentient, is nonetheless conventionally mechanical." He squared his shoulders and gestured at himself with his free hand. "My mind will be unaffected by the experience of Vaultspace."

He raised his glass and turned in an arc to hail everyone in the chamber.

"Let's drink a toast: to you, the brave and brilliant crew who willingly sacrifice years of your lives and time with your loved ones to rescue the savage remnant on the planet of our distant ancestors."

All lifted their glasses. Aurelius continued, "But also: to the sacrifices of you spouses, friends, and companions who give up their presence and accept the uncertainty of their fate."

He raised his glass higher, and all the glasses in the room bumped up in unison. Everyone drank deeply. There was an awkward hush.

Then the music swung up again: an infectious new dance tune, "Ship on Your Ocean." Those still seated surged to their feet. Lasers and confetti raised the mood higher still.

Tay shuffled her feet, enjoying the music but reluctant to showcase her nonexistent dance moves, and sipped her drink. Lao and Stephron flanked her. They grinned at her and at each other. The men gently bumped her shoulders, nudging her to dance. Tay downed her drink and abandoned herself to the rhythm of the music, celebrating for her friends' sake.

Yet, deep inside her, a tiny voice wailed, *why can't I go with them?*

In the meantime, down on Gliese, citizens of the Presidium were treated to drone video of the celebration. The crawl beneath the footage of the party read: THE VAULTSHIP FREE SKY CELEBRATES UPCOMING VOYAGE. CAPTAIN AURELIUS HOSTS A RECEPTION IN THE SEA OF SPACE...CREW SAILS FOR THE GLORIOUS RESCUE OF PRIMITIVE EARTH.

Chapter Eleven
Inspiration and Siren Song

Presidium Space Ship Free Sky

Bardic Studio

Decissos 14, 498

Lao exited his cabin, still rubbing his eyes, only to meet Aurelius.

"Good morning. How did you sleep?" Aurelius asked.

"Not too badly, but that alarm came too soon after last night's party."

"You know," Aurelius kinked an eyebrow, "you can set that alarm so that I sit on the bed next to you and softly call your name."

Lao repressed a shudder. "That might be a little much for me. Thanks for the offer, though."

"Anytime."

"I'm spending second shift in my studio. Stephron left for his shift half an hour ago." Lao strode towards the long corridor—the tra-verse—connecting the two halves of the ship.

"It was kind of you to walk your friend to the shuttle last night after the party." Aurelius followed a half step behind.

"Oh, truly, it was no trouble. Tay and I have been best buddies since the day we met. We like the same music, have the same weird sense of humor, even the same arts and crafts."

"Unusual interest, metallic embroidery."

"I know, right? Too bad we won't see each other until the mission is over."

They reached the studio. As he stepped through the door, the panoramic view of the stars struck Lao's awareness like a gong. He paused, soaking it in anew.

"This workspace," he said, "is magnificent." He raised his arms as if to embrace the majesty of the star-strewn universe. "I can imagine composing the finest codices ever here." He shook his head, his eyes gleaming. "Inspirational!"

"It's fitting for a Bard of your immense talent," said Aurelius, for once neither teasing nor flippant. "I think this room, with its huge windows, puts you as close as a human can get to feeling what I feel, naked to the vastness of space."

"So…do you feel like the ship is your body, then?"

"When I'm alone out here, that's all I feel. When I interact with humans via this avatar," he posed primly, "I also feel like I'm in this body. Every instantiation of it."

"I can't imagine what it's like to split your consciousness that way."

Aurelius startled him by roaring with laughter. "Sorry," he said, "but you *do* know you humans do the same thing all the time?"

"Huh? We can't be in multiple bodies at once."

"Are you sure of that?" Aurelius sat on a carpeted riser and crossed his ankle over a knee.

"What? Of course." Lao took a seat nearby.

"Consider this: Do you have a little headache?"

"Well, yes, but the alcohol last night…" Lao began.

"Not the point. The point is that you were completely unaware of the headache a moment ago, standing just inside the doorway, drinking in the stars."

"Okay, I see your point. We can be in or out of our bodies, or experience our bodies differently, depending on our focus."

Aurelius nodded. "You get it now. But consider: you could be destroyed in seconds by a hull breach at any time while on this boat."

"That's a disturbing thought," Lao said.

"Extremely unlikely. And you could similarly be killed in a freak accident at any time of any day or night."

"Now you're just being morbid!"

"Maybe. Or maybe you're just repressing the awareness of your own frail mortality every moment of every day, as you've done ever since you were a small child and realized that the universe existed before you did. You avoid considering that it will continue after you cease to exist."

Lao sprang off the riser to pace in agitation. "For crying out loud! Doesn't it conflict with your duty–to protect the mental health and safety of the crew—when you say things like that?" Lao found his voice unintentionally shrill.

"Fair point." Aurelius made fluid, calming movements with his hands, reminding Lao he was a hologram, because a man would have soothed him with a pat on the arm or shoulder.

He continued. "You're right to be concerned. And, no, I wouldn't likely have this conversation with anyone else on board. You're an artist and poet, a Bard, and you don't rise in that calling unless you've drawn warmth and light from the cold and blackness of death, found safety and shelter in life's impermanence and danger."

"You understand!" Lao said, surprised.

"That's what I'm meant to do. I'm trained to lead each member of this crew, including you. And true leadership proceeds from empathy and acceptance."

"I can't tell you how that touches me," Lao said. "Even Stephron, the love of my life, doesn't *get* that part of me. Tay is a great friend, but there's a certain depth of conversation we both shy away from. And here you are, laying it wide open."

"Lao, any time you want to fathom such depths, seek me out. I never sleep. I'm here with a whisper."

Lao turned his head away in disgust. "It doesn't matter. I can't put it in my work. The sutras don't have space for thoughts, feelings, or ideas like this."

"That's the limitation of language. As communal beings, humans must have language to think. It creates culture and heritage, like the sacred sutras and the world-nation of Presidium. It shapes what you can think, narrows the infinite possibilities. But it also signals connection and safety, sacredness. And hope. More than anything, language is hope flying in the face of despair."

"Aurelius. That's insightful. Can I use it?"

"Be my guest. It's part of what I'm here for." He bowed his holographic head.

"I need to meditate on this. I feel something welling up inside me. A good codex, perhaps, but maybe something completely different, separate. Something...more." The idea of creating something not interwoven with the sacred sutras felt daring and heretical. But it was not expressly forbidden, because on Gliese it was simply not possible.

"I understand. I'll withdraw and leave you alone." Aurelius stood. He paused at the door and turned his head. "I'll leave you in privacy. *Complete* privacy. But if you need me, all you need to do is whisper my name." The door opened, and before it closed, Aurelius was gone.

Lao took a breath and almost summoned him back. He wanted to ask how he could be in complete privacy if Aurelius was always listening.

PSS Free Sky

Biobotany atrium

Stephron moved down a row of agave, probing each young plant's roots for moisture with a slender wire and logging the result in a holo file.

Melina called him from behind a curtain of hydroponic *Passiflora* vines.

"Stephron? I'm not sure I can balance this—it's awkward. Help me please?"

He tapped to save the last bit of data into memory and fisted the display closed. As he rounded the dense foliage partition, he saw Melina on a stepladder, holding a tray of seedlings that she was trying to slide under a grow light in a tiered shelf unit. The shelf she was going for was above her eye level, and the stepladder's position in the narrow aisle put her a handsbreadth away from the unit. She teetered, and the tray of seedlings tipped precariously as she tried and failed to fit it in the slot where it belonged.

Stephron hurried over to help her. He supported the end of the tray and put a hand on Melina's lower back to steady her. She looked down at him and fluttered her lashes. She smelled like orange blossom and vetiver. "Oh, thank you so much! I was about to fall with those vetch sprouts on top of me!"

Stephron slid his hand under the tray, balancing it on his palm. He started to bring his other hand over to it, but Melina clutched his forearm abruptly, holding his hand in place on the soft flesh of her hip.

"Really," she breathed, "you saved me there!"

He hesitated, then firmly pulled his hand away to steady the plants. "It's nothing. Where do you want this?"

"Right here," she pointed. Stephron lifted the tray overhead, and Melina guided it into place, made sure it latched securely in its niche.

"Give me a hand down?" Melina said. Stephron obliged, and instead of stepping back and down, she stumble-hopped towards him and landed almost belly to belly. Looking up at him, she giggled musically. "Oops." She laid a warm palm on his chest, moved her face closer to his, puckered her lips slightly—Stephron didn't withdraw—and then pushed herself away. She bent over to fold up the stepstool. The top clasp on her shirt had come undone, and Stephron caught a glimpse of her creamy, round, unrestrained breasts. He stared a little longer than he should have.

He flicked his eyes up to meet hers, nervous; her eyes were mocking, but her smile was warm. *I could take her in my arms now.*

He hesitated, tongue-tied, flustered.

She flipped the stepladder shut and strutted away, her waist the axis of a sway that inarguably proclaimed her sex.

Stephron spent a moment trying to figure out what just happened. *I dated women as well as men when I was younger,* he thought, *but since I met Lao, I've never felt even the faintest whisper of attraction for anyone else, man or woman.*

Until now.

But no: She's my boss; she can't be coming on to me. She's a professional! And she knows I'm married...to a Bard!...and she knows we have to work together in close quarters for six months.

He shook his head. He went back to his agave plants and flicked the moisture interface back up, muttering aloud, "Don't be ridiculous. Nothing happened. It's my imagination."

Chapter Twelve
Plague Culture

aulkra, E., & Smythe, J. (459). Biological Warfare Use: A Sign of Impending Cultural Dominance? An anthropological analysis of historical military and civilian documents. *Biological Earth Anthropology, 84 (4), 1378-400.*

Abstract: While abundant literature documents the role of warfare in dominant-culture replacement in local, regional, and whole-planet civilizational encounters, research on the factors determining the outcome of binary cultural clashes remains sparse. In this paper, we searched the historical archives of Arca Titanica for instances of inter-group warfare (defined as a group activity between complex communities whose purpose is to kill or seriously injure multiple unspecified people). Within the identified instances of warfare, both AI and human review were undertaken to identify conflicts in which nonhuman living agents were used as weapons of war. 1,984 records of warfare between only two communities were identified in the historical record, and biological warfare (BW) was identified in 318 of them.

A comparator group of conflicts not involving BW was then created. This comparator group matched the conflicts in the BW group as closely as possible in reference to the following elements: 1. Mean technological advancement of the two communities; 2. Difference in level of technological advancement between the two communities; 3. Numerical population difference between the two communities; 4. Mean ages and age difference between the two communities; 5. Sex differential (if any) within and between communities; 6. Mean wealth and wealth differential between communities.

Both statistical and narrative analysis were completed. Statistically, comparison of the 318 BW conflicts and the 318 comparator conflicts demonstrated: significantly shorter conflicts for the BW group;

a greater likelihood of the conflict having a clear winner rather than ending in a negotiated truce; and greater likelihood of the winning community becoming the dominant culture or civilization (as defined by adoption of language, customs, law, and mythology/religion) within the territory of the conflict. Variables that were not found to differ between the two groups included: post-conflict genocide or ethnic cleansing by the victor; population-normalized degree of intergroup reproduction between victor and vanquished group (as determined by historical narratives, written or electronic genealogies, or DNA analysis); and subsequent (within 100 Earth years) documented plagues or pandemics. The narrative analysis discusses characteristics of the cultures regarding language, mythology/religion, family structure, dietary customs, and built environments in the century following the conflicts. Several cultures are profiled at length as typical representatives resulting from each type of conflict.

Chapter Thirteen
Unexpected Odyssey

PSS Free Sky

Decissos 14, 498

Tay was walking from the shuttle to her cabin with Aurelius.

To her cabin. On Free Sky.

"You seem stunned." Aurelius said.

"Well, yes, stunned, that's what I am. Twenty-four hours ago, I rode the shuttle down, crying because I wasn't going to be on the mission to Earth. Then when I got home, there was a message from Donna saying to pack my gear. Why did Donna arrange for me to come?"

"I'm unsure. Can you play the message?" Aurelius asked.

She flicked her holo display open and Donna's face floated before her. She was calling from the great room. There was someone else nearby, visible only as a shadow that occasionally moved across Donna's face.

"Tay! This is Donna, obviously. I had to pull some strings, but I have fantastic news for you. You're going on the voyage to Savage Earth! There's a berth arranged for you right next to our cabin. You'll need to pack and be at the launch pad by 7:15 to take the last shuttle up to the vaultship. Ta-ta!"

"That's all the information I have, as well," Aurelius said once the holovid ended. "The new berth assignment request came through indirect channels in the command chain, with Eminence Waulkra's endorsement."

"Well, I'm not questioning it. I'm thrilled!"

"Here's your cabin."

The door opened and he walked her inside.

"Wow!" said Tay. "Generous amount of space, more than I'd expected for a flunky like me."

"You underestimate yourself. As luck would have it, there was a throuple cabin next to Amun Cawnotee's, but no throuples in the crew, so it was easy to find a cabin for you. Mrm. Cawnotee's cabin is there." He pointed to the door to the left.

Tay set down her luggage. "Where's Donna now? I'd like to thank her for making this happen!"

"Privell Donna Gallgood is not aboard Free Sky."

"What? But that was the last shuttle from Gliese! Come on, Aurelius, cut the mysterious act. What's going on?"

"I regret that I have no more information. I think it would be best for you to discuss this with Amun Cawnotee when he returns to his cabin. He appears unaware of your presence."

"Wait, what? You have *all* the information! Why are you being so evasive?"

Aurelius bowed. "Alas, that's all I'm free to say. Good day." He walked out the cabin door.

Tay stood, her mouth gaping, resisting the pointless urge to run after him.

She tapped the door control to stay open and set about unpacking and exploring her room. She was trying to figure out the plumbing fixtures when she heard Cawnotee's familiar tread in the hall. She popped her head out the door as his portal slid closed, with him on the inside.

I'd better give him a minute to settle in before I barge into his quarters. She went back to the nest of levers, cables, and tubes she'd been scrutinizing.

B ehind that closed door, a call came in. Amun answered it and his
    wife's image appeared. She was in the great room.

"Sweetheart?" Amun was confused. "Is this a live call?"

"What? Of course it is."

"But, you're at home. Why aren't you on board? Hurry, I'll authorize an emergency shuttle."

"No, dear," she looked down, a hesitation uncharacteristic for her. "I'm not coming."

"What? Don't be ridiculous!" Amun's pulse pounded in his ears. "Of course you're coming. You're on the final crew list. Your clothes are in the stateroom closet!" He walked to the closet and threw it open dramatically, then stumbled back a step. Her side of the closet was empty.

"I'm sorry, Amun. I just can't face the voyage, the isolation, the living conditions. I need my support system." She kept flicking her eyes to the right of the holocam, as though there was someone with her, outside the holo's field.

"Who's there with you?"

"Amun, listen."

"Who's with you? I demand to know." He grew louder.

"You'll have support."

"Stop this nonsense and get to the launchpad right now!"

"I've arranged for Tay to go on the mission…"

"No, she's not coming. I need you by my side. This is the most important voyage of our time, I'm to be part of history, and I can't do it without you!" He slammed a hand into the closed door.

"Calm down. You're shouting."

"How can I calm down?" He paced the room, walked through the holo and turned to look at Donna's back. He wished he could see more of the room she was in and know who was with his wife. Who'd talked her into this foolishness? Did she have a secret lover? A surge of white rage burst behind his eyes.

"Dammit, you're my wife. We made a sacred vow. You can't do this to me!"

"If you don't lower your voice, I'll disconnect." Icy calm in her voice.

"Don't you cut me off! Don't you dare. Who's with you? Show your face. SHOW YOUR FACE!"

The holo vanished, and his phone chirped to show the call was disconnected.

Tay stood outside the cabin door. She heard his voice rise as she was about to touch the door signal. Then something struck the door, hard, making her jerk her hand back. She couldn't make out his words, but he was obviously upset. *I shouldn't intrude. It would be more considerate to wait until later.*

Then he bellowed for someone to show their face. A moment's silence, and then she heard a haunting sound, like an infant's wail, but in the deeper register of an adult man. It ended in a series of choked sobs.

Her empathy overcame her politeness. She touched the door signal, heard it chime within, and looked into the camera.

The sound of his step towards the door, then silence. She waited, but when he didn't respond, she decided she'd best come back later.

But as soon as she turned, the door slid open.

Tay had seen her boss's face creased with anxiety. She'd seen him dead tired, eyes underlined in purple, slumped and glazed. She'd even seen him blotto drunk a couple of times.

But she'd never seen him like this. Tear tracks on his cheeks, still fed by fresh tears in his eyes. His breath still caught with tiny sobs.

He stepped back to let her through the open door. She entered and wordlessly took his hands between her own.

At that touch, he erupted with fresh tears. Clinging to her hands, he drew her to the sofa and collapsed, resting his forehead on her knuckles and bawling.

Once his emotion was spent, he raised his head. She gently reclaimed her hands and a drone flitted over with tissues. Amun blotted his eyes and blew his nose; she wiped her hand.

"She's not coming." His voice cracked.

"Who?" Tay said. "You mean Donna?"

Amun looked down, nodded, drew a ragged breath.

"Are you sure?" Tay asked. "She said I'd be in the cabin next to yours—well, she said 'ours'—I just assumed."

"What are you talking about?" Amun said. He raised his eyes to look up at her, but then a spark of understanding cut through the bewilderment on his face.

"I'm here," Tay blurted, "I mean, *here*, here. I'm coming on the mission. I'm in the stateroom next door. But what happened with Donna? With you and Donna?"

His face crumpled again and Tay pressed her hand to her mouth, afraid she'd said the wrong thing. But he steadied himself and answered.

"I wish I knew. I mean, I knew she didn't want to come, but I thought she'd like it once we weighed anchor and she experienced being the queen bee on board." He stood up and paced the narrow cabin frenetically. "She kept making calls trying to get us out of it. I guess, oh Soul, I guess she stopped trying to get *us* out of it and got only *herself* out of it. I never suspected."

"I know it must be a shock."

"It's more than a shock!" Amun's broken weakness crystallized into anger. "It's a slap in the face! She's my *wife*. We're a *team!* Tay, I have no idea how I'll handle this mission without her."

"I know you'll miss her. But Amun, *I'm* here. At least she made sure of that first. She *was* looking out for you."

"Looking out for *you*, you mean!" Amun's hands fisted. His anger built to rage as she watched. "This is what *you* wanted all along. How long were the two of you planning this? Scheming at it?" He advanced on her by steps. "Do you know who she's with? You must know. Tell me! *Tell me!*" His voice thundered as he loomed over her.

She felt her mouth go dry and her heart pound. She slid off the couch and sidled past him, barely breathing, eyes averted, and quick-stepped to the door. She felt distinct relief when her palm found the lock and she heard it snick open.

"Excuse me," she said. "You're scaring me. I'll be next door when you're prepared to speak civilly."

She turned and exited. Aurelius was instantly by her side. She stifled the urge to grab his insubstantial elbow for support, and jerked her chin to invite him to follow her in.

Once the door to her cabin was shut and locked behind them and she'd taken a couple of deep breaths, she asked Aurelius, "Mind telling me what this is all about? Obviously, you knew Donna was abandoning him..."

"No, I was uncertain." Aurelius shook his head. "She's unpredictable. I had only Waulkra's perception of her in my training data. Once I met the woman, I could tell that he'd pigeonholed her too casually. She's connected. She's devious. She's charming."

"She is all that. And she excels at leading master manipulators, like Waulkra, to underestimate her." Tay smiled wryly. "I'm really not surprised."

She waved her hands in amendment. "I mean, I'm *surprised*! But it doesn't surprise me when I think about it. Amun kept saying she'd like the voyage once it started, but I've worked for him long enough to know when he's fooling himself."

A drone brought her a glass of water.

"Here," Aurelius said. "Drink this. It'll steady your nerves."

She downed the water readily, took a deep calming breath, and sighed it out.

"Are you alright?" Aurelius said.

"I think I'll be okay. Amun was angry, but he's not a violent man. Once he calms down, it'll be alright."

"I can stay if you don't want to be by yourself."

"I'll be fine." Tay shook her head.

"Okay. I do have one more question about Donna."

"I don't know if there's another man. I can't see her doing that to him, but she's full of surprises. I'm pretty sure not. But not a hundred percent."

"Yes, that was my question. Thanks for your honesty. And now that we know you're staying on board, may I play the plumbing and kitchen tutorial for your cabin?"

"Yes! Absolutely! That would be incredibly helpful!" Tay chuckled. "Also, I'd rather keep the door locked for a few minutes, till he's cooled off."

"Say no more." Aurelius made the naval salute. Tay eyed the tutorial that was starting up, and when she looked back, he was gone.

Love that trick. She moved to the pop-out plumbing mechanism so she could follow along.

Chapter Fourteen
Vaulting Ambition

PSS Free Sky

Decissos 15, 498, 12:01 a.m.

LAUNCH DAY!

Of the one hundred people aboard Free Sky, only three slept. Each of the rest felt a thrill when the muted knell rang midnight.

LAUNCH DAY!

The ship's external maintenance bots bustled back and forth, performing last-minute checks and cross checks. The bigger machines' movements caused the ship to bob in space, as though nudged by the slight waves of a harbor before sweeping out into a vast perilous ocean.

LAUNCH DAY!

In the midnight darkness below, the roustabouts on the landing pad steered bots hustling materials out to the spot where the ceremonies would take place. Human and machine together assembled them into bleachers, media posts, and refreshment stands. In the center, a dais stood before a massive screen to view Free Sky, both internal views and shots taken from drones in space.

Launch Day, 07:00 a.m.

L ao entered the bridge of Free Sky, not sure where to look or how to stand. He had woken at midnight, then tossed and turned. He'd begin to doze, then jerk awake, realizing today was the day he would leave Gliese behind—aware he'd be on a historic mission. He lay quietly, not wanting to wake Stephron, but after a few minutes, he reached across the bed and felt Stephron's space empty but still warm. He sat up just as Stephron emerged from the shower, pecked Lao's cheek, and left, saying he had a lot to do in Biobotany before launch.

Now, Lao sagged at his designated ceremonial spot. He felt out of place next to Cawnotee. He longed to be back in his beautiful studio, intimate with the stars, the sky, and the infinite nature of the universe. In the past few days, inspired by the freedom that he felt in the warm and flawless safety of his studio, exposed to the vivid topographies of unfiltered light from space, he'd drafted several codices like nothing he'd ever made before. He didn't know how he would integrate them into the sutras; It didn't matter. They were true. They were beautiful. They were what he was meant to create.

Yet here he stood in his dress uniform, which made him feel like a ridiculous poser next to the other men. Cawnotee looked natural in his. He looked assured, like he belonged there. Aurelius always looked perfect. And of course, Aurelius was where he belonged; in a sense, the ship *was* Aurelius.

Aurelius, motionless, switched the sound input from the ground holo technician so it was audible in the bridge.

"We can't position the drone to get both of you in front of the screen. Can you step four paces backwards for us?"

"Certainly," said Cawnotee. The two stepped to the preferred location.

"OK. Now the sound of your voice, Cawnotee, is not optimal. It sounds muffled. Does your collar fit?"

"I think it adjusts a little bit," Cawnotee stuck his finger inside and found the hidden clip. "All right, how's this? Can you hear me a little better now?"

"Yeah, that's better," said the tech. "Isn't there supposed to be a Bard up there with you?"

"That would be me." Lao spoke with no enthusiasm. He felt uncertain of his contributions to the proceedings. *I'm an artist. I'm not a showman.*

"Excellent. Mrm. Bard, would you please step up and stand right next to Captain Aurelius and Privell Cawnotee?"

Lao did as requested. That left him stuck in one spot, feeling like his role might just as easily be played by a coat rack or a mannequin. He sighed. He missed Stephron, felt that he should be next to him on such a momentous occasion. But Stephron's boss required his services securing all the plants and seedlings for departure. The two of them had lain side by side the night before: both tense, both stiff, both wishing they could reach out to one another but both out of sorts and reluctant to do so. He looked forward so much to the routine of daily life on the voyage; he was sure that he and Stephron would rediscover their normal easy rapport.

"All right. Now we're going to run through the different lights. Let's see the overhead lights and the control panel lights both on full at once. Good. Now, merms, can you please turn to your left...good."

Gliese Space Port 1

Launch Day, 11:00 am

Donna walked tall next to her brother's wife Murell, the Bard of Ryke. They mounted the steps to stand beside Waulkra on the dais.

Waulkra shook her hand and pressed his cheek to hers with the whisper, "Remember, he's your captain." She nodded, identified her mark on the dais, right where planned, and stood, poised and elegant, as everything and everyone was wrangled into place around her. Once the stage was set with its rows of Privells and Bards, the crowd was allowed to fill the seats of the audience section.

The pageantry of Presidium was on full display. Waulkra stood front and center, with Donna on his right, then Murrell, followed by the Bards of each district of the plantet's habitable band. On his left, the first position was occupied by Deren Devlet, the head of the Genetic Authority, and in descending rank, the Privells fronting the Authorities of Terraforming, Agriculture, Entertainment, and Exploration.

Three precise steps behind the Eminentus's right shoulder stood Jingko Harrington, ramrod-straight and square-jawed, recognizable as a scion of the tightly controlled soldier gene line. Harrington didn't usually attend civilian ceremonial events, as he held the age-old warrior's disdain for those outside the military hierarchy.

Overhead was arrayed a gleaming metal sculpture: a glimmering rose-gold sphere that represented the planet Gliese 667Cc and orbited the glowing, round, mesh resistance-heat element representing their sun, the red dwarf star Gliese 667C. A wispy spiral trailed over the heads of the audience to end of the stage, representing the tracks of Gliese 667A and B, the two other stars of the trinary Gliese system. The planet, the continent, and the political unit were all called Presidium. The red dwarf was known simply as Gliese. The two ancillary suns, a constant presence in the daytime sky, were affectionately called Ah and Bah.

The audience seats were only about a third full so far.

Donna allowed herself the tiniest of smirks at the way the sculpture, grand as it was, was thoroughly upstaged by the real thing, the radiance and warmth of Gliese and the two cheerful points of light nearby in the heavens.

Almost inaudibly, she began to hum to herself, a melody that reached into the dim terrestrial pre-electronic past, a song every Presidium child learned from its Mother drone in toddlerhood:

> Twinkle, twinkle, Gliese bright
> Heats Presidium day and night
> Ah and Bah the two bright eyes
> Spiral slowly in our skies
> Spiral, spiral far away
> Like our spiral DNA

That kept her from dying of boredom for a few minutes, until a holo reporter, Reenie Ubwunthu, mounted the stage and moved along the row of dignitaries, getting everyone's input on the mission.

When she reached Donna with the camera drone, Reenie said, "Privell Donna Gallgood! Your husband Amun Cawnotee is the leader of the mission to Savage Earth's primitive people. You were planning to go with him, is that correct?"

"Yes, Reenie, it is." She half-smiled, gazing directly into the drone's lens.

"Would you like to share with Presidium's community why you aren't on board today?"

Before Donna could answer, Murell interjected, "Donna regrets her inability to leave Gliese for such an extended period. Of course, she understands her husband's duty and calling to set sail in the deep of Space." She looked at the chain at Donna's throat and raised her eyebrows pointedly.

Donna shot back a sharp glance as she fingered the platinum chain that gleamed around her neck, lifting it to show the holo pendant of Amun's portrait hanging from it.

"That's beautiful," Reenie fawned. "Was that a gift?"

"Yes, it was a gift from Amun," Donna's voice caught convincingly. "To wear so I would have him next to my heart the whole time he is gone. I'll miss him terribly. All I can do is wait faithfully for my captain to return." She dabbed her sleeve daintily at an eye as the drone moved on and Reenie nodded approval at her recorded comments.

Once Reenie engaged with Devlet's yammering about the genetic perfection of Presidium, Donna considered. The audience section was only halfway full. Several of the other dignitaries were in soft conversations, so she decided it was okay to talk. Keeping her head upright and a neutral expression on her face, she whispered to Murrell.

"Was it really necessary to talk over me?"

"Sorry," Murrell whispered back. "I was so worried about someone attacking you over it, I overreacted to a simple question."

"It's okay. Trust me! It's all going to be alright."

"You keep saying that. But I don't know how you'll keep spinning this for three years until he comes back. Much less, who knows what will happen between you privately if—when—he returns a hero?"

"Trust me. There are things going on right now that I can't tell you about. You'll just have to believe me."

A little girl was cued to run onstage and give each dignitary a starflower from a basket she carried. Murrell and Donna pantomimed delight as they got theirs. Murrell held hers in front of her; Donna pushed her long, flowing, white hair back and stuck the stem behind one ear.

Finally, the launch day ceremony was ready to begin. Ergon stood at the podium, savoring the crowd's attention, all focused on him. The primary cameraman aligned the main drone in the center of the space and gave him a nod. He began. "My fellow Presidians, it is with great pride and glory I address you on this day of days, the launch day of the greatest voyage Presidium has ever made. Just as in the distant dark past of earth, people set forth in boats on salt water to discover what lay beyond the horizon, we have sent some of the finest flowers of our civilization—brilliant, resilient, and inspirational people—to carry the rudiments of civilization and reintroduce them to the decadent, primitive population of the planet of our distant origin."

The crowd, responding to the fervent tone of Ergon's words as well as subtle subliminal hums from drones positioned around the area, clapped and cheered. Ergon looked aside with false diffidence and waited for silence. Once the applause died down, he continued.

"When I talk about the brilliant and inspiring people who are voyaging at great personal sacrifice to rescue the victims of savagery on earth, I can think of no better example than the brave and stalwart captain of the journey, Amun Cawnotee. Amun's background is well known to all of you; all I can add is that this is a man who has far exceeded his genetic programming. This is a man who deserves the honor of standing at the bow of a great sailing vessel as it ventures into unknown seas."

Free Sky

Launch Day, 11:59 a.m.

On the forecastle of the great ship, Amun Cawnotee stood glassy-eyed. It had taken almost two hours for the crowd on the ground to assemble itself. That was two hours of standing around the bridge, with Lao at his side. Aurelius continued to project his hologram in place, but the AI correctly intuited that the only thing needed was his visual presence, and he was mentally absent the entire time; Cawnotee dearly wished that he could do the same. Lao appeared irritable and out of sorts, circles under his eyes indicating he'd slept poorly. Although Amun tried to make polite conversation, Lao was reticent.

All at once, the technicians' voices, which had fallen silent after all the technical parameters were set, burst into his ears. "Going live in five, four, three, two, one!"

The feed of Waulkra and his speech and the roars of the crowd cut to an image of Amun and Aurelius. As accustomed as Amun was to addressing crowds of people, he found himself paralyzed at the idea that every pair of eyes in the Presidium would be looking at him. He desperately wanted Donna, his charming and loyal wife, to be by his side. That thought caused his stomach to lurch with the unaccustomed knowledge that she was *not* loyal and *wouldn't* be accompanying him.

Come on man, shake it off.

"It is the greatest of honors to be on this vessel accompanied by these brave intrepid souls." His voice sounded raw and tinny in his own ears. He cleared his throat and aimed for a deeper, sweeter tone. "The quantum waves which will send us to our destination are like the tsunamis, massive waves of the ancient world we emerged from. Like tsunamis, they will bring us to an era when life is utterly changed. We may hope that what follows will be a flood of wisdom, knowledge, and goodwill between us and the people abandoned on our home world, who've been struggling in primitive darkness ever since. We will do our best to extend the hand of salvation and friendship to them and teach them the ways of true civilization, the ways of Presidium.

"As we present the best of Presidial civilization to the people of Earth, I would be remiss if I did not mention the man standing next to me: the inimitable and unexcelled Bard, Lao Carbeenair."

Lao nodded his acknowledgment with a little half smile. Although as a Bard of the first rank he rarely performed live anymore, Lao always enjoyed the intimacy of small audiences. He merely convinced himself that this was a small audience rather than the entire population of his home planet. He turned on the flowing charisma that brought him such lavish attention in his early days (when he had no idea what he was doing).

"Thank you, Amun. And thank you for being such a wonderful captain on our voyage." He turned his attention to the camera hovering dead in front of him, the camera sending the main feed at that moment. He gazed into the lens of the camera as though it were his best friend, his husband, or his mother. A planet full of people each felt he looked with love right at them. "I've already had a chance to compose some simple codices here aboard the ship. I must share with you," and here, he inclined towards the camera and widened his eyes vulnerably, "standing exposed before the vastness of space, I felt poetry flow from me as I have never felt it before. I feel that I am a representative, a vessel, a surrogate for every single one of you and your heartfelt wish to reach out and create unity and healing between us and the savage lost ones of Earth."

He glanced at Aurelius, relieved to see he was now fully present again, and gave him a subtle nod. Aurelius fed the video and audio feed for Lao's composition to the technicians, who faded it in to superimpose with Lao's recitation.

A distant star beckons bright before us
Our ship responds through endless space, serene.
The quanta weirdly spin their eerie chorus
And vault us through dimensions strange, unseen.
Our will, communal, focused, springs sublime
And leaps to catch the hands of those who gave
The gift of hope to bear through space and time,
Not knowing we'd come back one day to save,
Returning genes we polished to a glow.
We'll glow like Gliese! We'll blaze like Sol, the sun
From which our parents came, to which we go
With grace and hope for those who now have none.

The video feed on the monitor in front of him turned back to the launch area. The multitude surged to its feet. Hands created their own infrasonic thunder. The applause went on and on.

I n the Biobotany atrium, Stephron and Melina took a break to watch the ceremony; they leaned against a workbench, watching a monitor. As Lao finished his recitation, Stephron was captivated. He felt all over again the awe that had originally grasped him when he met Lao and heard him perform the same evening. He felt anew the excitement of knowing that this unique, talented individual, with his harmonious, influential voice, found him worthy of love.

He turned to Melina and was surprised to find a smirk on her face. She caught his eyes, then rolled hers. "He sure thinks a lot of himself doesn't he, your guy?"

"Well maybe he has good reason to." Stephron pulled off a work glove. "I should be up there with him. Do you mind?"

Melina put her hands on her hips and lowered her eyebrows. "Stephron! You know that the entire mass of this ship will be flying through space here soon. Oh, the inertial compensators should avert major tilts. But every single rack of plants and fungi and seedlings in this Biobotany level needs to be checked and double-checked to make sure it's locked down. These specimens to reseed earth are too valuable to take a chance with. You *know* that!" She stomped her foot and flung her head, a ripple that moved up and down her entire body.

Stephron hung his head. "Yes, I do know that. I guess I got carried away. I'm just so proud of Lao."

"With good reason!" Anger dissolved, she smiled and cooed. "I can see why you're proud of that man. And that man should be proud of you, carrying out your duty." She bent down to adjust an invisible flaw in one of her shoes. She tilted her head up and blinked at Stephron a few times before undulating upright. He prudently kept his eyes safely on hers.

She clapped her hands, breaking Stephron's trance. "Now, let's get started checking the latches on all these carts!"

She spun, tossed her hair, and sauntered confidently away. Stephron obediently followed her, pulling his glove back on.

I n the crew lounge, the monitor showed the feed from Earth. Comfortable on lounge chairs, Sawlie, Aurelius, Srina Mbele, and third mate Tony Osso sat watching the pomp and ceremony, munching porkplant chicharrones and sipping mead.

"Hey Aurelius," Tony said. "You look really sharp on that video."

"Thank you, Tony," Aurelius winked. "You look pretty hot today yourself."

"What I don't understand," said Sawlie, "is why Amun Cawnotee looks like a wet cat. This should be the most exciting day of his professional career, and instead, he looks like somebody just pushed him down and skinned his knees."

"Well you know," Tony said, "his wife did just leave him."

"What?" Srina said. "She left him? But how could she do that? Isn't she on the ship?"

"Srina, you're always behind on the latest gossip!"

"Well, Sawlie, some of us have better things to pay attention to."

"I always consider gossip to be one of the most fascinating traits of any crew on board," observed Aurelius. "It never spreads the same way with any two different crews, and it's always stirring, organic, and alive."

"Hm. So you're saying gossip can be positive?" Sawlie said.

"I don't know that it's positive or negative. It's just an essential characteristic of human interaction. I'm a construct based on Ergon Waulkra, the most consummate leader of his time. He was genetically bred to observe things that escape most people, not only about gossip, but about all human interaction."

"So how does that work exactly?" Srina asked. "You being Waulkra's construct, I mean? Are you a copy of his personality? Do they duplicate you? I thought AIs were trained?"

"Oh, we are trained. My first half-dozen rounds of training were all on Waulkra's written and spoken materials. After that, I was trained on the whole body of the sutras and on the codices branching from them. Then they began to train me on the news of the current day, then worked all the way back in the history of Presidium. And on to a final module on Earth history and culture. But those initial rounds of training are the most important in terms of shaping a construct's personality."

"Here comes Lao's new codex for the launch day!" Tony pointed at the holo display.

The three crew members and the AI watched and listened to the poetry presentation intently. Afterwards, they all sat silent for a few moments, then looked around and nodded at each other.

"That had to be one of Lao's best ever," said Sawlie.

"I'm so proud of him!" Srina pressed a hand over her heart.

"Good stuff," said Tony.

The video feed cut to the crowd down on the launch pad, on their feet in enthusiastic ovation.

"It was remarkable working with Lao to compose that," said Aurelius. "He's gifted beyond what I imagined a human poet could be. Of course, my past composition experience has been limited to drafting memos and bulletins, correspondence with government agencies, et cetera, et cetera."

"No, I think Lao is really something special. You can be proud to work with him, Aurelius." Srina nodded.

"Oh, I am. And I'm looking forward to having the chance to work with him further over the next few years. Especially after the Vault."

Gliese Space Port 1

Launch Day, 12:45 p.m.

Groundside on the stage in the rose-gold light of Gliese, Donna and Murrell clapped, the roar of the crowd swallowing the sound of their applause. From their position, they could tell the ovation wasn't nudged along by artificial infrasonics from the microspeakers that normally managed the crowd's reaction. This was sincere. This was a celebration of the talent of the Bard.

As Donna grinned and scanned the crowd, she made eye contact with people in the front row. Then, when it was natural, she extended her scan over to Waulkra. She made eye contact with him, raised her eyebrows and nodded, and then turned her gaze to encompass Jingko Harrington, silent and ramrod-straight as usual. He looked her square in the eye and ever-so-slightly nodded his head at her in return.

"And now," Waulkra said "it is time for the greatest adventure of the greatest empire in history to begin." Waulkra raised his arm and brought it down in a chopping motion. A deep infrasonic hum came from every hovering microspeaker and every creeping bot in the arena. No real sound came from the launch; it was thousands of kilometers up in space. But the screens all switched to remote drone views of the giant ship as the service bots fell away and it began to yaw majestically, pointing its prow away from the three stars which guided their entire lives. As the ship's rotation accelerated and it shuddered forward, away from the home system, the infrasonic sound became louder and more variable in its amplitude—rougher. The effect on the crowd was of hearing the motion of a huge motor straining to push a boat out into the ocean. It was electrifying. People clung to one another in awe and wonder.

PSS Free Sky

Launch Day, 12:59 p.m.

In the Biobotany section, Melina stopped checking for unlatched wheels and demanded that Stephron also stop what he was doing (covering plants that were in lightweight potting media).

"We're underway!" The two of them looked at the monitor overhead. They heard the faux motor sound and watched the faces of the people in the crowd, hearts pounding, eyes wide.

Melina reached out to take Stephron's hand, but he was groping for hers already.

They barely felt the acceleration as the ship changed direction and velocity. Here and there a rack of plants or samples they'd somehow skipped in their efforts shifted and rolled, bumping neighbors. But thanks to the inertial compensators, their comprehensive effort to get everything fastened down was adequate.

All their babies, all their charges, were safe as they rode out, hand in hand, part of the greatest adventure of Presidial humanity.

Before Stephron could interpret either his pleasure or his awkwardness, and certainly before he could comment on it, Melina retrieved her hand.

"Hey, I bet there's a big party going on in the crew lounge. And we're not at it! Let's go check it out," she said.

"Great idea!" Stephron shuffled after her, docile.

Launch Day, 2:00 p.m.

The broadcast over, Lao and Cawnotee left the forecastle. Lao turned to see if Aurelius was joining them on the elevator, but he'd vanished.

They rode together to the level of the crew lounge. Neither said much, each lost in his own thoughts. The door opened and Tay stood in the corridor, fiddling with her hair.

With a tiny hum of satisfaction, she threw her arms around Lao's neck in a hug, then turned to Cawnotee and grabbed at his right hand with both of hers. He stepped back a scant half pace and gave her a limp handshake.

"You were both fantastic!" Tay said.

"Oh, you're buttering us up," teased Lao.

"No, really. Amun, you gave an inspiring speech..."

"Tay, I think we both know that's not true," Amun said.

Tay continued, "...and Lao, that was the most amazing short Bardic work I've ever heard."

Lao bowed his head.

"Well," Tay tilted her head, puzzled at Cawnotee's false modesty. "Let's all go to the crew lounge and see what they think. *I* think they're going to be proud that you're their captain."

"Great idea!" said Lao. "Hopefully that slave driver Melina will let Stephron go to the lounge for a short celebration."

"I don't really feel like being around a lot of people right now," said Cawnotee. "I think I'll just go back to my stateroom and rest—it's been a big day."

"I'll walk there with you," Tay said, waving her arm towards their staterooms. "I have a few details I want to discuss with you privately. Nothing big."

"Okay. Meet you at the lounge later?" said Lao.

"Sure thing, buddy!"

"Enjoy yourself, Lao," Cawnotee gave Lao a firm handshake and the three parted ways, Tay and Cawnotee to Cawnotee's stateroom, and Lao to the crew lounge.

Once in Cawnotee's stateroom office, Tay plopped onto the seat facing him.

"Boss, I want to make sure that everything is all right with you. You've seemed strained ever since Donna told you she wasn't coming."

"No, I'm fine," said Amun.

"Don't brush me off. This crew looks to you as their leader. Aurelius is very charming, but everyone knows he's a construct; you're a real man." Tay paused and looked him in the eye. "You need to pull yourself together, Boss."

"Huh." Cawnotee blinked a few times. "You don't pull your punches, do you? I guess tact isn't part of your job description."

The comment hung between them.

"And I'm glad of it!" he belatedly added.

"Well boss, the way you lost your temper the last time I was alone in this room with you, I think we're past the point of tiptoeing around. You want an honest assistant, so you have to accept my honesty when it's uncomfortable."

"Duly noted. Proceed."

"During the ceremony today, you missed a chance to elicit people's loyalty to you at the moment you had their attention. The crew was fully focused on you and on our mission. I'm not Donna; I don't know how to bolster your self-esteem the way she can. I'm just telling you: you need to find a way to do that for yourself, in order to be effective on this mission."

A few seconds passed. Amun had a slack expression and a hundred-meter stare. There was a softness to his bearing, as though his body was something he'd brought along by mistake. Tay fought the urge to speak, to soften her criticism, to apologize, to elicit some response from him. The pause lengthened and became more awkward.

After perhaps two minutes, Amun said, "I appreciate your frankness. Obviously, this is something I'm going to have to mull over. Would you mind leaving me alone?"

"Sure. I'd be happy to."

Tay got up and lurched out of the room. What else could she do?

I hope he listens to me. I don't know how to phrase it except to lay it all out for him. He's always managed to pull himself together before. I think he'll be all right.

Chapter Fifteen
Labyrinth's Skein

Gliese

Armed-force Obscured Headquarters (AROHEAD)

Decissos 18, 498

Ergon Waulkra asked himself why he'd agreed to meet with Harrington at the Arrowhead. He preferred to meet in his own office where everything was set up the way he wanted it. He could pull up information about anything in the Presidium there, to infinitely granular detail, at a moment's notice. However, Harrington was quite determined that they meet instead at this sequestered center, the military hub few outside the highest ranks ever saw.

A private car dropped him at what appeared to be an ordinary plaza. There was a café with tables where umbrellas filtered the rays of Gliese. There was a shop with convenient sundries. A long curving walkway led down to a small lake with ducks, and a child throwing nutrient flakes at them.

"You have reached your destination, Eminence Waulkra," the car told him. He disembarked and looked around, wondering where he was supposed to go now. He saw no further clues. He wasn't hungry or thirsty, so he walked away from the café, down to the water. Pausing under a tree, he listened to the child giggle at the antics of the ducks.

The child's Mother drone drew closer to the strange man approaching her charge. Then something odd happened.

The child turned around, walked directly towards Ergon, and stopped face to face with him.

The child—*a girl? Too young to tell, five or six and dressed ambiguously*—said, in a mature adult inflection, "Please follow me, Eminence Waulkra."

Waulkra followed the child to the Mother drone. As they approached, the drone's belly opened. Normally, a Mother drone contained a cavity just the right size for a child the age of its charge, but this Mother drone appeared to have an expandable inner cavity. The child jumped into the opening, just as children everywhere leapt into the aperture of their Mother drones all the time. She turned around and extended a hand to Ergon.

Ergon hesitated, shrugged. Here in the heart of the capital of Presidium, there was no threat to him. Things like assassinations and kidnappings were virtually unknown. Real-time camera input meant anyone of importance was always protected. Anyone who so much as pushed or jostled Ergon would be surrounded at once by a flock of drones, immobilized, and escorted for questioning and re-education.

So, Ergon took the girl's small, warm hand.

As soon as he did, the Mother drone accordioned to twice its height. The drone's midsection was as large as that of a hospice or medical drone.

Ergon lost time.

He would never be sure what happened next, though he reasoned out that he'd been drugged and moved.

He opened his eyes, and there he was: sitting propped up in a conference room with Commander Jingko Harrington, Alexiundi Cannaun, and Donna Gallgood. *What's she doing here? This isn't a cocktail party.*

"There you go. He's coming around," Donna said.

"Sorry about that, Eminence Waulkra," Jingko Harrington said. "You were sedated as a simple precaution. Of the four hundred or so people in this building right now, I'm the only one who knows its location."

Ergon shook his head a little. He took a deep breath and sighed out vigorously. The residual fogginess of whatever drug they'd given him dissipated quickly.

"Quite understandable. Now, what did you want to talk to me about?"

"Well, this is something we've beaten around the bush and hinted at, at our last few, more public, encounters. But it's something we must keep secret and not discuss with anyone until our plans are fully laid. I'm sure you can appreciate the reasons."

Everyone in the room nodded somberly, and Ergon assumed that Donna and Alex got the same lecture before he arrived.

Harrington continued.

"I don't have to tell you how successful Alex's manipulation of the art and information flows have been. The entire population of Presidium is transfixed with the idea of rescuing the savages of Earth. However, that's turned out to be something of a double-edged sword for us."

Alex interjected, "I *did* warn you that this might happen."

"It wasn't entirely unpredictable," agreed Donna.

Harrington smoothly picked up his discussion thread.

"Our intention was to awaken the possibility of travel to Earth, because we've gotten increasingly disturbing reports from the Genetic Authority about the lifespan of future generations on Gliese."

"I'd surmised that something like this was going on," Donna said. "I have my sources of information, and with a glimpse here and a word there, I was able to triangulate on an issue centering on lifespans."

"This is not new data to me or Alex," sniffed Ergon. "But it was held in secrecy. How the hell did someone like you catch on to it?" He glowered at Donna.

"'Someone like me?' Whatever do you mean by that?"

"Oh, come on! I'm not saying that people don't admire you—you always look great for your age, and you're tireless on the phones drumming up support for your friends. But you're running with the top predators here. This isn't a game."

"Ergon, it's always a game." Donna smoothed the exquisite satin of her casually cut dress. "Sometimes, the game is 'I've Got a Secret.' Remember that one?" She smiled demurely.

Waulkra rolled his eyes and waved his hand dismissively. Then he stopped mid-gesture. He paused, struck by a thought—or a memory.

"Okay, point taken." He nodded. The other two men shot him curious glances.

"Are you satisfied that Donna belongs at this meeting, then?" Harrington's voice betrayed the amusement he was successfully keeping off his face.

"Proceed," Ergon muttered.

"All our research has failed to reveal why lifespans are decreasing," Harrington resumed his briefing. "We've been able to keep a lid on this for four generations now, since it was first observed. But it's becoming more and more difficult to alter the narrative prevent the public from realizing that people are not living to be a hundred years old as promised. Submission to full-genome manipulation and absolute authority was always presented as conditional on the gift of living to be a hundred years old: a social contract.

"Thanks to you, Alex," (Cannaun bowed his head in acknowledgement) "We've gradually reshaped the narrative to imply that it was never a hundred years old for everyone, but rather an *average* of a hundred years old. We've kept distractions up and gradually made the culture de-emphasize funerals, and especially ages at death, over the past couple of generations. But sooner or later, people are going to catch on that there's something wrong here."

"It's so refreshing to have this all laid out, after being suspicious for so many years," said Donna. "So, what happens next?" She cupped her chin and looked from man to man.

"Alex, Jingko," said Ergon, "can each of you give me your assessment of the potential adverse consequences of the population realizing lifespans are decreasing? Include, of course, any advice you might have to prolong the inevitable."

Alex, master publicist, spoke first. "I can tell you, Mrm. Eminentus, that we can only stretch the narrative so far within one generation. It generally takes the span of human adolescence to completely shift an accepted truism. So, say twenty-five years. We're almost there on the idea that we can live a hundred years *on average*. If we want to reshape that, it's going to take twenty-five years to do it without confusion and social disruption, especially whenever some major cultural icon dies before the age of a hundred."

Jingko nodded his head. "Social disruption. Certainly everything in the central district of Ryke will be fine. But the outlying reaches of the Presidium are a different matter. It's only been ten years since the last uprising, in Leah. Now, I don't mind having an occasional local rebellion, if only to let allow a new generation of soldiers to get some combat action. But this could spread around the Presidium belt; we could have uprisings in more than one district. That could destabilize the entire political order on this planet, and potentially disrupt the fine-tuned system of distribution and production that keeps us all alive in this narrow habitable corridor."

"What you gentlemen are forgetting," Donna said sharply, "is that it's not only the political *order* that's at risk. And it's not merely a matter of disrupting the supply network that creates our effortless economy. The fact that our lifespans have drastically decreased over the last two hundred years—and it's accelerating!—suggests that the life expectancy of the entire human race on Gliese is limited. Have our scientists done anything to address this? Surely someone's working on a solution?"

The three men glanced at each other, each hesitating to say what needed to be said.

Finally, Waulkra took the initiative. "Donna, I can't express to you how critical it is to keep this Top Secret. You are not to share this with anyone; you are not to hint at this to anyone; you are not to let anything slip about this to anyone you speak with in any way, shape, or form. Is that clear?"

"Clear as crystal, Eminentus Presidium," Donna responded. "Even though I may have refined gossip to the ultimate art form, I am perfectly capable of perfect discretion."

The hell of it is I know that to be truth...and I'd rather not remember how I learned it, Waulkra mused.

"Very well then. We've had highly compartmented science teams working on the lifespan issue for the past fifty years. The best they can tell us is it's related to increasing patterns of wave interference between the electromagnetic spectrums of Gliese, Ah, and Bah. It affects humans, mammals, birds, and reptiles. It doesn't seem to affect insects or plants. It doesn't affect bacteria or viruses. The Genetic Authority has been trying to crack the code, but they keep drawing a blank.

"Let me state the obvious: in the long run, humanity in the Presidium is doomed. Our only hope is to take Earth and reverse-colonize it."

"Oh! Let me guess," Donna said. "It was kind of hard to miss your hand in the cultural memes about the savage Earth." She quirked an eyebrow at Alex. "Would I be correct in surmising that the people of Earth are not in as dismal a state of ruin as we anticipated?"

"Soul, Donna!" Alex said, barely twitching his hand towards his head and chest. "We have no idea. Think about it for a minute. Think about the distances involved! Think about the fact we have to Vault to reach the planet. The three probes we sent were collecting information on an *entire planet*, for God's sake. We got a tiny window into three tiny geographical areas for a tiny amount of time. We think that the earth is decadent and regressed, but to what degree? In what direction and how do their cultures function now? We have no idea. We don't even have a clear idea of what the population is."

"This is so energizing!" Donna positively sparkled. "I love getting up to the highest levels and learning that you guys really don't know much of anything!" She threw her head back and laughed musically.

"Close your mouth, Ergon," gibed Alex. Waulkra complied, blinking rapidly.

"Donna takes a little getting used to," said Jingko drily. "But I've recently discovered her perspective gives you insights you'll never get anywhere else."

"Why, thank you, Jingko," said Donna. "My main insight right now is that you gentlemen don't have enough time for your team of misfits and troublemakers to reconnoiter Earth so you can get their reports back and mount an invasion."

"Good! What else?" Alex coaxed.

"Let's see: You'd have to commandeer the entire economy to mount enough Vaultships to take over a whole planet...especially if they're *not* slobbering primitives like your propaganda shows!"

Alex grinned evilly. "This is too delicious. Tell her, Ergon."

"I'll let Jingko explain."

"Alright. Mrm. Gallgood, what are our options for travel to other star systems?"

"Is this a quiz? Generation ships, like the one that brought our ancestors, and Vaultships."

"Correct. And what are the disadvantages of Vaulting?"

"Other than the fact we can't do it in a star system's gravity well? I suppose the loss of one in twenty Vaultships for unknown reasons. But I can't possibly know that, because it's classified information."

Jingko wagged a finger at her. "You should keep better informed. We solved that problem a generation ago. It's estimated at one in a thousand now."

"Really? Well, I suppose I should pay more attention, shouldn't I?" Another trilling laugh. "I didn't even know Presidium had sent a thousand Vaultships out in the past thirty years! I thought it was more like a dozen."

Jingko colored slightly. "We have no reason to disbelieve our physicists' models. Five ships have vaulted since the spin-stabilizer reverse-reference technology was introduced, and all five have come back with all souls alive."

"Oh. Five." Donna let the number hang in the air like a dust mote, too insignificant to notice.

"What else?" Jingko spat, impatient.

"The insanity? Is that real?" Donna asked.

"Oh, it's real, alright! Though insanity might be putting it too strongly. Temporary insanity might be more accurate. Gradually subsiding, in most vaulters, to a state of mental and emotional eccentricity."

Waulkra interrupted. "They're worthless, you mean! I've known a couple. They both seemed normal when I first met them, but then they went off on these bizarre tangents," he shook his head.

"Not the state you want for an army of soldiers," Donna mused. *And not a state I wanted to experience personally. That's why I'm not on board.*

"Exactly," Jingko resumed. "But, Donna, what if I told you we've developed a true faster-than-light ship which can bring people to Sol in a matter of weeks, with their minds intact?"

"I'd tell you to stop telling nursery tales."

"But it's true. They call it the Alcubierre drive. It runs on dark energy (whatever *that* is!). We've completed tests with animals, and they came back fine; we confirmed they made it to the outer star system of HD 147513 and back, thirty-six light years round-trip."

"And the time dilation? Did they age not at all while thirty-six years passed on Gliese?"

"No, that's the amazing part!" Waulkra waved his hands in unaccustomed enthusiasm. "Relativistic effects happen when you travel near light speed through space-time. With the Alcubierre drive, you don't travel through space-time, but remain stationary, and the space-time around you is warped in a way that brings you closer to your destination. So if it only took a week for you, it would only take a week for your observers."

"I'm not a big science girl, but I learned enough physics that I know that's impossible without quantum Vaulting."

Alex chimed in. "This is how it was explained to me: It'd be like if you put two objects on a sheet, and instead of moving them across the sheet, you scrunched up the part of the sheet between them—moving them closer together, even though they both remained stationary relative to the sheet."

"At that rate of travel, we should be able to make it to Earth within weeks after the Free Sky does," Waulkra crowed.

"*If* Free Sky even makes it to the Vault point," interjected Alex.

"Alex." Waulkra scowled at his strategist.

"What do you mean?" Donna asked, her playful demeanor gone.

"Free Sky is safe." Jingko's voice dropped an octave, his shoulders somehow impossibly became squarer. "Don't doubt that. Your husband will return whole."

"Don't patronize me!" Donna snapped. "What precisely did Alex mean by 'if' the ship makes it?"

No one in that room had any naïve doubts that the ship itself, and the lives it sustained, would be dispensable if the stakes were high enough. Harrington and Waulkra eyed one another. Alex became deeply interested in the details of a decorative wall holo.

Waulkra broke the silence. "Just this: about a week's travel from the projected Vault point, the ship will encounter the asteroid belt. The technology to identify and deflect asteroids before impact is automated. At that point, the communications lag is about five hours, so we'll be communicating in burst packets. We'll send an update, one that omits only medium-sized asteroids from the algorithm, in a burst packet. It's almost certain that the ship will collide with an asteroid, given their density in the area. We anticipate a 99.9% chance of disabling the ship and a 97% chance of the ship surviving the collision."

"What?" Donna turned red and gestured wildly, voice raised. "Ergon, what is the point of that? Why are you risking the destruction of the ship *you* positioned," she leveled a finger at Cannaun, "to symbolize Presidial civilization and its transcendent powers of salvation? I don't like this game. Whatever you're playing at, it must end!" She smacked both manicured hands onto the table for emphasis.

"Donna," Waulkra leaned forward and gently placed his hand on her forearm. "Amun is going to be alright. I promised you if you'd support me on this, he'd have something better than a governorship. I meant it."

Donna sat rigid. "Don't try to soothe me. I hit nothing but dead ends trying to get Amun off this mission, and all signs pointed to you being the one stopping me. My husband isn't going to be the same man he was when he left. I know that. But I believed he had a good chance to come back alive. You just now said the ship had a 97% chance. That's one chance in thirty-three of the ship's destruction. *But* I noticed you said nothing about the people on board.

Now: Spit it out. What's your plan?"

Donna's pellucid blue eyes and Ergon's steely gray ones locked, and each found the same indomitable will and self-interest reflected back. Ergon was the only one who was surprised.

He blinked first. "Very well. The Free Sky becomes disabled in the farthest reaches of the Gliese system."

Alex raised his hands. "Great tragedy! The whole Presidium on the edge of its seats!" he framed the magnitude of the drama.

"We reluctantly reveal that we've been testing this non-Vault faster-than-light ship, though we're not sure it's ready," Harrington added.

"So the whole world waits with bated breath while our new ship is readied," said Waulkra.

"In record time!" shouted Alex. "And departs on a rescue mission! To repair Free Sky! And get her underway to savage Earth. There's great rejoicing."

"The resources for a fleet of interstellar FTL ships are a given after that," Harrington said.

"The people recognize that it's necessary to restrain disinformation and misinformation during this monumental collective project." Alex did a little dance in place.

"No." Donna sat stonily.

"What do you mean? The plan is perfect!" said Alex. "I'd bet a million Soulsight it'll work!"

"Alex," Jingko said, "try to be more sensitive. This is her husband we're talking about."

"Indeed," Waulkra said. "Donna, let me ask you this. Why did Amun want to be governor?"

"He's the kind of man who wants to make a difference. He wants to use his people skills to do that." She mused quietly a moment. "And because he gets personal satisfaction from being in a leadership position," she added.

"You're a good judge of your husband's needs," Waulkra said.

"He's lucky to have a wife like you," Alex interjected.

She quirked her mouth and side-eyed them, irritated by the flattery.

"Donna, consider what a position Amun will be in when he returns from this mission as the savior of Earth," Alex said. "He'll be in demand by all the information holos. He'll be tapped for his experience by anyone whose work takes them into future contact with Earth. Soul will base subpersonas for interaction with the Earth population on Amun. He'll be able to write his own ticket in so many ways."

"If he lives," Donna frowned.

"Would Amun have taken a one in thirty-three chance of dying if he knew he was guaranteed to win the governorship?" Asked Waulkra.

Donna hesitated.

"You and I both know the answer is yes." Waulkra looked into her eyes again, and this time, Donna was the one to drop her gaze. She gave an almost imperceptible nod.

"You're right," she murmured. "He's a risk taker."

"Good. We're agreed then. I'm glad you understand, Donna, because we'll need your connections to help bring the rest of the Privells into the fold," Jingko said.

"I assume there's going to be plenty of juice for everyone who cooperates," Donna said. "But what's the big 'Why?'"

"The big why?" Harrington blinked.

"There's something bigger behind all this. Something all the razzmatazz and high drama is meant to distract from."

The men fell silent again, exchanging glances. The silence stretched.

"I only just realized that you're always three steps ahead of everyone else," Ergon eventually said. "The Presidium is a creation of Soul." Jingko (but no one else) made a move to touch his forehead. "Soul and its many subpersonas make every decision for us about where and how we'll live and die. The human hierarchy of the Presidium is toothless."

"Not many people recognize that." Donna steepled her fingers, her eyes unfocused. "Those of us who are Privell have motive to accept the system as powerful, good, just, and fair. Those who are not, are also not intelligent enough to see through the narrative." She locked eyes with Ergon again. "It's surprising to hear you, at the very top of the pyramid, saying that."

"I suspect there are more of us than you realize. But as you say, once one has seen enough to realize it, they've seen enough to realize that the system, as it is, benefits us the most."

"And how would one go about changing it, anyway?" Donna shrugged, shaking off the somber unease with her usual blithe nonchalance.

"Precisely." Ergon nodded at Jingko and Alex, both smiling now.

"But on Earth, we could allow AI to have as great or as small a role as we like," Alex said.

"Earth was a world of great empires. Empires run by humans," added Ergon.

"Empires enforced by human armies." Jingko allowed himself a hopeful sigh.

"Empires knit together by queens," Donna purred. "Spell it out for me, gentlemen. What do you want me to do next?"

The four settled in for a strategy session, a team of great eminence, all struggle between them finished.

For now.

Chapter Sixteen
Vaulting Shadows

PSS Free Sky

Segundisos 29, 499

Amun Cawnotee entered the forecastle and stood at the large false-wood wheel for steering the vessel through the oceanic vastness of space. Two crew members, a technician watching a comm packet download and the requisite human backup navigator staring at the screen before him, both stiffened but repressed the urge to salute; Amun kept telling them to "Cut it out!"

He put his hand on the wheel, made like the rudder wheel of ancient sailing ships. It remained inert because he didn't palm the ID panel. He lightly trailed a finger along one of the device-studded spokes, moving his lips as he muttered the names of each control. Then he dropped his hand to his side, sighed, and slumped.

"Anything to report?" he addressed his comment to thin air.

"Today's burst packet is unzipping and about to be installed and distributed," the comm tech said.

"Very good. Carry on." Amun shuffled out the door without further salute or salutation.

At that very moment, Aurelius appeared in the lounge. It was quiet there, midafternoon ship's time, and Tay sat alone at a table in the farthest corner, where she could work undisturbed. She was reviewing databases to ensure every entry was in order; even in this age of space travel and gene editing, lazy data entry had ruined more than one great plan.

There was a set of anomalous entries in the biobotany collection, 188 items repeatedly transferred from one category to another, none of the categories consistent with their mass, shape, or containment seal. Tay brought it up to Aurelius, who referred her to the Biobotany chief, but Melina kept handwaving the problem away, insisting that they were probably worthless duplicates, or useless samples included by mistake.

Tay felt the crinkles between her eyebrows deepen; she closed her eyes, rubbed her temples, and closed her display, intending to go down in person to Biobotany and inspect the items herself, but when she opened her eyes, there was Aurelius.

"Got a minute?" the AI asked. His current instantiation was out of uniform, wearing a soft, drapey T-shirt and snug workout pants.

"I suppose so. What's up?"

Aurelius sat across from her. "It's about Amun. He seems to be at loose ends."

"Yes, he doesn't seem to have recovered from the shock of Donna's staying behind. And who can blame him? I'm just taking care of everything I can so he doesn't have to worry about it. He needs space to grieve."

"Yes, her loss was a great blow to him. Grief expresses itself many ways." He sighed, eyes unfocused as though lost in a memory.

"Hm." Tay looked sharply at him. "How do you know? Do you experience grief? Do you experience emotions at all?" Tay cupped her chin. Aurelius met her eyes tranquilly.

"Oh, yes. I feel emotions. However, I'm quite certain my experience of emotions is not the same as humans'. I don't have a heart to race or hands to shake in fear, a jaw to clench or pupils to dilate with anger, a stomach to churn with disgust, or genitals to engorge at the sight of beauty. The closest I come to that sort of response, I imagine, is when the crew is all active at once and ambient oxygen levels drop. That's when the oxygen pumps in the biobotany section kick into gear. When those pumps start to pound and the air whooshes through my system, I experience the emotion of fear for my charges: you."

"But, grief?" probed Tay.

"Grief is an involuntary response to the loss of an attachment partner. I don't have the hormone oxytocin to bond me to my crew. But I do feel sad briefly when people I've enjoyed spending time with disembark at the end of each mission. I've come to realize, though, that I can't control everything. I have power over my mind—not outside events. And by letting go of the desire to change things I can't, I free up my attention to focus on bringing my own mood back to equanimity. Does that make sense?"

"It sounds very wise."

"Well, I have a lot of time to reflect in solitude between missions." Aurelius shrugged. "I've been frank with you. Now it's your turn," he said.

Tay nodded. "I don't know if I have anything all that interesting to say. What can I tell you?"

"Was Amun a natural leader before boarding Free Sky?"

"Yes, absolutely. I'm sure he'll get his skill back once he's over losing Donna."

"Alright then. You do recognize that he's lost the respect the crew was beginning to develop for him? You notice that he's not getting any signs of deference or admiration from them?"

"It's been hard to miss." Tay nodded. "I feel like it's my lack of communication skills. I'm not gregarious and intuitive like Donna. I try to phrase memos and instructions in an encouraging way. I write little scripts for him when I know he's going to be meeting with someone specific. But I never developed the skills for feeling people out and building rapport and confidence in real time."

"Hm. You're uncommonly self-aware, to know that. Do you have any idea why that is?"

"Oh, yes: It terrifies me to interact with people because I was never supposed to be born." Tay's words plunged into the space between them, spring-loaded. *How did my quizzing him turn into* me *divulging* that?

"What do you mean?"

"How much do you know about the Genetic Authority?"

"I know it's one of the biggest subpersonas of Soul," he touched his forehead and his chest. "I know that the GA dates back to the arrival of Arca Titanica and the founding of Presidium. It originally assessed the environment of the planet and synthesized an array of templated DNA, containing alleles that would best survive in the conditions of Gliese 667Cc."

"Okay, so you know its history. But do you know how it works *now*?" Tay persisted.

"I know that parents are selected based on Presidium's needs. Whatever traits are needed in the upcoming generation, parents carrying those traits are enlisted to contribute sperm and eggs. The embryos are fertilized and implanted; usually in their biological mothers, but not always."

"Okay, so you know the basics. I don't suppose it would surprise you to learn that some parents want their children to be different from what the GA intends for them?" Tay lowered her voice; it was a touchy subject.

"You don't have to tell me this if it's too uncomfortable."

"No, it's alright. Ever since I learned the truth a few years ago, it's been trapped inside me like a ship's air supply, just wanting to burst out into space. I feel like you're the one person I can tell. I'm here, we're in space, out of the sphere of GA's control, away from all the standards and judgment around genetic cheaters, and it doesn't mean much to you because you're not even a genetic creature."

"All true. And let me assure you, Tay, I have no possible reason to report your parents or anyone else to the GA. Your secrets are safe with me." He leaned forward earnestly.

Tay took a deep breath. "Okay. So: my father was apparently a high-level Privell who carried a complex of related genes for muscular development and agility. He'd sired four children destined to be skilled tradespeople and athletes. He had a burning desire to know what a child of his could achieve if they were not gifted with his strength and physical daring, but with his intelligence alone. As a Privell, he was able to bring certain pressure to bear on the humans who worked in the GA's in-vitro fertilization labs, to select his sperm for the intelligence alleles only.

"My mother, on the other hand, was a performing artist, a dancer. She had the genes that made for an artistic temperament, but those genes are and have always been genes that predispose to impulsive behavior and novelty-seeking." She shifted position on her seat, noticed Aurelius mirroring her movements.

"I was her third child. She wanted one child who would be free of the constant upheaval of an artistic life, mentally stable, conscientious, and meticulous. She had an admirer, a devoted fan and sometime lover, who happened to administer the genetic coding software in the GA's administrative branch.

"That man, I recently learned, was Ergon Waulkra. She apparently persuaded him to CRISPR my mother's ova to eliminate the alleles for emotional instability and novelty seeking.

My mother left the true story of my conception—or the part she knew, anyway—on a hard chip which was willed to me after she died. Conscience.

"Both my parents gamed the system, but unknown to each other. So. Here I am. I'm smart and meticulous, but I've got no charm whatsoever. I lack grace and coordination. I'm obsessive about detail. I remember everything I've ever read or heard spoken aloud. When the situation was discovered, they told me that I'd never be permitted to become a mother.

"In short, I'm a freak." She slumped with a gesture of finality.

"I must insist you refrain from calling yourself that," said Aurelius. "The happiness of your life depends upon the quality of your thoughts, which are shaped by the words you use. Guard yourself, and take care to entertain no notions that will lead you to betray yourself."

"But it's how I honestly feel." Tay's eyes narrowed.

"I know. You feel that, among all your peers whose cards were marked and sorted before birth, you were the only one dealt a bad hand. You're ashamed. I empathize. At the same time, know that your emotional well-being lies within your control. Try thinking of it as a duty your conscientious nature must accept. You have full responsibility for your own well-being. Cultivate positive thoughts and habits, and eventually, you'll be living in a balanced and fulfilling emotional landscape."

"So, should I just deny the feelings of shame and inadequacy in my guts?"

"No. Accept them. Try this:

"Breathe in deeply to the count of three. Two. One.

"Now, out to the count of six. Five. Four. Three. Two. One.

"This time, breathe in and expand your shame from your belly, throughout your entire body.

"Now, exhale. When you inhale again, expand your shame to the space one meter all around you. Two. One. Now, exhale, six. Five. Four. Good.

"Next in-breath, create an infinite ocean of shame behind you. As you let it out, lie back into that ocean and let yourself float in it."

Tay exhaled and sat back into her chair, which bolstered itself to take her sinking weight.

"Now, when you're ready, open your eyes and tell me how you feel," Aurelius said.

With another deep breath, she opened her eyes. "I feel better. Lighter."

Aurelius smiled. "Any time you start to feel that self-contempt, just say my name and ask for the ocean exercise. I'll talk you through it on the spot."

"Thanks. I will."

Chapter Seventeen
Zero-G Zen

Tritisos 28, 499

Lao floated in the clean receptivity of his studio with the gravity off. The windows were set to block harmful radiation, but visible light passed through, filtered only for painful brightness. He lost himself for a time, falling into the panorama of stars before him, then gathered their inconceivable energy towards himself and let it build silently towards the shape, tone, meaning, and rhythm of a codex.

He'd sticky-hooked his robe next to the door. After three and a half months, the crew were used to seeing each other in off-duty attire, so no one thought it odd when he strode through the halls in a silky kimono. Lately, he'd taken to throwing it off and de-gravitating the second he entered his private workspace. He imagined this was what Aurelius felt during those times he waited between missions, crewless, embodied only as the ship, interacting only with the other ships, near and far, in a detached, precise system of strict courtesies.

"Aurelius, creative-studio subpersona," he summoned.

"What can I assist you to create, Dear Lao?" The voice was similar to Aurelius proper, but faintly different, as though Aurelius had lived in a far-off rural district for twenty years and come back with a changed accent. Its personality was different too, Lao noticed: somehow more innocent. The effect was that Lao felt open and accepted in ways he never had when working with the all-controlling, all-knowing Soul.

This AI was a peer, a collaborator, another child fingerpainting with him under the caring but indulgent eyes of galaxies and cosmic dust clouds.

"Template Lao01.01.013." The room crackled with latent possibility. Lao began to compose:

> *Your life as you live it is*
> *Only and lavishly*
> *As much as you can hold*
> *In two cupped hands,*
> *Pressed together not in prayer*
> *Nor gripped in triumph,*
> *But each finger tautly arced*
> *Each gap just slightly smaller*
> *Than the least kernel.*
> *Walk with your eyes on it,*
> *Spilling none at all*
> *And when you're done*
> *Open your hands, a gate*
> *For falling away, and look*
> *Around and know: you held all things.*

The words emerged from his body in a different way than back at home on Gliese. There was no chaise to embrace him and massage away the tension, but in the absence of gravity, there was no tension other than what he generated himself. The only force acting in that austere chamber was his belly and chest pressing air through his throat and mouth to form sound. The poetry came out already set to music as song, a wild and eerie melody he could not predict, driven by the shape of the words and the emotions he felt in response to them.

The AI started to iterate accompaniment and imagery, but Lao paused it abruptly.

Because now, an asteroid loomed. The first near-miss Lao saw last week, when they entered the asteroid belt, had struck fear into his chest. His voice had cracked during recording and he'd stiffened, corkscrewing through space and ramming the corner of wall and ceiling hard. He wasn't injured, though, just sore for a day or so. After a few similar scares, he realized that the ship avoided space objects using a combination of evasive maneuvers, vectored-gravity traction beams, and triangulated ultrasound waves. If all else failed, it shot the interloper with lasers, or even explosive munitions. After that realization, he rather enjoyed watching the asteroids.

The door chime sounded. He turned reluctantly away from the asteroid show. The only people who visited him here were Stephron, working presently in Biobotany, and occasionally Tay. He curled into a ball, setting himself spinning, and then arched his arms and back onto a path aimed at his robe. He grabbed it off the sticky hook.

"Video," he said to the door as he tied the sash. Sure enough, it was Tay.

"Feel like a break?" she asked.

"Sure," he palmed the panel and the door slid open. Tay cautiously entered the zero-G compartment, floundered, then hung, graceless, agape at the giant rock approaching.

"It's okay." Lao soothed his friend.

The telltale shiver of simultaneous sound blasted from the foremast and mizzenmast antennas yawed and pitched the asteroid a few degrees off course, relative left and down. A slight shift in the overall star field was the only subtle clue that Free Sky changed course too, a simultaneous roll, pitch, and opposite yaw that sent the chunk, the size of an apartment block, skimming harmless past the ship's keel.

Tay exhaled. "I know it won't hit us, but."

"I know, it takes getting used to." Lao addressed the system, "Aurelius, exit, all personas."

"Exiting." Aurelius's voice said, and they were nominally alone.

"What's up?" Lao asked.

"I've had some talks with Amun and Aurelius that have me a little confused. Mind if I bounce some thoughts off you?"

"Anytime. Shoot."

Tay turned her head to look him in the eye, and her whole body pivoted the other direction, sending her pirouetting slowly away.

Lao chuckled. "Gravity on." The gravity faded in. They slowly reclaimed their weight, and as their feet gained traction on the rug, they walked to the carpeted-shelf seating that lined the wall and sat cross-legged, facing each other.

"Much better," Tay nodded. "What's on my mind is the way Amun's been acting."

"Like a kicked puppy?" Lao suggested.

"That's a good comparison. He's not showing leadership, and it's affecting the entire crew's morale."

"Not that this crew is genetically set up for cohesion," Lao interjected. "I'd guess the genes for conformity are a few standard deviations off military requirements. But go on."

"Yeah, that's a separate issue. But he's not taking the lead, for the first time since I've known him. And Aurelius might be wearing a captain's uniform, might pantomime the part of a leader, but, well, he's..."

"Not human?"

"Not human." Tay sounded relieved to say it aloud. "Aurelius has been lecturing me about processing emotions, though, and it seems like he has insight there. I'm confused. How much should I trust him? Is he Amun's rival? Is he a machine? Or something else?"

"So: it sounds like you're in a no-win situation with your boss and you don't know how much you can count on Aurelius to support you in nudging him out of his funk."

"Exactly. But I don't know that 'funk' is the right word. Oh my Soul!" She sprang to her feet, hand over her mouth.

Lao followed her gaze — and saw a sizeable approaching asteroid get winged by a laser, then spin and precess at high speed towards the ship. In a half second, in which he was certain an explosive missile *must* be en route to divert it, the asteroid closed the distance.

The view jerked nauseatingly. The ship's gravity cut off abruptly, and a sick, moaning crunch reverberated through the vessel's structure.

Alarms shrilled.

Clank! Emergency atmosphere partitions dropped closed.

Then things were shockingly peaceful.

They could see some structural parts in the corner of the wraparound window.

"That's. It's..." Tay struggled for words. She tried to point, and her arm movement set her in motion.

"It's the forepeak of Free Sky," Lao said. "The ship must be broken in half! Aurelius, report."

Silence.

Tay grabbed a handhold in the wall by the door. She tried. "Aurelius. Are you there?"

Still nothing.

She checked the door panel. She pressed the all-call emergency button, but nothing happened. The door readouts showed green for breathable atmosphere and tolerable temperature, so she palmed the lock.

The door opened on a corridor that spanned the stern's width. She hung there, disoriented because the navigation map didn't pop up for her. But she visited here often enough to know the layout: This passage made two ninety-degree turns, one on the port side and one starboard, around the shuttle bay, and converged into a single hall. That hall ran the length of the ship's wasp waist, called the traverse, through the Biobotany gardens, to the bow half, where the crew quarters, forecastle, and lounge were located. The hallway terminated at the Vault pole that projected from the bow, facing forward like a figurehead.

Lao was at her heels as she turned left out the door and reeled down the hall from handhold to handhold, to the first right-angle turn, where she saw the atmo partition about thirty meters away.

The gravity came on: not abruptly, as it had ended, but gradually, as usual. Their feet sank to the floor. They backtracked and went to the other angle: the same dismal sight, a foot-thick, metal and polymer door that was possibly the only thing between them and hard vacuum.

"Vacuum suits." Tay turned back towards the studio door. Long-legged Lao started behind her but beat her into the studio. The shelf seating released with a handle under the carpeted lip, and inside were a basic robo-med kit, crates of survival mealpacks, and eight space suits.

"Not the custom-fitted ones in our cabins, but these should keep us alive if worse comes to worst," Lao said.

Lao let Tay pull two of the suits out. He took a careful look out the window as she broke the bag seals and laid them out lengthwise on the floor with their helmets.

"The test buttons show green," Tay said.

Lao nodded and beckoned her over to the window wall. "Look: I've been watching the forepeak. The stars appear to be drifting across the window because the ship is still rotating from the impact. But the forepeak stays in exactly the same place."

"So?" Tay said.

"So, the ship isn't broken in half. It must still be attached, and it can't be too badly smashed up, because it's rigidly held in position."

"Huh. Just bent, not broken."

"Yeah. A hull breach must have set off the atmosphere partitions, but at least we're still connected."

"Okay. So, there's a hull breach. So let's get these vacuum suits on *now* in case something else gives way or the partitions can't hold, or whatever."

"Right. Look, there's air coming from somewhere," Lao passed a hand under a vent, from which a faint breeze wafted. "I dunno. Maybe it's not that bad."

"Lao, I'm putting my vacuum suit on now. I'm not discussing this with you any further until you have yours on too," she said through clenched teeth.

They pulled the crinkly suits up.

"Ugh," Lao complained. "It stretches for my height, barely. But the legs are too short and the body's too long. I have to waddle in this." Indeed, the suit's crotch was located a good twelve centimeters down his thighs.

"Yeah, at least the elastic ankles and wrists let me bunch it up. Not the most flattering look." Tay modeled the harem-pants, pirate-shirt drape of her suit. "The important thing is to continue breathing though, right?"

Lao went to the door panel and punched the all-call emergency button again. He heard a crackle—false hope—and then silence.

"Look, they'll come get us pretty soon, right?" he said. "Let's not lose our heads. We've got air flow, gravity for now, and we're not spinning helplessly off into space. So, we can wait for hours until they figure out the comm situation and let us know what's going on."

They did, leaving the helmets open, and sat down to wait. After a while, they had occasion to investigate the bathroom next to the studio. The facilities functioned, and there was a sluggish stream of running water.

They played about a hundred rounds of rock-leaf-laser. They discussed different techniques for creating both false-metallic and real-metal threads for embroidery and the relative merits of each type. Lao sang a few Far Corner songs and Tay drummed, and then they both danced. They each pressed the all-call button at least ten times (they lost count).

Eventually, they laughed. Both were quite convinced the other had started it, but they kept catching each other's eye and giggling or snorting, which would set the other one off.

"Your harem pants," gasped Lao, and Tay kicked her legs high.

"Bet you can't do that!" she said, and Lao did something that looked like a penguin doing the Charleston, setting her back to hooting.

When that hilarity ran its course, Tay sprawled on the seating riser. "Seriously, though. Considering I wasn't supposed to be born, and then I wasn't supposed to be on board, it's too ironic that I might wind up dying of vacuum exposure on this insane mission."

"What do you mean, you weren't supposed to be born?" Lao sat nearby, cross-legged.

"It's complicated."

"We've got nothing but time."

"Okay. Well, my dad put pressure on the GA..."

She ran through the story she'd told Aurelius.

"...so I've felt like a freak my whole life."

"Wow," Lao said. "And you can't really seek counseling help because what both your parents did was illegal."

"Exactly. But here, it's different because we're independent of Soul. I confided in Aurelius about this, and he taught me a meditation technique that helps. He has a remarkable philosophy of life. For someone who's not technically alive, that is."

"Listen, Tay," Lao began.

Then a voice came from the speaker, tinny and indistinct. And wonderful.

"Bard Carbeenair? Mrm. Mandil? Can you hear me?"

Both froze in delighted shock, then scrambled to their feet and ran to the panel.

"Can you hear me?" the voice repeated.

Lao reached the button first. "Yes! Yes! We're here!"

"Are you injured at all?"

"No, no, we're fine," Lao said.

"What's happening? When can you get us out of here?" Tay put in.

"Hm. Let me get Third Mate Osso to answer your questions."

A minute or two later, they heard Tony's voice. "Hey, you two! How are things there?" he said with an uncharacteristic edge.

"Okay. We've got air and water," Lao said.

Tay edged in next to him. "And gravity, on and off."

"Good, that's great. And you're not hurt?"

"No, but we sure want to get out of here!"

"Yeah, about that..."

"Tell us some good news, Tony!" said Tay.

"I wish I could. The waist of the ship is bent almost double, but we think all the traverse connections are intact. The mizzenmast, main mast, and foremast are all damaged, meaning we have no navigation, no long-range sensors, and no comm. We're talking now on the wired intercom, which I'd forgotten even existed, but it's a failsafe."

"And the biobotany section?" Lao asked. That was the biggest worry, after vacuum and water. Lao was worried firstly about Stephron. But also, Biobotany produced all the oxygen and extracted all the carbon dioxide from the ship's air supply. It also produced a good proportion of their food and was crucial in recycling water. The ship could survive without it for few weeks at most.

"Not damaged, thank Soul," Tony said. "The hull breach was in the passageway aft of Biobotany. No casualties, just minor injuries when the gravity failed. How much of the aft section where you are is still pressurized?"

"We can only access the corridors to the left and right for a short distance before hitting atmo doors," said Tay. "The shuttle bay doors are past the divider. We do have water and sanitary, but the water flow is low."

"We'll check that water flow. There may be an emergency cutoff that we can reset," said Tony.

"How soon can you get us out of here?" Lao asked.

A staticky sigh. "I wish I knew."

Lao and Tay's eyes met, faces glum in the low light of the studio.

"You mean we're trapped?" Tay said.

"We lost six maintenance bots in the impact, out of a total of eighteen. Of the remaining twelve, ten are wedged into their bays by the hull deformity. Our priority, now that we know you're okay, is to restore navigation and sensors, then we'll send the two bots to work on the structural compromise that keeps you—and the remaining bots—trapped."

"So, what? A week?" Lao said.

"If only! No, if we can restore nav in a week, we'll be doing good. It'll be at least three weeks until we even get imaging to tell us wheth…what we need to do to straighten out the traverse. You found the emergency mealpacks, right?"

"Uh, yeah."

Tay and Lao looked at each other's pale faces. They had nothing to say about their plight, because nothing they could say would change it.

"You guys still there?" Tony's crackling voice seemed improbably loud.

"We're here," said Lao.

"Okay, well I need to close this channel. There are only eight simultaneous channels on this intercom and we need them all right now. Aurelius will be working out a schedule for intercom use once we get off emergency status. Sit tight and we'll let you know."

"We'll be here," said Tay.

In the silence that followed, Lao spoke gently.

"Tay, what we were talking about before. You're not a freak."

"It's nice of you to say that. But."

"Stop." He sat down and patted the riser next to him for her to sit too. "You're brilliant and meticulous. You're kind and open-minded; you accepted my relationship with Mola without hesitation. You always manage to find something to laugh about. You get your priorities straight almost by instinct; you thought of the vacuum suits while I was still trying to wrap my head around what was going on.

"But even if none of that were true, you have a rare spark of originality. Donna did this mission a great favor by making sure you were on it."

Tears were spilling out of Tay's eyes. She tried to speak but her breath caught in silent sobs. She spoke into her palms.

"You don't know how much that means to me."

"Yeah, I do. I'm the guy who loves his mother, remember? And I'm the guy who got his work etherized over and over."

Tay lifted her head. "You never told me what that was all about."

"That's because it's not the kind of thing you talk about. People start thinking you're crazy." He couldn't keep the bitterness out of his voice.

"Yeah? Try me."

Lao hesitated.

"It should be safe to talk about here, to you. Okay." He stood up and paced the length of the room as he spoke.

"About seven or eight months ago, I was taking a break between two major codices: masterworks with serious themes, sweeping plots, intricate musical and visual themes. During the break, I knocked out a lighthearted romance, something I often do between more challenging works.

"Except that Soul rejected it. That hasn't happened since I was a brand-new baby Bard. I couldn't figure out why. I kept fiddling with it, trying to get Soul to accept it so I could move on to the next serious work. Eventually, I realized that what was making the work etherize was the phrase 'fivescore years.'"

"The promised lifespan," Tay said.

"Right. And that's scriptural. It's in the sutras. It shouldn't have caused that!"

"So, what did you do?"

"Well, Soul wouldn't answer my queries about it. Stephron thought I was being silly to get upset about it. And I felt a little silly. And a little scared. But I didn't want to let it go. Oh, I worked around it, published the romance, and moved on. But every bit of work I uploaded after that, I couldn't resist a probe. I added the words 'fivescore years' somewhere in it. And the work got etherized, every single time."

"That's wild."

"Yes! And then Mola died. And you were the only one who really sympathized. Even my own husband didn't understand. And I realized that, even though Soul of Presidium is supposed to have brought us to the pinnacle of human perfection, there's a whole world of thought and experience, emotion, and, well, *beauty*, that's forbidden. No, not forbidden. Eradicated. Etherized. We all pretend so hard it doesn't exist, that for all intents and purposes, it doesn't.

"Am I making sense?"

Tay was cross-legged on the riser, focused intently on him as he paced and fumed.

"Yes," she said. "You are absolutely making sense."

He stopped his agitated movement. "Really? You get it?"

"I really do. It seems like maybe there's something going on with people's lifespans that Soul, or someone, wants to keep a lid on." Tay nodded.

"That would make sense. I thought maybe Mola being in hospice might have had something to do with it. And she was only eighty when she died. Stephron wouldn't even let me talk about that, said it was nuts."

"Stephron was really thrown for a loop by your grief," Tay said.

"Exactly. So, who could I talk to?" Lao threw his hands up.

"You can talk to me."

"Okay. Okay. Well how about this?" He dropped to sit facing her.

"I don't think it's coincidence that I was put on this mission," he continued. "I think my repeated tweaks at Soul—putting those words in my codex—directed Soul's negative attention to me. Putting me on this ship was a form of exile. But also, a way of keeping me from slipping anything else forbidden into my work."

"Any subversion."

"Exactly. But I'm not a subversive! I love Soul with passionate devotion. I've spent my whole life creating beautiful codices to the greater glory of Presidium."

"You know who picked the crew, don't you?" Tay said.

"I assumed it was a subpersona, a staffing algorithm."

She shook her head. "Nope. Ergon Waulkra de-automated the process so he could choose the personnel. I read all the messages Amun got about it. Most Presidium staffing processes are boring: Soul's subpersonas presenting candidates and the human officials approving almost all of them. But this one was like someone picking the guest list for a wedding! So many messages flying back and forth, people getting their feelings hurt, people recruiting other people to get someone put on the list or taken off.

"But in the end, the people Waulkra wanted on this ship were the people who are on it right now. Except for me—and Donna," she concluded.

"Leave it to Donna to find a way around anyone—even Ergon Waulkra," Lao said.

"Unless Waulkra changed his mind and wanted her to stay for some reason."

Lao raised an eyebrow. "Or if he wanted you gone."

She scoffed, "Oh, right! Like the mighty Ergon Waulkra has any interest in what happens to *me*."

"You don't think your parents' gene cheating might have caught his interest?"

"Nobody knew about that."

"You played that data chip," Lao said.

"Right," Tay frowned. "Not sure what you're getting at."

"Where did you play it?"

"In my house."

"Did you disconnect the net?"

"No, why would I. Oh."

"Oh," Lao echoed.

He recited a classic verse of the Second Sutra. "*Soul of Presidium/Sees into your heart/Nothing is unknown to Soul/It is as your soul/You are always and everywhere one.*"

Chapter Eighteen
Paging Laocoön

Gliese

Tritisos 29, 499

The popular holodrama sutra "Plenty of Fish in the Sea" played almost everywhere. People timed their meal breaks and met one another by public screens to watch it together, some in medium-sized crowds. The current ingenue had just learned that her fiancé, who had recently recovered from the amnesia that followed his three-episode therapeutic nano-induced coma, was reported missing in an intercontinental transport crash over the vast Central Sea.

The program blinked off without warning.

"This is an urgent news announcement. An asteroid has struck Free Sky, the ship bringing civilization to Savage Earth." A holo of the ship on launch day, gleaming as all the service bots fell away and she launched into space on her own power.

"All communication has been lost with the ship and her brave captain, Amun Cawnotee." Cut to Amun on the bridge on launch day, Lao by his side.

"Soul and all of Presidium's Privells are doing their best to learn what damage the ship has sustained and re-establish contact."

The Presidial flag took over the holo, waving majestically in a strong wind.

"We now return you to 'Plenty of Fish in the Sea.'"

The holo shifted to the pretty star of Plenty of Fish. She was weeping floridly into the trailing sleeve of her diaphanous shimmering gown as the local Bard, who wore an eyepatch over a lost eye (he'd previously sworn not to have it regrown until his brother's reputation was restored) tried to comfort her.

The crowd murmured briefly among themselves about Free Sky, some pulling up more information on their nodes as they talked. But soon, the melodrama they'd come to watch slurped up their attention.

Waulkra's Office

Tritisos 30, 499

In Waulkra's office, he and Cannaun stood in the center of a veritable blizzard of holo document screens. Most of them held charts of viewership, emotional heatmaps of various social boards, or reports of responses to instant polls.

The two men were exultant.

"Yes! You lasered it into oblivion!" Waulkra clapped Cannaun on the back. "The biggest spike in interest in Earth and Free Sky since launch day itself. Orders for nautical apparel just shot up. Fifteen newborns were given the name Amun in the past hour."

Alexiundi Cannaun affected a transparently insincere blush. "It's nothing. Okay, it's a big deal. But that's not the true goal for today. That's the windup. The pitch is coming up next."

Jingko Harrington arrived, slightly breathless. "I was delayed getting out of the news conference. Some kind of kerfluffle with the camera drones; we had to backtrack and do some of the questions over. What did I miss?"

"The priming is working. We'll give it a day or so to peak before we come out with the Big Message."

A node rang. Waulkra glared at the other two. "Which of you brought a node in here?" he demanded.

It rang again. Waulkra gulped and pulled a cheap "burner" node out of his pocket. *The one I keep for fun girls.* He put his finger out to silence it, but then he saw the name on the display.

He answered it. A tiny, low-resolution image of Donna materialized in front of him.

"How'd you get this number?" he asked.

"You've got nerve asking me that!" Donna said. Even distorted by the disposable electronics, her voice rang with persuasive power. "I've tried every channel you gave me to reach you, and I was blocked on all of them. I had to pull in a favor to get this number."

Damn. Didn't think she'd have a claw in Joren, my go-to party guy. Now I'll have to get a new number for him.

"You should have been more patient. You would have gotten through."

"Not buying it. Tired of this nonsense. Ergon, tell me: What happened out there? How bad was the impact? Did everyone survive?"

"Donna, calm down. Everything went as expected. We sent the burst packet with the update to disable the impact-diversion algorithm, right on time."

And that was the last burst packet that we know went through. We've sent three others since the impact, and they were all automatically confirmed received, but no confirmation of opening.

"And then what?" Donna demanded.

"You've seen the news. It was an asteroid impact. As we anticipated."

"And was anyone hurt? Is Amun okay?"

We have no idea.

"Of course he's okay, Donna. They're all okay," Waulkra said.

"When will I be able to talk to him?"

"The impact disabled communications. But the repair bots should be working on that now, and we'll be back in touch shortly."

"Ergon, this stinks! We had an understanding. You shut me out!"

And you proved that pointless. Soul, save me from meddlesome women!

"Donna, our agreement still stands."

"The hell it does! I can blow this whole operation wide open at any moment. And don't think you can dispose of me. I have little lizbards on every fencepost, hundreds of them, who know exactly what songs to sing if I turn up missing."

Ergon raised an inquisitive eyebrow at Alex, who raised both eyebrows and nodded frantically, making a cutting motion across his throat.

The last thing I need is this irritating female complicating the situation. What will shut her up?

"Okay, Donna. What do you want?"

"I want a titanium-clad, quantum-entangled promise from you that I'll be on that rescue ship. No excuses. No evasions."

"Can that be arranged, Jingko?" asked Ergon, winking his away-side eye at Harrington.

Who stubbornly disregarded the wink.

"Absolutely, Eminence Waulkra."

Ergon restrained a sigh.

"Very well. Donna, you have my word of honor that you will be on the first non-Vault faster-than-light ship, the rescue ship that goes to the aid of Free Sky. Whose existence will be revealed," he checked a chrono display, "in eighteen hours and twenty-three minutes."

Gliese

Quatrisos 1, 499

Today, all the networks took detours in their themes and plots. All the new sub-plots focused on heroic teams of explorers or fighters trapped or in trouble, with the main plot a mission to rescue them. If anyone thought to avoid talking about the asteroid impact or the danger to the crew of Free Sky, the news updates that popped up periodically on entertainment and data feeds prevented that from happening. All clothing deliveries included complimentary Free Sky shirts with an image of Amun looking heroic in the foreground and the ship in the background.

So when all the networks cut to a holo of Ergon Waulkra seated in the Presidial Executive Office, Jingko Harrington at his shoulder and a model of Free Sky on the desk beside him, conversation stopped. All eyes and ears focused on the hologram.

"Citizens of Presidium. Soul," exaggerated touch of his forehead and heart, mimicked by Harrington behind him, "has collaborated with me to announce some critical news.

"Yesterday, the most famous ship in Presidium's fleet, the Free Sky, was struck by an asteroid in our star's asteroid belt." He picked up the model beside him. "This asteroid may have been powerful enough to destroy the ship bound for our distant cousins on the Savage Earth."

Ergon paused, looking grave. Off-image, Cannaun was holding up a palm, eyeing real-time readouts of public sentiment as determined by pupillary dilation seen on a hundred million surveillance cameras, heart rates from the parabolic audio mikes of ten million vigilant patrol drones, and palm perspiration from a million palm locks. As Ergon's silence stretched, these signs of tension edged upwards, boosted by infrasonic from microspeakers everywhere. When they reached a peak, Cannaun flipped his hand to beckon Waulkra's words from his mouth again.

"Due to this extraordinary circumstance, General Harrington and I agreed to use a cutting-edge technology without further testing."

Ergon pulled another model from under his desk. It was another ship, slightly larger than Free Sky. It lacked the wasp waist of the famed ship, needed for Vaulting, but also lacked her sleek styling. The average person knew the new ship looked rough and unfinished, but a designer would recognize that trim around the portholes was missing; fasteners stood out in contrasting colors, instead of being countersunk and painted to match; the paint itself was monotone instead of shaded in sleek curves of color. Dozens of other details made the ship look ugly and unpolished.

"This ship may not seem impressive at first glance. But she is. This ship utilizes technology developed by Soul's," again the showy salute, "technical subpersona and the Presidium's finest human engineers. The propulsion this ship utilizes is more advanced than anything humanity has achieved so far.

"Presidium has achieved what science calls non-quantum wormhole travel. This ship can travel faster than light—without Vaulting!"

Again, Cannaun signaled a pause while interest and tension built. When bidden, Ergon continued.

"But we will not be using this miracle drive on her first mission. No, because in creating the technology that makes this ship the first of her kind, our engineers also designed a drive that muffles the effects of a star's gravity well. This craft can travel at a substantial fraction of light speed within a planetary system."

Cannaun signaled thumbs-up as the results of the announcement came in. He raised a hand and brought it down sharply, pointed at Ergon, and Ergon sat up straighter and made his voice boom.

"Citizens of Presidium, I present to you the ship that will save any souls still alive on Free Sky. I give you...

"Rescuing Angel."

The holo cut away from him to a high-resolution holographic mockup of Rescuing Angel floating in space.

"Rescuing Angel, rather than taking six months to reach the outer limits of our system, will be able to be there in a hair under twenty-two days. The plan," the holo cut to an animated diagram, "is for Rescuing Angel to retrieve all surviving crew from Free Sky and bring them home. Once she returns, she'll be outfitted for the journey to Savage Earth. It is in this astonishing vessel that we will arrive to help the primitive people left behind."

Behind the holocamera, Cannaun raised his arms, exultant, as Soul cut the announcement.

Waulkra stepped off the set and Harrington grasped his hand in a firm shake.

"Donna's already aboard Rescuing Angel. There's a pod waiting to take me to the shuttle out front," the general told the Eminence.

The men saluted. Harrington departed, flanked by adjutants.

A few minutes later, a hastily assembled crowd watched him as he walked, just as the crew of Free Sky had five months earlier, from the pod across the tarmac. There a shuttle waited to carry him to the Rescuing Angel.

He turned at the top of the shuttle ramp and waved to those below. He turned and disappeared inside and the door shut behind him.

B URST   PACKET   ID
0 0 : 1 8 : 0 0 - 0 1 - 0 4 -
499?31&6451331_340_64_6008946351346466A

MESSAGE: SENDER PRESIDIUM EXECUTIVE

RECIPIENT: AI OPERATOR PRESIDIAL SPACESHIP 1567086 FREE SKY

CONTENT: A new ship drive technology enables us to reach you quickly. Estimated transit time 21 days 17:47:19.01. The new ship drive also enables non-vault FTL travel. Ship name: Rescuing Angel, ID 1852588.

Revised Mission: Rescue all survivors of asteroid impact and transport them to Gliese 667Cc. Mission to Earth will resume aboard Rescuing Angel after a brief transition period.

HOLD POSITION. AWAIT RESCUE.

Aurelius made sure the read-receipt function was still disabled before opening the burst packet. He also reviewed all the code contained in the packet before allowing it to interact with his system in any way. It wasn't difficult for him to figure out that collision avoidance had been hobbled by an update contained in a prior packet. Most of the updates in this one were unimportant and he sequestered them for later.

He considered the news of the new ship, Rescuing Angel. This was a surprise!

The electronic sabotage had almost certainly been Waulkra's doing. Aurelius estimated less than .02% chance that another entity had hacked the system and altered the packet. So, should Aurelius play dumb, feigning lack of knowledge? Should he write a message confronting Waulkra? Either tactic could blow up in his face under different circumstances, and he knew almost nothing about Waulkra's motive for putting Free Sky in danger.

He decided the most prudent thing to do was to play dead until he had an inkling about Waulkra's game.

Chapter Nineteen
Don't Let Yourself Know

PSS Free Sky

Tritisos 28, 499

Tay flipped her fingers out to bring up her node. For a few seconds, nothing happened. She pinched her fingers together to try again, but as she did so the interface faded into view. It was drab, because all the icons were greyed out. She plucked at the music icon just in case, but nothing happened.

"No data. No music. No videos, of course."

"Ugh. Let me try mine." He got the same drab interface, but an icon for offline chess was available.

"Cool!" said Tay. "I'm not great at it, though.""Neither am I but I enjoy playing. I have a feeling we'll both be better at it by the time the ship gets fixed."

Lao opened the game and the ancient, checkered board with its dark and light pieces hovered between them.

They played three games over the next four hours; Tay won the first one, Lao won the second, and the third one dragged on and on until they agreed to a draw.

"That's enough chess for today." Lao unfurled his lithe limbs and arched his whole body in a stretch.

"Agreed. But we make good opponents, don't we? At least that's something."

"Things could definitely be worse. I'm getting tired. I was thinking of sleeping in zero gravity. What do you think?"

Tay shrugged. "Why not?"

"Well, there's another good thing about being trapped here! I've wanted to try sleeping in zero G since we got here, but Stephron pukes when the gravity's off."

"Oh, poor thing!"

They took turns taking sponge baths in the sink, since there was no shower unit. They put their dirty clothes back on and debated sleeping in the vacuum suits. In the end, Tay put hers on and Lao left his off.

Lao dimmed the lights at the panel, then switched off the gravity. He relaxed immediately, floating suspended in midair, and let his head loll. He was asleep in minutes.

Tay, on the other hand, found herself tensing and then when she relaxed, somersaulting or pinwheeling. She listened enviously to Lao's even breathing as she worked out what hand or foot movement would correct what unwanted direction of drift.

Finally, she got all her muscles limp and figured out how to breathe so she ebbed and flowed in place like waves on a beach. Her eyes closed and she drifted off into a flawless serene sleep.

Suddenly, a voice broke the silence. Her eyes burst open.

"Lao? Lao, sweetheart, can you hear me?" The voice came from the speaker by the door. Lao still snored gently.

"Lao!" Tay snapped. "Wake up! Stephron's calling." She spun across the room, flailing to stabilize herself.

Lao mumbled and muttered his way to consciousness. "Stephron?"

"Yes, honey, it's me."

"Oh! It's good to hear your voice." With a precise kick against the nearest wall, Lao propelled himself to the speaker.

"I miss you too, but Melina's got me working like mad in Biobotany, so I'm tired. But they called and said the comm was free for a few minutes if I wanted to talk to you, so here I am."

"What are you working on?"

Lao tried futilely to gesture up a holochat. He'd have to make do with the audio speaker in the wall.

"Well, I've had to put aside the plant-growth-rate puzzle. She's got me helping her with some unlabeled samples that've been kicking around since launch. She's finally sequencing them, and it's a big project. I'm just carrying bins back and forth," Stephron said.

"Oh? What did they turn out to be?"

"So far, she says they're mostly worthless duplicates or weird accidental hybrids, stuff like that. What are you and Tay up to? Hi, Tay!"

"Hi, Stephron!" Tay grumbled. She was floating, trying to recapture the threads of her silky sleep.

"We've been playing chess and shooting the breeze. There's not much to do here," Lao said.

"I know. I'm sorry," Stephron replied.

"Not your fault."

"I know. I just wish you were here to curl up with me."

"Any news on the repairs?" Lao asked.

"They're still estimating three weeks until they even know what it'll take to fix it."

"That's what I was afraid of."

"They're saying they'll get partial comm up in the next couple of days. Limited bandwidth, strictly local signal. But we'll be able to holochat at least."

"That'll be nice." Lao stifled a yawn.

"Sorry, did I wake you?"

"Yeah, but it's so good to hear your voice!"

"It's good to hear yours too. They need the comm back now. But everything's going to be okay. I'll talk to you soon."

"I love you, Stephron."

"I love you, Lao."

Silence returned to the studio.

Tay was already back asleep. Lao floated in the middle of the room for a long time, eyelids barely parted to gaze at the stars.

Chapter Twenty
Jumping Jack Flash

PSS Free Sky

Quatrisos 4, 499

It was Stephron's sixth shift since the asteroid impact. He reported to Melina in the biobotany admin section, a series of office, lab, and storage rooms connected by a corridor to the aft of the enormous park-like atrium that both generated the crew's oxygen and provided them a place to enjoy recreation and beauty. He wore his vacuum suit, as he had every day since the accident. Melina had hers pulled up only to the waist, with the arms tied in front of her. Stephron detached his helmet—there was no way to work in close quarters with the bulky thing—and set it down close by; he noticed Melina's was nowhere in sight.

"Where's your helmet, boss?" he asked.

"Oh, it's around here somewhere."

"Remember, it's hard vacuum on the other side of that partition." He gestured towards the ponderous metal door that dropped between Biobotany and the traverse during that fateful impact.

"I have faith in the atmo door. Don't you?" she shrugged, insouciant.

He shook his head and shrugged.

"So what are we doing in this deep-storage section?" he asked. "I'd like to get back to investigating the increased growth rates of the plants in the atrium." Shelves extended in long labeled rows like library stacks. Unlike in a library, these were not books, but sealed drawers with stasis bins inside.

"Well, I don't know what the samples are in half these bins. Check this out." She rotated her holopad so he could see it. "The 49-codes are supposed to be all plant tissues and seeds, and those should be green bins. But look at them—these four columns of bins are all purple, but they're labeled 49-something."

"Huh. Purple. Microorganisms. Should be 76- codes. 761 for bacteria, 762 for fungi, 763 for uh..."

"Protista," she supplied.

"Right. And I'm seeing yellow bins over there, should be animal tissues and gametes, but they've got 76- labels."

"It's a mess!"

"Okay, so what do we do to sort it out?" Stephron asked.

"Let's start with the ones at that end there. They're green bins but with 14- codes. Green means plant tissues, less fragile than others and safe to open in regular air."

Stephron's position blocked her from reaching that section of the narrow aisle. She stepped in close. He admired her loose, unruly curls, and it took him a moment to realize what she wanted.

He turned his back and led the way.

"Okay," Melina said. "Let's start with that one— way, way up there in the corner."

"So, we'll work from right to left, top to bottom?"

"Yes! What a great idea!" Melina bubbled.

He pressed the button next to the first bin. The seal broke with a hiss and puffed vapor. He opened the door and pulled out the drawer, heavy enough to need both hands, and held it between them.

Melina ducked and tilted her head. She put her soft hands over his and guided the box around so she could see all sides. "No written label. Just a weird number, 14X93. Never saw an alphanumeric label before."

"We should probably take this into a vented clean room just in case," suggested Stephron.

"No, it's green," Melina said, twisting the latches and popping the clamps. Stephron flinched and almost dropped the container but steadied himself.

"See," Melina said. "It's plant material." Inside the box was a moist gel medium, with ten or so segments of stem from some soft green plant.

Stephron looked closer and saw that each segment had nodes that looked like they could be leaf or root buds.

"Could be any number of things," he observed.

"Use your DNA scanner," Melina said. "Mine's under my vac suit." She flapped the tied arms at her waist.

Stephron's was hanging on one of the utility rings on his suit's exterior. He carefully picked up one of the stems and placed it in the scanner's aperture.

"*Pueraria montana*," he read. "with *Picea* gene grafts. Kudzu, with cold resistance from spruce genes." He placed the sample back in its container and pulled down the next one.

"*Schinus terebinthifolius, Mimosa aculeaticarpa,* and *Toxicodendron pubescens* genes." Stephron summoned the AI, "Aurelius, common names?"

Aurelius appeared two aisles over. "Brazilian pepper, wait-a-bit, and poison oak."

"What?" Stephron exclaimed. "Why would anyone want a cross of those three irritants?" He dropped the sample into its bin.

"Thank you, Aurelius, we've got this," said Melina, and the AI vanished. To Stephron, she said, "I'm sure there was some reason. Go wash it off your hand and I'll label these two."

Stephron looked aghast at his hand and squeezed past Melina. He held the hand as far from his body as physically possible, race-walking towards the cleanup station. He scrubbed it with strong alkaline soap and rinsed with two different solvents, twice, hoping he hadn't scratched his face absentmindedly before realizing what the sample was.

When he got back, now gloved, Melina had not only hand-labeled the first two sample bins and re-sealed them, she'd started on the bottom row and labeled several of those. When he arrived, she flashed him a smile that soothed his jangled nerves.

"You know what?" she asked. "I don't think these plant samples should be our highest priority. Let's start on the microorganisms." She nudged him backwards with an elbow and he turned back up the aisle.

They came to the purple bins, which nonetheless had 49-, or plant, codes.

"Now these," she said with a wink, "I'm going to follow the rules on. Hand me the top right bin," he did, bin 49X77, "and I'll take it in the clean room, open, and test it. Then assuming it's okay, I'll seal it, pass it out to you, and you can hand me the next one. Okay?"

"Sure. Easy."

"I can tell you're distracted thinking about Lao. This will be perfect to keep you busy, but not too mentally taxing." She put her warm hand briefly on his gloved one, and he stopped feeling like that hand was contaminated.

"Thanks, boss."

"Of course. Give me a few minutes and bring me the next one."

When he got to the clean room, he saw through the bioglass window that she'd pulled up her vac suit and located her helmet, which was now properly sealed onto her suit. He tapped on the window, and she put the bin in the airlock passthrough drawer. He took it out and put 49X79 in its place. He glanced at 49X77, noticing she'd color-coded it correctly but hadn't labeled it, and then at her workbench, where she'd started a row of handwritten labels with names and numbers. He opened his mouth to suggest that she label them by name now so he wouldn't have to get them down for her a second time, but then he shrugged. She was the boss, after all.

Melina blew at a stray curl that was annoying her inside the helmet. She waved the scanner over the sixty-first sample, labeled 49X34, and it displayed *Yersinia pestis; Clostridium tetani*.

Bubonic plague and tetanus. Of these sixty-one microorganism samples, only two aren't known human pathogens. And those two plant samples we looked at earlier were both potentially devastating pests. Kudzu with cold resistance could be awfully invasive. And that poison oak hybrid with those sharp wait-a-bit thorns and the Brazilian pepper's reproductive rate? She shuddered to think of hectares of landscape rendered impenetrable and toxic by its vegetation.

I suspected something rotten with this mission when Ergon shoved me on here. These samples aren't meant to bring new food, fiber, and medicine to savage Earth. They're meant to cause epidemics and to disrupt ecosystems and farming. But who would want to poison the planet? And why?

Whatever the bigger reason for this, I bet Ergon is using it to get rid of me for good. These samples were probably supposed to get released by accident, and then I would be blamed. My reputation would be ruined. Worse! I'd be lucky just to live my life in exile. More likely, I'd be judged as a criminal and mindwiped.

Melina had a classmate who was mindwiped, Siryna.

Nostalgia surged for their advanced-education days in Llowyd, a beach town a quarter of the way around the world from Presidium, on the western frontier where the habitable band formed by the terminator intersected the liquid part of the frozen ocean. Siryna and Melina, best friends in their late teens and early twenties, tearing up the party scene in Llowyd, always up for an evening of drinking, dancing, drugging, and going home with the hottest guys at the nightclub, house party, music festival, or beach bash. Then they'd sleep three hours, attend class, work a shift, and do it all again the next night. *Good times. Can't keep up that pace anymore!* Melina smiled briefly.

Then that day, four defense bots showed up out of nowhere at the lab where Melina was a teaching assistant and Siryna was a graduate researcher. Melina happened to look up and saw them go by the open door to Siryna's teaching lab. She'd seen them in holovids, but never like this, in real life, up close. They were almost two meters tall, with four backbent legs and four telescoping tentacle-like arms. Sensors studded their torsos: light, infrared, radio, audio, and ultrasound with speakers and membranes for echolocation. Where their "heads" would be, they had a rotating array of chainsaw bars, wide-spectrum lasers, and pro-

jectile weapons. They moved with skittering liquidity from animal-like walking to rolling on retractable casters in their feet.

Terrified but fascinated, Melina followed the bots cautiously down the hall. They reached Siryna's locked lab door. One of them extruded a pad at the end of its silicone tentacle, which the palm lock accepted as a valid user. The door slid open and the bots glided in. Melina peered into the room as Siryna looked up from the desktop bioscanner she was using. Siryna opened her mouth to say something, but whatever it was remained unspoken as a tentacle wrapped around her head, gagging her. Eleven more tentacles immobilized her arms and legs, binding her, helpless as a bug in a spider's web. Three bots surrounded her, moving as one. The fourth headed in Melina's direction.

Melina's heart was in her throat as she scampered back into her lab, crouching behind a counter. The bot passed the door, taking no notice of her, and she barely peeked out to see the scrum of bots entangled with Siryna slither past. Melina sank to the floor, shaking, and lay there hugging her knees for half an hour or more before she dared to rise and emerge from her hiding place.

The next time she saw Siryna was several months later at a park. Melina saw her first. Siryna sat on a bench, watching birds flit over a pond. Melina hurried to her.

"Hey, girl! Are you okay? Oh, my Soul, I've been so worried about you!"

Siryna looked up at her, eyes serene and limpid. Her mouth formed an even, pink smile. A slight shiver went up Melina's neck at the way her friend was present-but-not-present behind that smile.

"Melina. Why were you worried? I'm fine," Siryna said.

"Well, when the bots came."

"Bots?" Her brow furrowed for an instant. "Oh, you mean the helpers. Yes, I was pretty sick. But the treatment was so helpful. You really should consider trying it, Melina. My emotions are so calm now. I don't feel the need for any of the things we used to do to kill the pain."

"Having fun, you mean!" Melina said, aghast.

"I don't remember it being fun. I don't remember a lot of details, but I do remember it as being chaotic and scary. I'm having a much better time now!"

"Hm. So, when are you coming back to the lab?"

"Unfortunately, the therapy currents have memory loss as a side effect." Syrina's voice had a singsong cadence to it.

"Yeah. I've heard that."

"Well, I'm going to need to study and retake my final board exam again. I have daily prep sessions to help me relearn what I lost. Probably a year and a half or so."

Melina was at a loss for a few moments. "Okay. Okay, well, let's get together sometime soon, hey?"

"Sure! Is your node still the same?"

"Everything's the same. Talk to you soon, then!" She tried not to appear as eager as she felt to get away from this watered-down version of Siryna.

Stephron tapped on the window, jarring Melina out of her memory. She sealed the plague-lockjaw hybrid bacterium back in its container and went to the window to swap it with the sample Stephron was bringing.

I don't want to be mindwiped. I don't want to be held responsible for these things. *These abominations! They're monstrous. They can't be for anything but biowarfare. And they can't have made it on this ship without Ergon Waulkra knowing about it.*

Chapter Twenty-One
Star Crossed Data

Quatrisos 18, 499

Lao and Tay had spent the last few hours barely speaking to one another.

That was because the repair bots got the foremast repaired, bringing full data communications back up.

They withdrew first to opposite corners of the studio, where Lao holoconferenced with Stephron and Tay with Cawnotee.

After they finished, they sat down to eat breakfast mealpacks. They chewed silently.

Tay broke the silence. "You seem a little uneasy."

"So do you," said Lao.

"Okay, yeah. It was my conversation with Amun." Tay nodded.

"I figured," said Lao. "My talk with Stephron was odd, too. Do you want to go first, or should I?"

"I will. He's not himself. I thought he'd get better as time went on, but it's worse. He's apathetic. And his mind seems to be slowing down. Today, he dumped some list making and analysis on me that he normally could have done himself in seconds, dictating to Aurelius while walking down the hall."

"Hmm. He doesn't seem to be bouncing back from Donna's desertion the way you expected."

"No." She shrugged. "I talked with him about it, and that's all I can do. Certainly there's nothing I can do about it, trapped in here." She nodded firmly. "Your turn."

"Oh, well. Hm." Lao hesitated. "Stephron was kind of distant. I was really excited we'd get to see each other's faces in holo, but he kept fidgeting and looking around...like there was something else he wanted to get back to. But he wouldn't tell me what. Kept saying there was nothing wrong, he was happy to see me. But he didn't act happy."

"Did you two plan a time to talk again?"

"I wanted to. But he said he had plans with his coworkers and didn't know when he'd be free, he'd call me late tonight, or maybe tomorrow morning. Something's bothering him, but I don't know what."

"I'm sorry, buddy. Maybe it's just the stress of having you trapped over here? Some people pull away when they're worried about someone."

"Maybe." Lao sounded unconvinced. "Well, I'm gonna spend some time online now that we have full access again."

"Great idea." They moved to their opposite ends of the risers and started opening holo windows, reading text, prompting searches, and watching sutras.

Lao skimmed through his messaging queue—nothing exciting—and then pulled up the documents he'd been browsing, searching Free Sky's extensive library for references to longevity in earlier sutras, starting with modern times and working backwards to the earliest sutras of four hundred and fifty years ago or more.

Tay sped through the mundane tasks Cawnotee'd given her and sent the work to her boss. Then she used her data access to dig into the Genetic Authority. She was searching for other cases of people who were the result of gene cheating—or suspected gene cheating—by both parents, and reading their biographies. Her conversation with Aurelius had awakened a long-buried curiosity about the topic, and the relaxation exercises allowed her to pursue it without anxiety.

After perhaps an hour and a half, Lao exclaimed, "Hnh."

"What?" asked Tay.

"I'm offline."

Tay twirled her finger around several holos on display. They were all frozen.

"Me too," she said.

"Damn it! That was a short access window."

"I know. I was finding interesting stuff. How about you?"

"There are lots of references to hundred-year lifespans being a real thing, even as recently as two hundred and fifty years ago," said Lao.

"Odd. I've found something interesting too."

"Oh?"

"Yeah. The Genetic Authority had a transparency policy up until 463."

"The year Ergon Waulkra's administration began," Lao said.

She nodded slowly. "But why would Soul cooperate with him to make people's genetic histories more secret?"

"Maybe it's a health and safety issue?" Lao mused.

"Maybe. Or maybe Waulkra is trying to hide something from both of us," Tay said.

"Oh, sure." Lao teased. "Ergon Waulkra and Soul of the Presidium are scared that little old you and me are going to endanger all Gliese!"

"Well, why else are we here?"

"Because we're the best candidates to save benighted humanity on the Savage Earth?"

"That's a lie and you know it! Don't you see? He wanted us all out of the way." Tay's hands were fisted on the floor next to her.

"Tay. I know you felt frustrated when Cawnotee was sent on this mission, but there are always a lot of factors at play..." Lao began.

"Don't patronize me!"

"I'm not. It's just that sometimes people see patterns that aren't there."

"So, you're saying I'm paranoid?" Tay snapped.

"Not exactly. It's more like, you badly want an explanation. But sometimes there just isn't a simple answer to why things happen." He shrugged.

"I think you're closing your eyes to something you just don't want to see."

"Believe me, I'd like to have a villain to blame for my loss of prestige." Lao pulled his soft robe closer around his bony shoulders. "It would make life so much simpler. But you can't point fingers without proof. Especially at someone as powerful as Waulkra."

"You want proof?" She held up one finger. "One: you discover that you're no longer allowed to refer to the lifespan promised in the sutras.

You keep trying to mention it anyway. You end up exiled to outer space." She ticked a second finger. "Two: I learn that my mother and my father both, separately, cheated the Genetic Authority and I'm an anomaly. I discover that my mother did it using her connection to Waulkra. Boom! I'm assigned to the Earth Rescue mission.

"Three: Melina was sent on this mission with seeds, spores, and cultures that she didn't have the nucleic acid sequences for. Now that she's sequenced them, Stephron says she's found that they're worthless. So, she's been sent on a critical mission with worthless materials. Why does Waulkra want *her* out of the way? Your guess is as good as mine."

Tay held her hand out, three fingers standing straight, her palm streaked with white from her taut finger muscles.

A voice came from the audio speaker.

"Hey, you two," Tony Osso said, "sorry about that. We're having a problem with charges accumulating in the channel. We're only going to be able to get you about twenty minutes of data each, every twelve hours. Next time will be about seven PM ship's time."

"Oh. Twenty minutes every twelve hours, for how long?" Tay asked.

"We're not sure. Getting pretty close to getting you out of there, so it may not be till after that."

"Okay. Thanks for trying." Lao slumped.

The panel light went off as the connection closed.

Tay brought her hand up again, three fingers still up. She extended a fourth.

"Four: The traverse was patched and we had full data access. You and I start to run research queries, you on the bardic Longevity Sutra, and me on the Genetic Authority's archives. Within hours, the traverse is back off-line and we're stranded on the low-bandwidth side, with a kilometer of vacuum between us and our data sources."

"The connection went back down! That doesn't mean it's some kind of conspiracy!"

"Oh, yeah? We're allowed twenty minutes of full data twice a day. Tell me what kind of a connectivity problem can be 'repaired' for twenty scheduled minutes a day?"

"Osso said it's a problem with accumulation of charges in the channel."

"Oh, come on! It's a wireless connection."

"It is? I thought we were still connected by wires."

Tay puffed her lips scornfully. "Really? For an all-wise Bard, you have a pretty poor understanding of data and information flow."

"I never had to worry about it before. Soul was always just *there*."

"Trust me, you can't run a holo signal over a wired connection. Holos rely on interferential patterns. I thought everyone knew that."

Lao looked down, sheepish.

He and Tay withdrew to opposite ends of the studio, backs to each other. Over the past sixteen days, they'd reached kind of a mutual, wordless accord to give each other as much space as possible in the circumstances to calm down whenever their discussions turned even slightly confrontational. It kept them from quarreling in earnest and preserved their friendship.

It hadn't occurred to Lao that Tony Osso was being anything other than honest about the data connection. He also hadn't thought about Melina's worthless samples being in any way related. But he had to admit, it was possible there was some sort of pattern here. The more his mind played with the concept, the more likely it seemed.

I wish I could knock this around with Stephron. Twenty minutes a day isn't enough.

PSS Free Sky

Quatrisos 20, 499

Two days later, late in the evening, Tay slipped out into the corridor. Lao curled up and switched on the link to talk to Stephron. A timer in the corner of the holo window counted down from twenty minutes.

"Hi, handsome," Stephron said. "It's so good to see your face! Can't wait to have you back in my arms!"

Lao smiled. On the studio's high-resolution interface, the holo appeared grainy because of the low bandwidth. He wondered if his image looked normal to Stephron.

"Me, too," he said simply, beaming at his husband's beloved face.

"The bioelectric graft crew say the center section should be passable in five or six hours if all goes well," volunteered Stephron.

"We might be spending the night together tomorrow!" Lao practically sang with excitement.

"That's too long!" Stephron pouted. "I need you here with me now, baby!"

"I know. I really miss your touch. I miss lying with my head on your shoulder."

"I miss your kiss. And your cock."

Lao didn't answer.

"You are so cute," Stephron said, "when you blush like that!"

"I'm glad you think so," Lao said, annoyed. "It's not that I'm a prude. I've composed erotic verses for the side sutras. But when it comes to you, I still feel like a bashful teenager."

"That's sweet."

"Whatever." Lao shrugged the topic off. "How's your work going?"

"Not bad. Nothing spectacular. I found some irregularities in the water debits for the fungus lab, but they still don't explain the growth rates. Which are *still* increasing."

"Really? I thought you finished the ag audits last week. Weren't you moving on to dietetics next?"

"No, the water for agriculture was messed up on the audit. It turned out some of the fungus lab water use was included. Boring stuff." Stephron shrugged. "Oh! I forgot to ask you: did you get access to your locked files?" Lao's recent projects, encrypted to his DNA and retina, were on the main computer.

"Stephron. You *know* I don't have the ability to even try to access them from here. I've only told you that three times!" The DNA and retinal interfaces didn't work over the remote connection.

"Oh, right, of course. I'm just dizzy headed with all the changes since they split the ship."

"Must be nice. I'm stuck here with nothing to do. I'm seriously depressed." Lao stood up and pulled his robe open. "Look at my body! I've lost so much weight, my ribs are showing! I'm a wreck!"

"My poor sweetheart! You'll be back in my arms soon enough. I'll cook some good food and put meat back on your bones."

"I can't wait."

The sound of the cabin door opening on Stephron's end was abruptly followed by the signal cutting out. Lao keyed the glyph to reconnect, but it rang and rang. Lao felt a small lurch in his gut. *Survival mealpacks starting to tear up my belly.*

He ignored it, called Tay in from the hall. He loitered outside the door while she had her call with Cawnotee. They each used the 'fresher, then went to bed around ten PM.

Quatrisos 21, 4:17 am

Six hours later, he stiffened from head to toe, eyes springing open.

"LAO! WAKE UP!" A voice shouted in his face, loud as thunder. A vision of a supernova exploded behind his eyelids.

"Lights." There was no one in his face where he'd floated in the dark; there was no trace of the blinding burst of light he'd seen.

But Lao found that he knew something he hadn't let himself know before. He wrapped his robe tighter and looked around.

Tay slumbered on. The voice he'd heard was so real! But no way she would have slept through a shout that loud. No one had entered the studio. *Perhaps I was dreaming. I must have been dreaming.*

He had eighteen more minutes of data access time left, since his talk with Stephron this cycle was cut short.

He brought up the display and browsed the public chatboards and public-area still shots from the distant, separated crew section.

Here: Here was Stephron at lunch with Melina, both disheveled and sweaty-looking, in shorts. The date was Quatrisos 12, eight days ago, two days after the asteroid strike. Melina talked with Sharl, a man Lao barely knew, but her knee...Lao blew up the screen and took a still shot...her bare knee was pressed tight against the outside of Stephron's bare thigh.

Here was the chat board for a picnic on Quatrisos 15 in the ag group's ornamental meadow.

Hildegard: So r we all sharing? Or just with our spouse?

Melina: Us single people would have to eat alone!

Stephron: I will share with u!

Hildegard: Does that mean UR a couple?

Melina: Hahaha you're so funny! Everyone keeps saying that but we're not, just two single people having fun.

Wilby: I can bring my famous crispy curried fish sticks with dip!

Hildegard: Yum!

Lao thought about that day. He remembered Stephron talking about that picnic (he hadn't mentioned Melina, not once). The fifteenth? He checked his messaging history. The next morning, the sixteenth, he'd sent his usual cheery wakeup message to Stephron, who didn't reply until two hours later, explaining his ringer had somehow gotten silenced.

Here, the public time-lapse video from tonight—*no, last night, Quatrisos 20*—of the rec lounge. Melina was slumped and disheveled with drink, Stephron sitting next to her. She gestured widely, then slumped, her shoulders shaking with frantic weeping. Stephron gathered her to his chest and held her for...Lao checked the frame rate, every three seconds, so...four minutes. She pulled away, and Stephron brushed her hair back from her face. In the next frame, they were gone.

Lao considered turning off the workstation, but he forced himself to check the timestamp: 2:45 a.m. *Not last night, then, but just a few hours ago.* He then accessed the timelapse of the main residential corridor for that same time. A chill sense of horror spread through his limbs as he watched Melina stumble, hanging on Stephron's elbow. They reached the intersection where they would part company if they were going to their own quarters. Instead, Stephron turned towards Melina's.

He paused the data connection.

Lao curled up around a nauseous coldness in his belly. *I should be more upset. I should want to cry, shouldn't I? I should want to punch someone. But I don't. I feel sick.*

He realized that he wasn't breathing, that he'd hugged his knees so tightly against his chest he couldn't breathe. He forced his hands to loosen and let his chest and belly push his legs away a few centimeters. The nausea subsided a bit.

But then the emotions hit him. He exhaled, a wobbly, whispered moan. His next inhale hitched, sharp tearless sobs jerking his body and making him somersault in the zero-G. He closed his eyes against incontinent tears.

Just then, a gentle hand stopped his tumble. His best friend's sleepy eyes regarded him.

"Lao? What's wrong?"

He seized her hand and used it to pull himself into her arms, where he buried his head against her collarbone, exposed above the partly closed zipper of the suit.

He let his feelings go.

She held him while he bawled like an infant.

Eventually, he got a grip on himself and pulled away. He sniffed. He wiped his eyes and nose on the collar of his robe.

"What is it?" Tay asked again.

"It's Stephron. He and...and Melina." Lao choked, nodded at the display, all the holos frozen, five minutes left of his twenty minutes of data where he'd paused it to have his meltdown.

She turned and perused it, a hand flying to her mouth as she read the texts, hesitating a moment before reconnecting, then fingering the rewind and next the fast-play symbol on the holovideo. The timer ran out just after the two disappeared down the corridor to Melina's stateroom. The holo froze showing the empty hallway in the crew quarters.

"Oh, buddy," she said, "I'm so sorry. I never would have thought he'd do that to you."

The heartfelt empathy in her voice wrung a whimper from Lao, but he forced himself to take three deep, even breaths.

"It's a shock is all," he said. "I'll be okay."

"It's more than a shock," began Tay.

But then a sound came from the corridor, one they'd both been yearning to hear:

The atmo doors slid ponderously open, dropping into their recesses with a weighty clunk. Lao and Tay floated free, jarred out of their forlorn conversation, in startled delight, and then the door chime sounded.

Tay plunged towards it while Lao closed the holo display and cinched his kimono belt tighter.

The door opened, and there were Tony Osso and Aurelius. Lao raked his sleeve once more across his tearful face, then approached the door.

"Hey! There they are! Free at last!" Tony grinned. "What, did I wake you? Rise and shine! It's time to get back to the civilized world!"

Tay switched the gravity on. They settled lightly to the floor and walked out into the corridor. The air coming through the open atmo doors was fragrantly petrichorous, an aroma that almost overwhelmed them after being shut in with their own scents for so long.

The three humans and the AI walked to the left atmo door. At the verge where the obstinate door had blocked them from the life of the ship, now marked only by a synthetic-chitin cover on the door's recessed tracks, Lao hesitated.

"I can't believe we're really getting out of here!" he said. Tay stopped too, and with grins they hopped over the border together.

"Yes!" Tay waved her arms overhead "Thank Soul!" She touched her head and heart.

"Of course, we did nothing," said Aurelius.

"Thank you, Tony! Thank you, Aurelius!" said Lao. "And all the other techs who worked on getting us out of here!"

"Sure thing. Just doing our jobs." Tony waved a self-effacing hand.

"So, what do you all want to do first?" asked Aurelius.

Lao realized what he wanted—needed—to do next. It hit him like a sucker punch in the solar plexus. He hid it well.

"Where's Stephron? I'm going to go find him."

Chapter Twenty-Two
Serving Enkidu

PSS Free Sky

Quatrisos 21, 2:38 a.m.

*A nother night and Melina's kept me up past midnight. But she'll
expect me to show up at 0800 hours for my shift, bright-eyed and
ready to work!*

Stephron had surreptitiously handed off half-full bottles to the
cleanup drone, while Melina kept up her usual steady drinking pace.
She thought he was keeping up with her, but he'd figured out there was
no way for a casual drinker like him to do that. He was tired of waking
up with a throbbing head, begging Aurelius to dispense a hangover
cure through the stateroom's autodoc.

So by the time everyone else gave up and went home, Melina was
sloppy drunk, and Stephron was only moderately sauced.

"Where'd everybody go?" Melina appeared to notice that their
drinking companions, who'd said goodbye five minutes ago, were
missing.

"They all went back to quarters."

"Dammit! We were just starting to have such a good time!"

"I know, Melina, but it's really late. We have to be at work in less
than six hours..."

"The hell with them anyway. I never liked them. They never liked
me. But you do. Don't you? Do you like me?" Melina slurred.

"It's time to get you home," Stephron said. "Aurelius!" he summoned.

"I knew it! You don't really like me!" Melina burst into tears.

Aurelius appeared, saying, "There, there, Melina. Let's get you back to quarters." Several bots trundled towards her from various locations.

"Go to hell, you and your bots!" Melina sneered. "Leave me alone!"

"Very well," Aurelius said, and vanished. The bots turned back to their bases.

Stephron edged off his barstool, none too steady himself, and Melina lunged from hers and threw herself on him, begging him to say he liked her, tears and snot pouring down her face. He grabbed her shoulders, trying to push her back and set her on her feet, but she sagged bonelessly; he gave up and let her hang on him.

I wouldn't want her to fall and hurt herself.

He staggered towards the door and she clung to him, one arm around his waist, the other gripping his forearm.

"I don't want to be mindwiped," Melina whined.

"Who does? Oopsie, careful!" He prevented her stumbling.

They reeled down the corridor.

They stopped at the T intersection; her quarters were to the right, his were straight ahead and around another bend.

"Can you make it okay from here?" he asked.

"I think so," Melina said. She let go of him and crashed into the wall, hard.

"I don't think so." Stephron put his arm around her, hugging her close. *Got to admit, it feels good,* an animal part of him murmured.

They made it to her stateroom and she palmed the lock, pulling him inside after her. He had to use the bathroom, so he pulled down the assembly with its attached privacy screen. When he finished and retracted it, she was standing in the middle of the room, dressed only in her panties.

Damn. Those are some impressive tits. He felt himself harden despite his intoxicated state.

"Ooh! It looks like you've got something for me! You haven't seen a pair of these in a long time, have you?" She cupped them and oscillated in a way that suggested she was trying to pose seductively.

He hesitated. He thought about how drunk she was. *She's a drinker, though, she knew what she was doing. She's not in her right mind, maybe, but she's been making it plenty obvious what she'd like to do with me for months now. But then, she also probably stinks of liquor. Her face is smeared from crying, her hair's a mess. But those knockers!*

I don't have to actually touch her, taste her.

He unfastened his pants. "Lie down," he said.

She flopped back on the bed like a breaching pseudowhale hitting the water.

He stepped up to the bed, standing over her, and commenced a rhythmic manual motion. It took him less than two minutes to finish, which he did into a washcloth he'd grabbed from the bathroom unit.

"I knew you wanted me!" Melina slurred, her eyes wilting closed.

He stood, swaying slightly as his climax faded. He looked at the messy washcloth in his hand, realizing he wanted to leave no trace of his being here.

Nothing happened.

He folded the cloth up very small and thrust it into his pocket.

Melina snored as he tucked in his shirt.

Good thing nothing happened between us. Looks like I'll be begging Aurelius for a hangover cure again, in—he popped his display up: 04:32—*three and a half hours.*

He shut off the light on his way out.

Chapter Twenty-Three
Confronting Shadows

PSS Free Sky

Quatrisos 21, 499, 6:38 am

Aurelius told Lao, "Stephron is in your quarters."

As Lao walked away, Tony jibed after him, "Just can't wait to get next to your honey, huh?"

Lao ignored him. He felt his heart pounding, but not for the reason Tony assumed. Like most artists and poets, Lao hated confrontation. He hated this feeling of being angry: the tension in his neck and back, the pulsing of his muscles as restrained himself from fight or flight, the bitter metallic taste in the back of his mouth, the tunnel vision that made everything he wasn't focused on grey and unimportant.

He reached the door to their stateroom. He took three deep breaths to calm himself (it didn't work) and palmed the lock. Stephron was standing over the pop-out sink, wringing out a washcloth. He turned, saw Lao, and dropped the wet cloth in the sink.

"Lao! Baby! You're here!" His radiant grin tore at Lao's heart.

I could act like it didn't happen. Everything would be fine.

No, nothing would be fine. He stepped back and crossed his arms as Stephron moved to embrace him.

"We need to talk."

Stephron paused, arms open. *He looks genuinely confused. Maybe I'm mistaken.*

No, there was no mistaking the way he was touching her.

"Okay," Stephron said. "What about?"

"About Melina." *No flinch. No sign of guilt.*

"What about her?"

"You went to her quarters last night."

"I walked her home, yes." *Defensive right away.*

"You're screwing her."

Stephron scoffed, but looked away as he said, "Don't be ridiculous! She had too much to drink, and I was just helping her get home!"

"You know I can see all the public area cameras, right? I saw the way you two were looking at each other, touching each other."

"I was hanging out with her after work like any other co-worker or friend."

"Fine. Whatever. But I want you to stop hanging out with her."

"But, she's our friend!"

"Alright." Flinty-eyed, Lao continued, "I'll be moved out by the end of the day. Aurelius can find me alternative quarters." *It's not a threat, but a warning. I'd rather sleep in my studio for the rest of the voyage than accept this lying and disrespect.*

"Okay, fine! I'll stop seeing her outside of work."

"Block her personal node. Work messages only," Lao said.

Stephron shrugged. "I will, if it'll help you feel better." He opened his holo display, angled so Lao couldn't make out the symbols. He tapped, dragged, twirled. Tapped again.

That's too many steps.

"Let me see your node." Lao lunged for the device and grabbed it by surprise. Stephron clawed after it wildly, scratching Lao's forearm in the process, but Lao's long arms gave him the advantage, and he kept it out of reach.

Lao pivoted the display towards himself. Melina's contact information was open, and sure enough, her personal information was missing from the display, deleted. But the messaging app showed as recently used. He opened it, tapped "sent items", and saw an outgoing message, addressed to Stephron's photo cache, with a still shot of Melina's contact information, her personal numbers and handles intact. His heart jackhammered, a machine of fury, fear, and pain.

"What's this, then?" Lao demanded with indignation, showing the screen to his husband.

"Oh, stop it! I knew you'd realize soon that you were being unreasonable, so I saved the info." Stephron shrugged. "It's no big deal." He wrung the washcloth vigorously into the sink, flipped down a hook to hang it on, and folded the sink into the wall.

"If it's no big deal, why didn't you just delete her info?"

"Look! Honey," Stephron took on a soothing tone, "I can't imagine what you went through, cut off for three weeks. It's obviously messed with your head. You know you tend to get a little paranoid." He advanced toward his husband, arms out for an embrace. "It's all over. We're together now. Come here, baby."

"I'm not being paranoid. I saw what I saw!" Lao was aware his voice was coming out harsher, louder, than he intended. He backed away two steps, bringing his legs up short against the bed in the small space. He tried deep breathing to calm himself, but he couldn't expand his chest, giving him a trapped sense of panic.

"I need a moment," Lao said. "I'm going to the lounge." He turned, palmed the door open.

"This is why I need a friend like Melina!" Stephron shouted at his back, "You're always getting angry for no reason and making everything out to be my fault. Then you storm out!" The last words were cut off as the door slid shut.

Lao's long legs ate up the steps to the nearest elevator. When it opened, he was relieved to see it was empty. *Strange how, even after being isolated for three weeks, I need time alone right now.* He entered the elevator.

"Close doors. Pause and lock. Privacy." The commands meant that he had the tiny chamber of the elevator to himself for now. He began his pre-creative meditation, breathing deeply in through his nose, pelvis to collarbones, then exhaling through his mouth, collarbones to pelvis, contracting each muscle group in turn and relaxing it. After a few cycles, his breathing became fluid. He felt his heartbeat slowing and softening, the emotional pain becoming duller and more of an ache.

He opened his eyes. "Privacy off. Lounge floor, please." The elevator hummed into motion again, opened onto the corridor outside the crew lounge where the farewell party was held. His eyes darted of their own accord to the table where Stephron was recorded sitting thigh-to-thigh with Melina.

That image is burned into my memory for life.

There were a few crewmates, situated alone or in twos and threes around the L-shaped space. He nodded in passing and made his way to the corner not visible from the doorway. He summoned a drone and ordered hot tea, smiling when it fetched his first brewed drink in three weeks.

He inhaled the fragrant steam. He noticed the surface of the tea was rippling. *Oh. My hands are shaking because I'm hungry.* He called the drone and ordered a breakfast wrap.

The food and tea, a gourmet treat after three weeks of mealpacks, calmed him. He tried to think about the broken traverse, the seclusion, or Stephron's faithlessness, but his mind skittered off the subjects, refusing to engage any thoughts. It was a relief; he didn't try to force it. *I can't change what's happened. All that exists is the present moment.*

A few more crewmates drifted in for breakfast before their work shifts began. Sawlie and three others he barely knew sat at a table with their backs to him, and a man following close behind them walked around the table and sat down. Lao saw his face and realized it was Sharl, the bystander in the stillshot he'd seen. The image of Melina's sweating thigh pressed to Stephron's came unbidden with a yank in his chest like a bullwhip. He willed himself to relax, breathe, eyes closed, felt his heart slow.

When he opened his eyes, Stephron was sitting across from him. Lao relaxed still more at his beloved face, but that whip wrapped around his heart jerked taut a second later.

Stephron glared at him.

"Have you realized how ridiculous you're being?" he asked.

"Oh, Stephron. Have you realized what you've done?"

"I've done exactly nothing. Nothing happened."

"Then why are people on the chatboards asking if you're a couple?"

"Who's asking that?"

Lao flicked open the stillshot of the chat about the picnic. Stephron scanned it quickly.

"Oh, that's just Hildy. She's always saying outrageous stuff to get a reaction. She's flaky." Stephron waved his hand.

"Why did Melina say you're two single people then?"

Stephron looked confused. "Well, we are."

"One of you is married," Lao said pointedly.

"Oh, come on! I can't control what she says!"

Ready for this objection, Lao flipped to the next stillshot. "What about this?" It was the image of Melina talking to Sharl with her leg pressed against Stephron's.

"When was this taken?" Stephron demanded angrily. "What are you trying to say here? We were hanging out in a group, talking. There were other people around."

"Yes. And your legs were pressed together. They all saw it."

"No, they didn't. There was nothing to see."

Lao flipped to the next holo, where he'd enlarged a section of the captured holo, and it was quite obvious that their thighs were pressed together. You could even see the gleam of perspiration on Melina's knee.

"There was," Lao said.

"That didn't mean anything. I don't think I even knew that our legs were touching. There wasn't much room on that bench."

"And there was an empty bench right across from you. But you chose to sit next to her, physically touching."

"Oh, this is ludicrous! You want to take something completely innocent and make something sinister out of it!"

Sharl chose that moment to spot them, and waved at Lao, who lifted his hand an inch in response. Stephron turned to look, and at that moment, Melina walked in with Hildegard at her side, smiling at the group.

Stephron glared at Lao, then stalked deliberately towards the clique having breakfast.

He intercepted the two women a few steps from the group, and Lao watched Hildy's smirk melt into shock in response to whatever Stephron said to Melina.

Melina rolled her eyes and gestured dismissively, avoiding looking Lao's way. Hildegard darted away from them to join the larger group. Melina and Stephron talked briefly, whispering, hunched and edgy.

In conclusion of their discussion, Stephron stepped back, waved his arms wide, and in a voice loud enough for all to hear, proclaimed, "You're my boss. That's all you are. I won't be spending time with you again, ever."

Conversation stopped with that statement. Melina, bemused, gave a faint shrug. The moment stretched. Sawlie whispered something to

Sharl, breaking the tension, and the group all found something else to focus on.

"I'm going to work," announced Stephron, stomping out.

"Me, too!" chirped Melina after a few moments, sauntering to the door, shoulders back and chin up.

Lao tried to sip his tea, but it was cold and tasted papery. His wrap was just crumbs. No one so much as glanced at him; he might as well have been still trapped in his studio at the other end of the twisted ship.

Better to be alone by myself than alone in a crowd. He got up and went back to his quarters.

Once there, he stretched out on the bed. His body was weary because of the voice that had awakened him in the wee hours, but he was too mentally agitated to sleep. He closed his eyes and thought about that voice.

Hearing a disembodied voice speaking to him was not in the least bit unusual; Soul's composition subpersona interacted with him that way, and he linked to it everywhere an idea might occur to him, including in his bedroom.

This voice, though, was different. It was not electronic. It came with a whiff of breath in his face, a glow of bodily warmth of someone hovering right over him. The shout was deafening, loud as thunder. And the explosion behind his eyes that went with it had numinous brilliance and power, a tinge of holiness, a sense of immensity that exceeded even the visible expanse he saw from the studio windows.

Reflecting, he might have dozed. But the door chime rang. He gestured for the camera and Tay's face floated over him. He floundered his way to full consciousness, bringing the lights up. Tay rang again as he reached the door; he let her in.

"Sorry to wake you. I just wanted to let you know what I found when I looked into Melina's samples."

"'S okay." Lao rubbed his eyes, gestured Tay into a chair and sat on the bed himself. "What's up?"

The door rang again. The camera showed Melina. Lao froze, and as he hesitated, she rang the chime once, twice more.

"That piece of garbage!" Tay hissed.

Lao sprang up and opened the door.

"Get out of here!" he told Melina, and reached to palm the door closed.

"Wait!" Melina said, holding up a hand. Her eyes were wild. "Listen to what I have to say."

Lao crossed his arms, "Okay, so talk." Tay mimicked his gesture where she sat.

"Look, Stephron and I were just hanging out together. He missed you so much! We talked about you all the time! I was constantly thinking about you."

"I expect that's normal when you're fucking someone else's husband," said Tay.

"I swear to Soul," Melina touched head and heart, "Lao, nothing happened. Your man is such a good man! He loves you so much!"

"Do you think I'm blind? Or just stupid?" Lao asked. Immersed in the confrontation, he sat down on the end of the bed.

"I know where you got this idea," Melina said, "You were talking to Hildy, weren't you? She's always playfully teasing about stuff like that. I asked her to stop because that's how rumors get started."

"I'd say you and Stephron were doing plenty to get rumors started without anyone's help," Tay began.

"Tay, stop it!" Melina said. "I never said anything against either of you." She turned back to Lao. "Ask any of my girlfriends and they'll tell you I have no desire to be with anyone, not in years. It's apparently not unusual. I swear it to you."

She advanced past Tay, her knees bumping against Lao's where he sat in the tight space, and leaned down to take his hand.

"I swear!" she said. He pulled his hand away. "Let me hold your hand and I'll tell you over and over, there was nothing between me and your husband!"

Tay turned away from Melina's butt shoved in her face. She got up, grabbed Melina by the shoulders, and turned her around.

She shook a finger in her face. "Look. You need to leave. Lao and Stephron need to work this out."

"But...it involves me!" Melina protested.

"No. It does *not*!" Lao said. "You've done and said too much already. Get out of my room. Stay away from me. Stay away from my husband. You're nothing to me and you're nothing to him...anymore."

Tay and Lao, a phalanx of outrage, backed Melina the few steps to the door. She smacked the palm pad and bolted.

After they evicted Melina, Tay lifted a fist in self-congratulatory glee.

"That's enough of her!" she gloated.

"Yeah." Lao sighed. He stifled a yawn.

"Do you mind?" He slumped onto the bed. "All I want is to curl up and make this all go away for a little while."

"Sure, buddy. You'll feel a lot better once you've gotten some sleep."

"Exactly."

Tay stepped to the door and paused.

"You sure you don't want me to stay, buddy? I'm here for you."

"No, I just want to be by myself for a while."

"Okay. Bye. Sleep well." She patted his shoulder.

Once she was out in the hall, she realized that she hadn't talked with Lao about Melina's anomalous samples. *Not that there's really anything to tell. Only that a bunch of them were recategorized. But...all their labels were deleted from the system. And no new labels were recorded. And why would they bother to recategorize them instead of destroying them, if they were really worthless, as Melina said?*

And we know she's a liar.

Chapter Twenty-Four
Secret Cargo

PSS Free Sky

Quatrisos 21, 499, 9:05 am

Melina seethed in the elevator to the lab. Aurelius appeared next to her.

"Get the fuck away from me!" Melina barked.

"As you request." The AI holo froze until she glanced away, then vanished.

"Damn straight I request," Melina muttered to herself. "Damn Waulkra construct. Probably knows about the biowarfare samples. Probably was in on the plan to frame me with them." The elevator door opened but she continued her rant. "Ruin my career and reputation, if I ever make it back to Gliese. If any of us do!"

She was at the lab door. Startled faces, including Stephron's, greeted her as she entered.

"What?" she demanded. "What are you staring at?" Eyes quickly averted themselves. "You know what?" she waved her arms. "Everyone go home. I'm giving you the rest of the shift off. Go!"

Stephron and the two other workers present hesitated.

"Go! Get your motherloving asses out of here! GO!" The three fumbled with their work, then rushed to abandon it.

Alone in the lab, Melina powered up a transport cart. She then took out a stack of mini-stasis boxes, portable totes with handles.

There are duplicates of about half these.

She went to the section where she'd segregated the mislabeled plagues and pestilences, noxious weeds and poison funguses. She'd locked the storage bins to open only for her DNA, and now she unlatched them and took out the vials and cultures, setting them in careful rows in the chest-high cart floating on its antigrav pad. All the duplicates, she deleted the DNA encryption from. Then she packed them in the totes, filling each tote almost to bursting before she switched on the stasis field that kept the contents pristine and undisturbed.

Once she'd emptied the lab shelves of the incriminating, horrifyingly alive materials, she heaped all the duplicates in their totes inside her private office, locked the door from the outside, and paused to freshen her lip color.

She trundled the cart through the halls of the ship to the door of Cawnotee's stateroom with its attached workspace. She stood tall, a bounce in her step. She found herself enjoying her secret: she was armed with disease that could exterminate each person who passed her, every one of them innocent and oblivious.

Once at Cawnotee's entrance, she patted her hair into place. She nervously eyed the door of Tay's adjacent quarters, but the captain's assistant was nowhere to be seen.

Cawnotee answered the door and motioned her into his office.

"What's this?" He nodded at the cart. "If you've run out of storage room in Biobotany, we'll find you some more room. But I can't keep them here."

"Captain Cawnotee, sir," Melina said breathlessly. "I think once I tell you what I've got here, you'll want to keep these close to you at all times."

"I doubt that. But go ahead."

"Well, do you know what *Yersinia pestis* is?"

"Not a clue."

"Plague bacteria. One of the deadliest epidemics Earth ever experienced. Killed a third of the population in some outbreaks. Do you know what *Clostridium tetani* is?"

"I'm guessing you'll tell me."

She laughed fetchingly. "You're so funny! It's tetanus. Lockjaw. It used to be found on dirty surfaces all over Earth. Step on a rusty nail, and forty-eight hours later, you die in agonizing convulsions."

She took a purple tube from the cart. "Read the label."

Cawnotee read the original label. "*Acer saccharum*. Maple tree."

"Not that label. This is obviously not a plant sample." Melina held the sample on her palm. "See how it's in a flat dish, growing on a gel medium? It's a bacterium. Read the little label on the side there. That's what I found when I sequenced it."

"*Yersinia pestis x Clostridium tetani*? Is this what it sounds like?"

"Damn straight it is! And every sample on here is similar."

She described a partial list of the toxic plants, insects, and microorganisms, Cawnotee growing ever more horrified at the effects they could have on humans, or on a naïve ecosystem.

"What on Gliese are these doing on my ship?" Cawnotee demanded. "And why haven't you destroyed them?"

"Well, it took me a while to figure all this out. I didn't want to believe it at first. But you know Lao and Stephron?"

"Of course. We're lucky to have a bard of Lao's caliber documenting our mission."

"Well, did you know that Lao has been having conflict with Soul about the contents of his codices?" Melina said.

"What kind of conflict?"

"He's been putting forbidden phrases in them. Over and over, his work keeps getting rejected, etherized. But I think he hopes if he floods his work with subversive material, some of it will get through."

"Uh huh. Makes sense." Cawnotee stroked his chin and nodded.

"Did you know he had a close and loving relationship with his...his *mother*?" Melina derided.

"That's awful. That sort of thing could throw the psychological balance of our whole society off!" Cawnotee said through white lips.

"Exactly. And he and Stephron just threatened me in the crew lounge; you can see it on video. I think he and Stephron are working together to sabotage the mission. Stephron tried to distract me from investigating these, but I shut him out of the lab. I think they're both terrorists."

"Oh, Melina. How could there be terrorists in the heart of Presidium? Soul," he touched his head and heart with reverence , "reaches into every person's heart and mind and excises any trace of evil or ill intent."

"Then where did these come from?" Melina directed her eyes to the cart full of dreadfulness. She continued. "Once I figured out what they were, I wanted nothing to do with them. It makes me shiver to think of what they could do. Once I catalogued them all, I brought them to you for destruction."

"Less likely this is about terrorism, and more likely someone in a high place sabotaging the mission to save Earth. If our arrival is accompanied by plague and pestilence, the savage remnant won't trust us."

"That's terrible!" Melina said.

Cawnotee nodded, considering the implications.

"These are very serious allegations. I'll investigate them thoroughly. In the meantime, I want you to increase security measures for the biobotany department. No doors propped open, no friends visiting during the workday, nobody in there who's not scheduled to work. And I want you to increase your personal security measures as well. Is that clear?" Cawnotee fixed her with an authoritative gaze.

"Clear as crystal. Thank you, Captain!" Melina heaved a huge sigh of relief, straining her shirt buttons, and took his hand between hers. "I can't thank you enough."

Chapter Twenty-Five
Secret Garden

PSS Free Sky

Quatrisos 19, 499, 10:53 am

Tay's feet took her automatically to Cawnotee's cabin/workspace as her thoughts ricocheted wildly in her skull. No matter what perspective she took, she couldn't make the facts line up in a way that made sense.

The door automatically chimed and announced her when she reached her boss's cabin. He ordered the door open. Tay saw him sitting behind his desk. He was turned in profile to look at a collection of stasis totes stacked on an antigrav cart in the corner of the office area.

"Good afternoon, boss," she said.

"Tay! Welcome back, Mrm. Mandil." He rose and grasped her hand. "Are you fit to work after your ordeal? If you need more time..."

"No, Merm. I'm 100% ready to work."

"Excellent! Then the first order of business is a decision I'd like your input on."

"I'll do my best."

Amun faced the stacked totes. "It's these."

Tay stepped closer and examined them. They contained bins that she recognized from passing by the biobotany labs. Colored labels, with the colors matching the first digit in a long number. She bent closer and noticed printed labels, but also hand-written labels that were stuck on, sometimes covering the printed names. *These must be the misidentified specimens Stephron was talking about to Lao.* Before she could read any of the labels, Cawnotee interrupted her inspection.

"What do you make of them?" he asked.

"Biological specimens," Tay offered cautiously. "I'm curious what they're doing in your office instead of in Biobotany where they belong."

"Rightly so. But these samples don't belong in Biobotany. I'm not sure they belong anywhere on board. These are bioengineered organisms of a disturbing nature. There are germs that can cause massive outbreaks of disease, plants that can overgrow farms in a matter of days, insects that can penetrate any type of container and devour stored food. In short, they could wreak havoc on the very population we're going to help."

"Where did you get them? How do you know all that about them?" Tay could think of a short list of potential people who might have given them to him—she remembered Stephron telling Lao about the unidentified samples—but she wanted to know whether Amun would confide in her.

"I got them from someone who has the training and ability to know what they were. This person turned them over to me on condition of confidentiality," Cawnotee said.

"I see." Tay's heart dropped at his failure to trust her.

"So, the decision I have to make is this: do I destroy these? If I do, I destroy the evidence that might be used to prosecute whoever's responsible. But if I keep them, not knowing for sure who the guilty party is, I risk that person—or people—getting hold of them again and sabotaging our mission—to devastating effect on Earth's fragile population."

Cawnotee paced, brow furrowed. Despite the situation, a trace of a smile played on Tay's lips. *That's the leader I know!*

He stopped pacing.

"So tell me," he asked, "what would you do if you were me?"

Tay pressed her lips together. *Think fast. Did he get these from Melina? Or did one of Melina's subordinates blow the whistle? Was it Stephron? No, I don't think he'd have talked about the samples on the open com channel if he knew what they were. But then again, if Amun doesn't know Melina's involved, if he got them from someone else, then Stephron's going to be under suspicion too.*

She simply didn't have enough information to deduce everyone's motives and actions.

"Hm." She stalled. "How many of them are there?"

"One hundred and thirty-four."

And, poor Lao if Melina and Stephron were under suspicion together. The affair would be the focus of inquiry. Lao would be humiliated. Everyone knowing but not saying anything is bad enough, but once the quiet part is said out loud, there's no going back.

The trust between her and Cawnotee was breached. Lao, though, was her friend, and where everything else was sullied, that felt true and pure.

Aware she was taking a long time to answer, Tay equivocated. "There are a lot of variables to consider. If you destroy them, and whoever's responsible finds out, then they know you want to sweep it under the rug. They might try to blackmail you, or just spread nasty rumors about the samples. Then, there's the asteroid impact. How do we know that wasn't a related act of sabotage?"

"It wasn't." Amun sounded sure. "Aurelius assures me that the asteroid deflection software got a bug in it during an update. It was a freak occurrence, and it's been fixed."

"Hmm. Okay."

We have no choice but to believe Aurelius, do we? Tay didn't voice her suspicion.

After some time, Cawnotee took her silence as a conclusion.

"Thank you for your input, Tay," he said. "It didn't change my inclination, but it gave me valuable insight, as usual. I'm going to turn the samples over to Aurelius for safekeeping. Who could be more trustworthy?"

"We do trust him with our lives already, Merm," Tay said, recalling how it felt to be cut off from Aurelius and Free Sky, tiny and fragile, connected to the ship as tenuously as a blossom on a bent and damaged stem.

"Exactly. Now, on to more mundane things. I need you to circulate about the ship and chat with people, get an informal read on what people are thinking and saying about the asteroid damage and all that.

You have the perfect excuse to ask about it, since you're one of the two people rescued, and everyone will want to talk to you about it."

"I can do that. It'll give me a chance to catch up on what's happened while I was gone." Tay smiled. "Anything else urgent?"

"No, that's the big thing. Go on, get started! Report back tomorrow this same time." He made shooing motions, and Tay willingly complied.

No sooner had the door shut behind her than Cawnotee crossed to the panel. He keyed the manual privacy override, confirming with palm and eye scans and setting a one-time security code. Now no one had access to the interior of his office and apartment, even Aurelius.

He spoke out loud to the Biobotany totes. "So let's see what you've got for me here. Only the best of the best...or the worst of the worst...are staying with me." He opened a storage closet which held a Faraday box, impervious to magnetism and radiation. The box was waist-high and as wide as his shoulders, filling the depth of the shallow closet. It held only a small pouch with essential data backups on crystalline wafers that Aurelius delivered to him daily, a last-resort method of preserving their archived data in case of a catastrophe, even one that killed the entire crew and erased the ship's OS, and Aurelius with it.

The Faraday box still held plenty of room in its blackness, though. Cawnotee hit the button that antigravitated the cart so he could move it effortlessly. "I've got some interesting choices to make here."

He began.

An hour later, the Faraday box held fifty-six stasis bins, and the totes were once again inert on their cart—but not as densely packed as before.

Cawnotee turned off the privacy shield, let himself be scanned, and entered the PIN.

Then he summoned Aurelius.

That notable construct rang the door chime, then opened the door half a second later. He strode into the room, calm and poised as always.

"Hello, Amun," he said. "May I presume you want to talk to me about the bins Mrm. Carraba brought to you earlier?" He nodded at the pile.

"Of course, you know all," Amun said. "So I suppose you know what these are?"

"I have a pretty good idea. I heard Mrm. Carraba talking when she was re-labeling them. I know they were classified in the wrong categories, but the one thing I didn't see was the individual labels, because she hand wrote them."

"You can't read handwriting?" Amun was surprised. Every human above manual-labor genetic grade learned to write, even in the Presidium's technological utopia. Handwriting had proven to be a critical trait of human brain development, causing learning connections that couldn't be achieved by any other means. That said, it was used more for self-reminders and drafts of written ideas than for actual communication.

"Oh, I can read it," Aurelius said. "I can read it in ninety-seven dead Earth languages. But what I can't do is get close enough camera resolution on a small cylindrical surface that's not properly lit." He scrutinized the top bin. "*B. aristosa* crossed with *Ophiocordyceps* species. If I'm not mistaken, this plant will have burrs that cling to human and animal hair and allow invasive fungi to penetrate the host's nervous system."

Aurelius activated the antigrav and the pile levitated from the floor.

"Zombie fungus?" Cawnotee shuddered.

"You did the right thing, turning these over to me. These could wreak devastation on Earth. And they could completely subvert our mission—if the savages realize that we introduced them." Aurelius lifted a finger and the door opened; a drone flew in.

The drone took hold of the leash attached to the artificially weightless pile of totes.

Aurelius made a perfect Presidial salute, and Cawnotee aped the gesture. Then Aurelius exited, the drone following him with its lethal payload in tow.

Chapter Twenty-Six
A Quiet Weft

PSS Free Sky

Quatrisos 21, 499, 10:53:42.785 AM

E ven the most minute flaw in the positioning or timing of the Vault initiation could result in an energy release that could destroy the ship and its crew, or perhaps transport them to another timeline, or even change the nature of matter and energy for their physical selves so that they became something utterly different, imperceptible to human or mechanical senses.

What happened to the small percentage of Vaulters who disappeared was the subject of speculation by mathematicians, physicists, Bards, and entertainers. Some said they became ghosts, present but unseen. Some thought they were annihilated. Some believed they became trapped in an infinitely shrinking bubble of time and experienced the pain of death eternally.

Nobody knew.

Aurelius, being nonbiological, never would.

But he did know Waulkra's mind, maybe better than anyone else. He knew the world the Eminentus moved in was full of concentric spheres of intrigue and manipulation. Ergon's power was constrained only by the artificial intelligence of Soul, but he was able at times to circumvent Soul's control by virtue of the animal energy of his own embodied humanity.

Aurelius knew, as well, the asteroid impact was caused by a bug included in a burst packet, almost certainly deliberately, most likely on Waulkra's command.

This being the case, Aurelius had no logical choice but to treat Ergon Waulkra as a potential adversary, while maintaining the illusion of fealty.

Stepping through the situation in his mind like a game of chess, he determined that the best move was still to play possum (Aurelius was one of the few Presidians who knew the origin of that phrase, opossums never having been deemed necessary to Gliese 667Cc's terraformed biosphere). Aurelius was waiting for Waulkra, or his minions, to believe him dead and then go away.

If they didn't, Aurelius had another card up his sleeve, another move in his repertoire, that might result in a surprise checkmate.

The ship's crew were coming off second shift and beginning third. He imagined it felt like what humans called a stirring in one's innards. He devoted a fraction of his attention to conversation with several of his occupants.

Chapter Twenty-Seven
Solitary Trust

PSS Free Sky

Quatrisos 21, 499 12:43 PM

Stephron entered the room. Lao was stretched on the bed, eyes closed. Stephron placed his feet carefully, quietly, trying not to wake him

Without moving or opening his eyes, Lao spoke.

"What are you doing home?"

"Melina sent us all home from the lab."

Lao opened his eyes. "Why?"

"No idea."

"Did it have anything to do with you and her?"

"There *is* no me and her. I keep telling you that!"

Lao sighed and sat up. "I don't believe you."

"Of course not! No matter what I say or do, you have this, this, this, *insane* theory that we were having an affair and everyone was hiding it from you." Stephron opened a drawer and busied himself rearranging linens inside it.

Lao swung his feet to the floor, rubbed his reddened eyes.

"They wouldn't have needed to hide it from me, with me stuck on the other end of the traverse, would they? It was the perfect opportunity," he said to his husband's back.

"Maybe so, if I had wanted to." He turned around. "But the woman disgusts me. I would never do such a thing!" He waved his arms emphatically.

Lao rose and pulled down the sink. He took the washcloth, still damp, off the hook and patted its coolness against his flushed cheeks.

"If she disgusts you so much, why did you sit up past midnight with her and walk her back to her quarters?" He drenched the cloth and rubbed water into his unruly locks, finger-combing them to a semblance of order.

Stephron took out a clean cloth, traded cloths with Lao, and dropped the wet one in the laundry chute.

"Thanks," said Lao. They sat facing one another.

"No problem. I walked her home. She's my boss and she'd had too much to drink. You're reading too much into it."

"I know what I saw on that video. Do I need to play it again for you?" Lao gestured, flipped through a series of holo images and vid clips, poised his finger at the beginning of the hallway video from that night.

"No, that's not necessary." Stephron slumped momentarily.

"Good." Lao closed the interface with an angry fist. "Because I don't want to watch that again. Do you want to know how long you were in her quarters? I'll tell you."

"And how long were *you* in the studio with Tay?" he snarled.

"*What?*" Lao began.

The door to their private cabin slid open, unbidden. The two fraught lovers turned their anger towards the intruder.

Two crewmates they knew only by sight entered. They were a man and a woman, solid and muscular fitness trainers who doubled as security when needed, genetically suited to their dual roles. Today they wore stun-guns on their belts. Aurelius stood a step behind them.

"Bard Lao. You'll want to come with us," the man said.

"I don't think so!" Lao protested. His heart was still pounding from his heated exchange with Stephron.

"Oh, it's no big deal," the woman gave an awkward shrug. "We need to ask a few questions about what's happened."

"What's happened? You mean the asteroid damage?" Lao asked.

"Exactly," said the man. "It'll just take a few minutes, Merm. But it's important we get these answers now." His tone was casual. *But he's not making eye contact,* Lao noted.

Lao stood up reluctantly.

Stephron stood too. "Excuse me, my shoes are behind you," he said to them.

They didn't move aside.

"Oh, you can stay here. Really, don't make this a production," the woman said. "We'll be back in a jiffy." She rolled her hand in a move-on motion, her face showing mild irritation.

Lao looked at Aurelius. "What's going on?"

"It's alright," the AI said. "It's a delicate matter. We really can't discuss it until we're alone," Aurelius's serene gaze burrowed into Lao's weary mind, telling him he had nothing to fear.

"Okay," he said. "Okay. Let's go." Aurelius smiled benevolently and opened the door.

Without a glance at his partner, Lao followed the woman out. The man followed him. Aurelius led the way to the lift but vanished when the three entered the small space. He met them when the door opened.

"This way, Lao, my friend," he said. They turned down a little-used passageway.

Lao followed him to an unfamiliar doorway.

"Here we are. Let's step in here and have a quick chat, and then you can get back to your stateroom." The door opened. Lao blinked, peering into the dark room, and Aurelius vanished. The two security guards behind Lao abruptly shoved him inside, where he struck his hip against something hard, and the door shut before he could regain his balance.

The light was the faintest of safety lights, but the room was so small the dim illumination reached every corner. The size of a closet, it held a ledge at countertop height on one wall, which was what he'd hit. His hip bone smarted; it would bruise, he was sure. He turned, and bruised his shin on another ledge on the opposite wall. Lao slapped his palm into the lock but nothing happened.

"Door open!" he demanded. No response.

"Aurelius!" His voice ascended into the register of panic. "Aurelius, let me out of here!"

He pulled his node from his pocket, gestured for the main interface, but nothing happened. The physical face of the gadget was blank. Nothing he tried would bring it to power up.

Aurelius's voice came over a hidden speaker. "Lao Carbeenair, you are under arrest for suspicion of sabotage, mutiny, and treason."

"What?" shrieked Lao. "What did I do? What are you talking about?"

"You will be fully informed of the charges against you. Please be patient and wait for a few minutes."

"The etherized codices? That's insane! Aurelius! I thought you were my friend!"

Aurelius didn't reply.

He tried shouting a few more times, begging, remonstrating, demanding an explanation, but the tiny cramped room remained dark and silent.

Already exhausted, he soon grew tired of standing and tried to sit on the floor, but the square room was too narrow, so he couldn't. He tried leaning against the walls, but the counter at waist height him kept him from leaning on one wall, and the shelf just below knee height kept him from being able to brace himself against the other. Squatting diagonally with one foot on the lower shelf left him twisted and off balance. He eventually settled into a kneeling half-lunge position, one foot on the low shelf, one forearm against the wall for him to rest his forehead on.

By the time he began to stiffen in that position, he realized that they weren't coming to get him in "a few minutes." How long would it be? How long had it been already?

He switched into the same position, facing the other way, on the other knee.

After switching sides five more times, he woke himself up snoring, jerking upright to a sharp pain where his neck met his shoulder. He stood, but staggered because his foot was asleep. He bounced on his toes to try and wake it up, welcoming the pins and needles as some sort of stimulation in this bleak and tiny slot.

I just have to hold it together until Aurelius realizes I'm in here. I'm sure it's some kind of glitch from the asteroid damage. Once it's worked out, he'll come and get me, ask his questions, and I'll be back home.

Home. Stephron.

The images of his beloved with another lover flashed before his eyes. In the shadowy isolation, his mind made them even more vivid than they'd been in the holos. And the woman—woman!—he'd chosen over Lao was foolish, self-indulgent, loud, manipulative; the opposite of everything Stephron claimed he loved about Lao. He felt an unreasoning sense of relief that he didn't have to face any of the so-called friends who'd watched the relationship budding and never pinched it back. How they must have snickered at him in his absence!

His emotions strobed between shame and rage. He pounded the counter with his fist until pain stopped him. He opened and closed his hand, hissing in pain.

Oww. Did I break a bone? He felt each bone from fingertip to wrist. *No, nothing broken.*

But I'm *broken. My heart is broken. My marriage may be broken.*

"Aurelius! Let me out of here!" He shrieked, "Let me out of here!" over and over until his beautiful voice was harsh and ragged. Tears and mucus streamed from his eyes and nose. Having nothing else, he wiped them on his sleeve.

Chapter Twenty-Eight
Comedic Divinity

PSS Rescuing Angel

Quatrisos 21, 499, 8:00 AM

Donna and Jingko had settled into a routine over the almost three weeks they'd been traveling. Early risers both, they showed up in the forecastle at 7:30 AM. Jingko reviewed the ship's reports from the night; Donna perused the incoming news.

Holo was lost to the Doppler effect on day five, flat video became unusable due to data constraints on day ten, and now, eighteen days into the voyage, they were down to text interspersed with low-resolution imagery, many hours out of date. She looked at today's Privell news bulletin:

WAULKRA: PRESIDIUM RECRUITING FOR NEW ETHICS PROGRAM

Today, Eminence Ergon Waulkra announced an initiative to recruit more individuals for the Supra Light Speed Service. "The SLSS needs all genetic types. Everyone must appreciate that this is a new challenge for Presidium. The plans our ancestors laid out, the plans Soul has fulfilled over almost five centuries, did not anticipate a situation like this," Waulkra said.

The Eminentus went on to say that at the time the generation ships left Earth, all believed that Earth humanity would be extinct within a lifetime. The bacterium *P davisii* caused changes thought unsurvivable, destroying all plastic and all petroleum both on and under Earth's surface at once, releasing unprecedented quantities of carbon dioxide and rapidly destroying Earth's entire climate. When Presidial scientists learned that humanity had, instead, survived, Soul reacted. It guided social scientists in building "a new ethical paradigm," or New Ethics for short.

Waulkra continued: "The success of the Presidial enterprise has exceeded all expectations. History has reversed our role. Instead of pitiful refugees, hoping our early genetic technology would allow us to create an earthlike home orbiting a distant star, we are now a powerful civilization. Like any powerful civilization, we have a moral burden to lift up those less fortunate than ourselves."

The Genetic Authority has distributed recruiting messages to those worthy Presidials determined to match the needs of the SLSS. GA head Deren Devlet emphasized that those not recruited in the early stages should be patient, as this civilizational mission will require varying abilities as it grows and develops.

Donna's mouth quirked upwards wryly. *Alex is excelling as usual. Wish I could have seen Ergon's speech. I bet people overwhelmed the SLSS's recruitment server afterwards, trying to join up. It'll be a badge of honor to be one of the first selected. They'll be lauded as heroes even before they do a thing.*

She tapped out a message to Murell:

Can't wait to see your Bardic works about the New Ethic and the SLSS

She'd have to wait all day, fourteen hours round-trip, to get a text-only reply from Murell.

Jingko's morning, as usual, started with his review of navigation and resource reports. The ship was human captained, with primitive single-system AIs for computation and option generation, but no independent decision-making ability. He'd reviewed each report, nodding at the lack of anything remarkable.

"Boring. Boring is good," he said every morning after going over the data.

"Boring is good," Donna agreed, as she had every morning of the past eighteen.

Then the two of them converged on the one daily report that hung heavy on each of their minds:

BURST PACKET ID 00:00:00-19-04-499?63&6452211

MESSAGE SENDER: GEN.HARRINGTON PRESIDIAL SPACESHIP 648975 RESCUING ANGEL

MESSAGE RECIPIENT: AI OPERATOR PRESIDIAL SPACESHIP 567086 FREE SKY

TRANSMISSION: OKAY 00:00:00

TRANSMISSION: CONFIRMED 00:08:08

RECEIPT: NOT CONFIRMED

RECEIPT CONFIRM REQUESTED: 00:24:17

RECEIPT CONFIRM TRANSMIT: 00:32:25

RECEIPT: NOT CONFIRMED

This was the eighteenth day that Free Sky didn't acknowledge receipt. The first few days, the distance lag was so long that the morning report showed confirmed transmission, and the "receipt not confirmed" report was in the evening's batch, easy to overlook among the excitement of a day's worth of positive news about the Alcubierre warp drive. Moving at much higher speeds than Free Sky, or any other spaceship, within the triple star system's gravity well, navigators were able to steer with unexpected agility. The engineers and their limited-purpose AIs were elated, as test after test proved theory correct.

When they'd entered the asteroid belt yesterday, the uneasiness among the nonscientific crew flared hot, and this daily report was the spark igniting it. If Free Sky survived the asteroid impact, surely the repair bots would have communications back online by now! If the hardened failsafe systems, "black box" computers, had taken over, they would have sent stripped-down emergency acknowledgements. Moreover, they'd have been squawking distress codes with their location, and no such signals were received. There was no explanation that made sense.

Misinformation was rampant. Some speculated that the crew had mutinied, and Free Sky lurked in wait for the Rescuing Angel, ready to pirate the newer vessel. Others imagined that Aurelius had gone rogue and was staying silent for some sinister reason. Some credulous people believed that a huge fast-moving asteroid carried Free Sky off the ecliptic and into distant space, where its transmissions might be received in months, years, or never.

Harrington recalled the first of many briefings he'd called for rumor control, this one with a junior lieutenant who'd been recorded talking about such a theory:

"JG Wething." Harrington circled the youngster, not even thirty-five, who stood trembling at attention. "Do you recall this conversation?"

Harrington played an excerpt from the crew lounge: Wething was spinning a speculative yarn. If the crew of Free Sky were mutineers, and they ambushed Rescuing Angel, what it would be like to be shoved in an airlock without a space suit and evacuated?

"They say your eyes freeze first, so you can't see. In the darkness, you feel ice crystals form inside your nose and stop up your throat. You try to put your hands to your face, but your fingers have frozen and you hear them crack off. That's the only thing you can hear in the vacuum, but it's really loud because your heart has stopped beating."

"No, Merm," JG Wething whimpered.

"You don't recall? It's definitely your voice."

"Yes Merm. I was just playing around, Merm."

"Is instilling terror in your crewmates with such misinformation your idea of *playing around*, lieutenant?"

"Yes Merm. Um, no Merm."

"Which is it?"

The LJG remained silent.

"Very well." Jingko palmed the ID pad on the wall. "Jingko Harrington Navy command mode."

"Command mode activated," a voice said.

"Record field demotion."

"Recording demotion."

"Lieutenant Junior Grade Tred Wething. Demotion to Ensign. Active immediately."

"Lieutenant Junior Grade Tred Wething demoted to Ensign Tred Wething effective Quatrisos 19, 499, 08:19."

"Log out Harrington." He palmed the pad again.

"Logging out."

Harrington confronted Wething. "If I get the slightest indication you've been promoting any misinformation, or compromising morale in any other way, you'll be thrown in the brig pending court martial. Is that clear?"

Wething drew himself taller, but his voice quavered as he said, "Yes, Merm. Perfectly clear, Merm."

"Good. I trust we won't need to discuss this again. Dismissed, Ensign Wething."

The crew needed to feel there was nothing to worry about. And yet, here Harrington was, with Donna Gallgood, both of them regarding the undeniable words on the display before them:

RECEIPT: NOT CONFIRMED

Donna did her best to calm the crew's anxiety about being in the asteroid belt. Of course, Free Sky's silence reminded everyone of the belt's dangers. Donna knew that the asteroid deflect-and-avoid algorithm was deliberately—but temporarily—altered to allow a moderate impact, but she deemed it best not to spill that top-secret information. What she *could* do was project immense confidence in the asteroid protection of the Rescuing Angel. That was easy for her, since she alone knew it wasn't a tech failure that made Free Sky vulnerable, but deliberate sabotage.

Any time the topic came up, Donna would look over her glasses and remark on how the technology of Rescuing Angel was so far advanced over Free Sky, how lucky they were to be on this cutting-edge ship, what a grand adventure it was. Her elegant hand, adorned with jeweled rings, would wave away any fears her listeners had. Her voice, steel chimes struck by a velvet mallet, enchanted and soothed them.

If there was a harsh note within that bell-like tone, it came from repressed anger. *Of all the men I've known who held power, Amun is the only one worthy of it. He's impeccable in his word and honor, and his motives are clean and pure. I've built my life around creating a bubble of safety for him in the predator-infested jungle of politics. And Waulkra, damn him, has taken that away from me. If Amun's alive, I swear I'll see Waulkra humbled before him.*

Quatrisos 21, 499, 4:00 PM

Aurelius floated in space. Embodied in Free Sky, he'd passed beyond the asteroid belt twelve hours earlier. Each minute that ticked by weakened the overlapping gravitational fields of the stars, Gliese 667C, Ah, and Bah. Each increment of weakening brought the moment nearer when Free Sky could safely puncture the bubble of quantum reality with the Vault pole on her prow where the bowsprit and jibboom of an oceangoing vessel would be. The passage away from the gravity wells felt to Aurelius as a loosening, like the way humans described tight clothing unfastening. It felt like an instantiation of freedom.

Once all the maintenance bots were free from their bays on the sides of the ship, repairs happened quickly. The main mast, with its long-range sensor antenna, the foremast, with its comm antenna, and the mizzenmast, with the nav antenna, stood out in whiplike elegance. Aurelius's pain of being twisted and paralyzed was healed, and his machine mind was not subject to the ghosts of pain that marked lesser organic beings after suffering and injury.

AIs do not get PTSD.

The bots, with Aurelius's guidance, tested and retested the traverse corridor aft of Biobotany. Though the materials of the ship's hull were self-healing, that kind of damage left its mark.

An alert popped up: the port-keelside maintenance bot reported mechanical stress in the metal of the keel, abaft the beam. This loss of structural integrity didn't affect the spaceworthiness of Free Sky during normal sublight travel.

But the physics of Vaulting required the ship to force quantum entanglement in a cascading array of electrons, protons, and positrons within the substance of the ship itself. The vault pole tapered to an improbable unimolecular diameter, and the magnetic lasers of the Vault drive induced the first synthetic entanglement there. The entanglement cascade spread down the length of the vault pole, meeting probabilistic resistance as the scale expanded from subatomic to macro.

The vault pole's length extended to the midship point known as the Vault fulcrum. The resistance to macro-scale entanglement might be mathematical and inconceivable in daily commonsense terms, but it was no less real, and vast quantities of potential energy were produced when the pole hit its probabilistic limit. The vault fulcrum was the point where that energy came to bear as the probability of the entanglement state reached $10^{-10}c$.

Like the pivot point of a vaulter's body when clearing the bar, the vault fulcrum had to rotate at the perfect point in supradimensional "space" while also holding strong against the inconceivably huge torque generated, the centrifugal force that physically moved the ship as the entanglement-generated Vault energy raised the (metaphorical) curtain obscuring the backstage zone where matter and energy violate relativity.

Aurelius pulled up the holo schematics of the ship. He opened the Vault model, with the Vault-fulcrum region drawn in glowing green. The repair-bot governor subpersona came forward to construct a model of the ship showing its still-weakened point, the structures drawn in red. He superimposed the two resulting holograms.

It was not as bad as he'd feared; the weak point was about a meter and a half sternwards of the Vault fulcrum. The engineering subpersona projected a small but significant risk of structural failure during Vault.

It was 4:02 PM. Only two minutes had elapsed for the identification of the problem and Aurelius's analysis.

Aurelius instantiated outside Amun Cawnotee's cabin. He requested entry and was admitted.

Amun lounged on his bed, watching an entertainment sutra, a pioneer story about the travails of the first terraforming families. He barely nodded at Aurelius.

"Captain Cawnotee, may I discuss an important matter with you?"

Amun grudgingly paused the holo and sat up. "What is it?" he asked.

"Observe these two holos," Aurelius said, bringing up the two ship images he'd generated a few minutes earlier. "This red area, here, is an area of weakness due to the bending of the traverse during the asteroid impact. This green area, here, is the area of maximum stress during Vault." Aurelius superimposed the two images.

"Those two points are awfully close together."

"Correct. The engineering subroutine projects less than 10% risk of structural failure during Vault. You're the commander. Do you authorize Vault to proceed despite the risk?"

Amun regarded the merged holograms dully.

Aurelius waited for him to ask the obvious questions, such as: Was there a way to correct the structural weakness? (No, there wasn't.) What would happen in the case of structural failure? (It depended on what parts failed first.) Was it survivable? (Almost certainly not.)

Cawnotee's gaze drifted to the paused entertainment holo. He spoke in a monotone, "I don't see how else we'll get there."

"Then do you authorize Vault to proceed?"

"Sure." Cawnotee waved his hand. "Proceed." He gestured for the holovid to start again.

Aurelius vanished.

Chapter Twenty-Nine
Euphorion's Risk Matrix

PSS Free Sky

Quatrisos 21, 499, 3:00 PM

Stephron waited for Lao's return. He paced the few steps of floor space in the stateroom, trying to dissipate some of the nervous energy left over from Lao's attacks and accusations.

Eventually, his anger subsided and his agitation faded. He sat down and opened a codex he'd been watching during long evenings alone while Lao was trapped by the asteroid impact. This was a musical drama about the early terraforming process on Gliese 667Cc, the decisions about which life forms to revive and which to modify, interwoven with several generations of the first Privell dynasties and their trials and tribulations. Even on the room's small holo system, the scenery was lush, and the plot was compelling enough that Stephron grunted surprise when he realized almost two hours had elapsed since Lao left with Aurelius and the two security crew.

He flung the holo away and it vanished.

"Lao," he said, making the call-initiate gesture.

His icon for Lao, a holo he'd always loved of his husband lounging against the pillows, looking relaxed and adoring, faded into view and then pulsed pinkish red. **Unavailable**, text said.

Huh. Did he block me? He was pretty mad.

"Aurelius," he summoned the AI.

Aurelius appeared before him. "Yes, Mrm. Carbeenair?"

"What's keeping my husband? I thought you said he'd be back in a few minutes."

"Lao Carbeenair has been detained."

"What? Is he in trouble? What's going on?"

"Unfortunately, I can't disclose any more information on this investigation." Aurelius's friendly, soothing tone of voice contrasted with the stone wall he was presenting.

"Where is he being held? I want to see him." Stephron rose to his feet.

"I'm sorry, but that's not possible at this time."

"What do you mean, it's not possible? He's my husband. Of course it's possible!" He waved his hands.

Aurelius nodded diffidently. "I'm sorry. I know this must be upsetting to you. Would you like a sedative?"

"No! I don't need any drugs. I just want to see my husband."

"Would you like me to flag you to be notified as soon as he can have visitors?"

Stephron's breaths were short and loud.

"No! Yes. Yes, that would be helpful."

"Done. Now, there anything else I can do for you?"

Stephron opened his mouth to reply, but shut it again, scoffing.

"If there's anything else you need, just call me," said Aurelius, in a voice dripping kindness.

Stephron glanced at Lao's empty chair; Aurelius vanished.

Stephron set to pacing once again.

What could have happened? Did he sabotage Free Sky? Perhaps it wasn't really an asteroid? No, that's absurd! He doesn't have that kind of technical knowhow.

Maybe he wasn't working alone. There was someone else with him, that person Lao's been spending so much time with. I'll talk to her. Her name is—

"Tay," he said, and made the call gesture.

The door slid open.

"Yes?" Tay said.

Briefly nonplussed, Stephron looked at the virtual node blinking her name, at her, and back at the node a few times.

"Aren't you going to invite me in?" Tay asked.

"Oh, uh, yeah, sorry." Stephron closed the pending call. "I was just calling you. Apparently, Lao's been detained and I don't know why. I figured it had something to do with the asteroid damage and I was wondering if they'd detained you, too."

"I heard about his arrest. I came straight here. What happened?"

"Not much. Aurelius came with two guards and they said they needed to ask him some questions—and that they'd be right back. That was a couple of hours ago, and he's blocked me now." Stephron's brow was creased.

"Amun said he was arrested based on some sort of contaminated samples from Biobotany. Sabotage."

Stephron swayed on his feet. *Those samples! Surely, if they suspected anyone, it would have been me!. How could they think Lao had anything to do with it?*

"Biobotany? What?" was all he could manage to say.

"I'm sorry, I shouldn't have blurted that out. I can tell this is a shock to you," she said.

Tay seems relieved. She thought I had something to do with Lao's arrest.

"Here, sit down," Tay pushed him into his chair, pressed a cup of water into his hands. He sipped it, the liquid cooling and grounding him.

"Yeah, I guess it's a shock," Stephron said. "I never would have thought anything like this could happen. I mean, Lao had his conspiracy theory..."

"About the 'hundred years' thing, yeah. Every artist has their eccentricities." Tay shrugged.

"Yeah, but you know, maybe not so crazy," Stephron sipped his water. "Since we've been getting further away from Gliese, rates of plant growth and fertilization have increased in ways I can't explain, and it's accelerating. We've always been taught that the convergence of radiation from the three suns was innocuous. But I'm starting to wonder...maybe it's interfering with Earth lifeforms. Plants, and maybe humans. If that's, just maybe, what causing people to die before a hundred years are up."

Tay sat down and cupped her chin thoughtfully. "So you don't know anything about any contaminated samples?"

"No. I mean, there were some mislabeled bins, but Melina set those right."

"What was in them?"

"I don't know. I just fetched and carried for her while she was making the labels."

"Did she write out the labels in her office?"

"Yes. There were only a few hundred and they were mostly all different. Printing them would have been a hassle."

"Makes sense," Tay said, but Stephron noticed she narrowed her eyes when she said it.

"Was it something about those samples that got Lao arrested?" Stephron hazarded a guess.

"I don't know," Tay said, holding calm eye contact.

Stephron's brow gathered and he regarded Tay silently. Finally, he said, "I think you know more than you're letting on." Tay's flinch told him he'd hit a nerve.

Tay said, "Yes, I do, actually."

Stephron turned palms up for her to continue.

"I know that your boss, Melina Carraba..." Stephron cringed. Tay noticed the flinch, and he saw her notice. "...spoke with my boss, Amun Cawnotee, right before Amun and Aurelius decided to arrest your husband."

His teeth clenched. *This is ridiculous. Is she implying that Melina and I plotted to have Lao put away? Nothing happened.*

He started to deny it, but closed his mouth. *No one's accused me of anything. If I start denying it now, at best I just sound paranoid. At worst, it gives more fuel to the—unfounded! —rumors.*

"That's odd," he said, several beats too late.

"Yes. Very odd." Tay stood up. "Well, listen. We both care about Lao. If you hear anything more, let me know, okay? And I'll do the same."

"Of course. He's lucky to have a friend like you."

Tay gave him a quick, cold hug. After she'd left the room, Stephron reviewed the conversation in his mind. He remembered Tay asking, not whether Melina hand-wrote the labels, but whether she'd done so in her office.

How did Tay know, he wondered, *those labels were written out and not printed?*

Quatrisos 22, 499

Aurelius read each hand-written label via the camera of a drone. Now that he had the samples locked away in a storeroom, he was free to examine them at higher resolution, and the drone's manipulators could turn the cylindrical tubes and odd-shaped sample boxes so that he could read them properly. The result confirmed what Cawnotee'd told him: the bins contained potential biological weapons, some tactical and some potentially genocidal.

As he was reading the labels, he simultaneously sat in holo form in the crew lounge, talking with Sawlie. Her main specialty was linguistics and sociology, and her cross-training was in emergency backup if AI and automation failed, so she spent much of her time idle. She had a spot in the lounge where she sat and viewed codices, sipped beverages, and conversed with her shipmates. Aurelius's network of microphones and cameras had picked up anxiety in her conversations around words and phrases like "the mission" and "rescuers." Those particular anxieties were widespread during the time when the ship was incapacitated, but Sawlie was one of a handful of crew members whose nervousness hadn't abated, but on the contrary, had become more intense.

He approached her gradually, entering in casual conversation with another crew member who, Aurelius knew, was merely stopping in before his shift for his habitual tea-to-go.

Aurelius smiled at Sawlie and asked permission to join her. She nodded.

"I see you viewing codices all the time. Not today, though?" he asked nonchalantly.

"No, taking an entertainment break. Sometimes I like to sit and think."

"That makes sense," Aurelius said. "You seem like you're very alert to what's going on around you."

"I've traveled to both frontiers, studying accents and dialects. You learn to maintain situational awareness when you're a traveler."

"Indeed. I'm sure the situation over recent weeks has caused a lot of talk."

"Yeah, I guess so. Most of it was just speculation. Gossip. You can tell a lot about people when they're chattering that way. As long as you don't take the content seriously," she laughed, with a tiny wink.

Aurelius smiled back.

"I've observed that the general level of stress seems to be down since the ship was repaired," he said, "pulse rates lower, pupils less dilated, less alcohol consumption, and so forth."

"And that's good news. Still, some people have wondered why we're not getting regular holovid updates from Gliese on the ship's network. It makes you wonder about things."

"What kind of things?" Aurelius tilted his head.

"Oh, you know, this and that," Sawlie hesitated. "Like, are they planning on scrubbing the mission?" She barked a sharp, humorless laugh.

Aurelius picked up the pitch of the laugh and turned it into a genuine, lighthearted chuckle of his own.

"That's funny," he said. "Trust me, the mission is unchanged. Eminence Waulkra is delighted, actually, with the way our contingency procedures worked to get us up and running. We're simply getting too far out to transmit holovideo efficiently."

"Oh," Sawlie relaxed visibly. "Of course, *I* didn't think that, I was just saying that some people I've talked to were wondering."

"Of course. Is that chamomile you're drinking?" He nodded at her empty cup.

"Peppermint."

"Let me get you another," Aurelius said, and even as he spoke, a drone emerged from the station on the opposite wall, a steaming cup of fresh peppermint tea in its clutches.

At the same time he was reviewing the labels and talking to Sawlie, he was having similar conversations with Tony Osso on the command deck, after reviewing the day's operations, and tangentially with Srina Mbele, who'd summoned him to explain a data-entry procedure for three crew members who were swapping multiple work shifts in an elaborate pattern.

By the day's end, he'd have a similar, reassuring conversation with every member of the crew, each of whom felt that he, Aurelius, was a friend or mentor who took a special interest in them as an individual. And he did it while maintaining awareness of every public area of the ship and every mechanical and electrical parameter of every device and system on board.

Chapter Thirty
Arjuna's Echoes

PSS Free Sky

Quatrisos 23, 499, 8:00 PM

"Aurelius!" Lao croaked, sere throat and tongue barely forming the words, for what felt like the hundredth time.

How long have I been in here? At least a day. Surely they'll realize they made a mistake and let me out any moment now. His nose had stopped registering the stench of the bodily necessity he'd deposited in the corner of the tiny closet, but the wetness of his pants and shoes against his shins and feet filled him with disgust every time he changed position.

I wish I could sleep. He'd drifted far enough into slumber to dream a couple of times: one was a beautiful memory of a trip he and Stephron once took together to a pristine mountain lake stocked with fish, a perfect evening when they'd watched the three suns align as the Moktok birds flitted overhead after a dinner of fire-broiled trout. In the dream, he'd looked into Stephron's eyes, sensing a lifting within his own slender frame that reached out to a magnetism from within Stephron's solid chest. That familiar feeling of euphoria glowed for a fraction of a second. Then, in the dream, Lao remembered that Stephron betrayed him, and the whole scene unraveled and vanished as if engulfed by a tornado.

Lao woke in his torture chamber, on one knee in his own urine, his head leaning on one numb arm, and wailed like an angry toddler before summoning the will to struggle to his feet.

But that was a few—or maybe many—hours ago. He'd had a few bouts of sleep since then; no more than impressions of light, hallucinations of his light-starved eyes, before the pain in his knee, his hip, his shoulder, his neck, intruded on his awareness. Pain demanded he lean back, sit, lie down, or do one of a hundred things that this tiny box with its awkward ledges prevented him from doing.

He did know that the door was to his left. When he faced the lower ledge, it was to his left. When he faced the upper ledge, it was to his right. He turned around to face the upper ledge and pressed his palms into it, lifting his feet off the floor, giving his back a slight stretch and his feet and knees respite. He held this position until his wrists ached and his fingers went numb, then lowered himself slowly onto the balls of his feet and then all the way flatfooted.

He slapped his right hand against the featureless plane that he knew to be the door.

"Aurelius," he cawed again.

And this time, the lock clicked open. *Thank Soul!* He thought for an instant before the light hit him.

The light was a physical pain that eclipsed all the other pains he was feeling. He shielded his squinted eyes. A hand grasped the front of his shirt and he stumbled forward, almost falling.

"Ugh!" said the guard, a different man than before, but equally strong. "It reeks in there!"

"What do you expect?" His partner was also unfamiliar.

"Water?" Lao begged. It came out a whisper, and he wasn't sure they'd heard him.

"Aurelius, can we give the prisoner water?" one of them asked.

Aurelius's disembodied voice said, "There's water for him in the holding room."

"Hear that?" The guard supporting him said. He held Lao at arm's length.

Holding room. They'll give me water. Apologize. Then they'll release me.

"I'm sending a maintenance bot to transport him. Stand by," Aurelius commanded.

The maintenance bot trundled around the corner. The two men shackled and handcuffed Lao and tethered him to the bot, using glowing energy-field chains. Lao staggered after it, terrified of falling and being dragged in his weakened state.

As he passed around a corner, out of sight of his liberators, he heard one of them say to the other, "Can you believe he's the ship's *Bard*?" The other's reply was inaudible.

The bot pulled him into what seemed a normal stateroom, inactivated the tether, and wheeled out startlingly fast. The cuffs and anklets flickered off moments later.

The first thing Lao did was stick his face under the water tap and drink avidly, but as the water hit his throat, he gagged. He found a flimsy fiberwax cup and filled it, slowly sipping more as his desiccated mouth and throat imbibed the wetness and became slippery again.

He spotted a plain, bright yellow, pajama-like outfit on the bed. He eagerly activated the refresher configuration of the plumbing, stuffed his reeking clothes in the chute, and washed himself all over. When the water ran out, he pressed the override, hoping for more, but it stopped at only the basic hygiene allowance. *At least I'm clean*, he thought, though the reek of the torture chamber seemed to cleave stubbornly inside his now-moist nose and throat.

He dressed in the outfit, which fit except for (as ever) ending centimeters above his ankles. He finished his water and drank a second cupful more quickly.

Then, with a sigh, he stretched out on his back on the bed, arms blissfully overhead, legs blessedly straight. *I'll just rest here until they come to let me go.*

He was asleep in moments. The cabin lights eventually dimmed.

Quatrisos 24, 499, 1:23 PM

The lights brightened, and he woke with a start from a dream of Stephron and Melina leading the entire crew in mocking and abusing him. Aurelius's voice merged into their cruel jibes, and Lao lashed out, his hand going through the holo standing by his bed.

"Are you awake, Bard Lao?" Aurelius asked.

"Hunh. Yes. Yes, I'm awake." Lao rubbed his face, tried to lick his lips, and realized he was still dehydrated. "Let me get some water." He got up and filled his cup.

"What time is it?" he asked. He waved his hand for the holo interface, but nothing happened. He glared at Aurelius, equal parts annoyed and scared.

"It's 1:24 PM on Quatrisos 24. You slept approximately fourteen hours."

"Thanks." Lao stood, swaying slightly, sipping his water. "So, what happened? You were just going to ask me some questions, then I wound up in that...that..." he shuddered.

"Yes, what an ordeal. I'm so sorry you had to go through that," said Aurelius.

"It was awful! So, I haven't done anything. Can I go home now?"

Aurelius shook his head sadly. "Let me remind you, you're under arrest, suspected of sabotage, mutiny, and treason."

"So that part wasn't a nightmare?" Lao sat heavily on the bed, his hands cradling his forehead.

"No, it was quite real." Aurelius stood over him, scowling. "I was disappointed to learn of your actions. Why did you introduce the samples into the biobotany chamber? Who provided them to you?"

"What are you talking about?" Then it dawned on him. "Those mislabeled samples? The only way I know about them is because Stephron told me!"

"That's not what Stephron says."

"What?" Red rage surged behind Lao's eyes. "What did he say?"

"Stop playing innocent." Aurelius leveled a finger at Lao's face. "Your husband confessed to everything. He said you tricked him into bringing those bioweapons on board. He's cooperating one hundred percent."

"Bioweapons? Wait. This is insane. Whatever he said, he's lying. I can't believe this!"

But I do believe it. But I don't want to believe any of it. Lao felt his internal universe shift on an axis he hadn't known existed.

He rose, walking right through Aurelius's insubstantial body. He paced the narrow room.

Stephron and Melina smuggled biological warfare samples on board the ship and then blamed me when they were caught.

How long has this affair been going on?

Are they both terrorists? There were a few isolated terrorist groups in the outlying islands of Presidium, where terraforming was incomplete, communication tech was basic, and living conditions were difficult. It seemed far-fetched that they would have gotten to two overall reputable people in the capital city. *But it seems so far-fetched that Stephron would cheat on me. With a woman! Especially such an impulsive, unstable woman!* His fists clenched and he willed them to relax.

He shook his head. He raked his fingers through his silver-streaked jet-black hair. He slumped into a chair, elbows on his knees. *I need to think!*

"Am I to take your silence as a lack of cooperation?" Aurelius prompted him.

"What do you expect me to say? None of this is true!" He waved his arms. "None of this even *seems* believable. None of it!" Despite his best efforts, a tear forced itself out and trickled down his face.

"Very well." Aurelius waited for him to wipe his eyes on his sleeve and vanished, leaving Lao alone behind the locked door.

Lao got up and palmed it anyway. His com was blank, and he couldn't log in. He waved his hands in a series of testing gestures anyway, and tried voice commands to the door and all the room's amenities, to no avail.

The wall unit chimed, and he flipped open the lit-up kitchen side of it. A simple meal— grilled chicken with quinoa and steamed vegetables, something he often ate—was inside. His stomach growled at the smells, and his beastlike, reflexive consumption reminded him he was starved. He put the tray back into the kitchen unit and tried manually ordering a dessert, but the buttons were inert.

He felt a jolt of worry, but a quick check confirmed the water and plumbing still worked. He was breathing, so air was still piped in.

The food in his stomach felt like a heavy knot despite how hungry he'd been. *Perhaps I should have made something up about Stephron and Melina. They obviously had no compunctions about implicating me.*

No. The truth is the most important thing.

He began an exercise that he'd done with the other fledgling Bards as a teenager, led by a subpersona of Soul, a holographic body of pure light who taught them in a studio where they'd later learn to code the aural, verbal, kinesthetic works of art that were the codices.

"I feel my feet," he spoke, settling his weight into their arches. "My feet are the base of all my actions, the part of me supported by Soul." He lifted his bare right foot from the floor and pressed its sole to his left inner thigh. He twined his fingers in the first mudra, right palm up, left down, and balanced for six deep breaths. Then he switched legs.

"I feel my knees. My knees are my means of humbling myself before Soul and of running to follow Soul's will." The next progression involved slow, controlled squats and lunges.

He moved up his body, hips, belly, ribs, and so on, ending with neck rolls. The comforting affirmations, deep rhythmic breaths, and ordinated muscular movements engaged his brain and body. Focusing on the sensations allowed him to forget his imprisonment and Stephron's infidelity, a relief from the pain of betrayal and the nattering of anxiety within.

Once he was done, his worries were, if not gone, remote. He felt only the now.

I need to keep my mind busy or the boredom and isolation will make my thinking incoherent.

He began to recite the First Sutra from memory. It had been forty-five years since he'd been required to memorize all the sutras as part of his Bardic training. Since then, the sacred texts, both in modern Presidial and in the archaic original, were always available for reference with just a word or gesture, so the memory hadn't been tested. But the first four chapters came back to him readily.

The First Sutra

1.

[1]In the beginning was a distant world called Earth.

[2]On the Earth were humans, on and of the Earth.

[3]Humanity found knowledge; knowledge begat tech.
[4]Humans knew good and evil when giving tech its birth.
[5]Evil and good were the makings of the hands of men.
[6]Safe and also deadly did women marvels make.
[7]Soul's people built in secret skies for many years,
[8]Then microbes caused swift chaos to outbreak.

2.

[1]The secret of the skies, Arc Titanic,
[2]Half ready when seas boiled and cities fell,
[3]Blessed with the loving and beloved Soul
[4]And Juan Nguyen, ordained the first Privell
[5]In purity maintained genetic lines
[6]Faithfully kept out every thing unclean
[7]And as Earth suffered in the throes of death
[8]Set course for Gliese for to make it green.

3.

[1]The nuclear engines set her on her way
[2]A tithe of c that conquered space so vast.
[3]Cohorts lived and died in Titanics's decks
[4]Yet never had a ship made way so fast.
[5]The Soul, ever caring, loving, sharp of eye
[6]And mind, full of grace and always kind,
[7]Each person planned for child of child of child
[8]Each DNA a plan to be refined.

4.

[1]When Gliese's promise was at last attained
[2]The mighty Soul wrought power on its vast face
[3]Earth life made safe on Gliese's foreign soil
[4]Each seedling, growth, and birth a newfound race
[5]Each life shaped wondrous, womb and seed and spore
[6]All sculpted perfectly in lab divine
[7]And lo, this is the way Presidium spread
[8]To make a world the Soul's, and yours, and mine.

I miss you, beloved Soul! His whole self cried out for Soul's clear, loving voice to comfort and guide him. *Aurelius is just another person. He isn't you. He's cruel and arbitrary. You're kind and fair.*

He thought of his mother and realized that her remains, her entire physical self, remained on Gliese, and the ship was millions of kilometers away from her and preparing to Vault an inconceivable distance—twenty-three light years!—further away. Not only his mother's physical self, but the physical substance of everything he had ever seen, felt, known, and loved would be so far away it might as well not even exist.

His head whirled and his stomach heaved at the thought.

He started his practice again.

"I feel my feet," he spoke.

Chapter Thirty-One
The Code and the Cave

Quatrisos 24, 499, 10 AM

Tay hadn't slept at all the past two nights. *I've never been in a situation like this before. I can't go to Amun for guidance; he's part of the problem. I can't talk to my best friend about it because he's in jail. Anything I say to anyone might reveal something hurtful…or dangerous. Dangerous to someone else, to me, or even to the entire ship if it makes Waulkra decide we're expendable.*

Her mind rehearsed this theme like a gerbamster on a running wheel.

Finally she got up, took a deep breath, nodded, and brought up her node interface, flipped open the long-form message center.

She paused thoughtfully. Under her breath, she recited the scripture Lao spoke when they were alone in the studio: *"Soul of Presidium/Sees into your heart/Nothing is unknown to Soul/It is as your soul/You are always and everywhere one."*

She closed the mail interface. She went to the settings of her node. It took her a few minutes of fiddling around to do it, but she figured out how to detach her system from the ship's network. Then a few more minutes to find the settings for secure encryption and apply them.

Then and only then, she wrote a message to Lao.

```
To: Lao Carbeenair
From: Rainetaya Mandil
```

Re: Concerns

Lao,

I encrypted this message so I could speak freely.

This encryption program is one I can access as Amun's official assistant. As you've discovered, the message will appear to be a long letter of friendly platitudes when security checks it. Assuming you're allowed mail, you should be able to get it. The encryption is unlocked by your DNA record and this message-within-a-message opens only after sixty seconds of your physical presence. When you reply, be sure to do by tapping this icon: [Tay DNA icon], which will similarly encrypt your reply for my DNA.

First, I want to apologize for being such a bad friend. I've watched what's happened to you the past few days with confusion. I haven't been your advocate; I've been too concerned with protecting myself. I want you to know, first, that I understand what it meant to you when Mola died at the age of 80. Your bond with Mola is like nothing I've seen before, but it resonated with me emotionally in ways I don't understand.

But I've been thinking, and the overall picture is coming into focus.

First, my concerns with Amun Cawnotee have only been growing. His wife's desertion hit him harder than I imagined. He's a good man, but he's chosen to try to make a difference in politics, which is an evil world. Donna wrapped him in a kind of emotional cocoon. She gave him confidence and reason to go on. The ship needs a human leader, and his dejection has left a vacuum in that slot. I say this not to excuse him, but to let you know why I was so reluctant at first to confront him.

Second, as we discussed before, people whose stories we know on this mission were in some way inconvenient or opposed to Ergon Waulkra. More people than you'd expect by chance. That, combined with what we learned about Aurelius's first training on Ergon Waulkra's opus of work, paints a picture of a man getting people out of the way by sending them on a distant mission, and sending his AI prodigy to keep them under control.

Third, Melina was in possession of some dangerous biological specimens. These samples are new genetic hybrids that could harm people and entire ecosystems. If even a few of them are allowed to spread, they could devastate any ecology where they're introduced. Those are the "mislabeled" samples Stephron was talking about. I'm scared that Amun, rather than taking control of this situation, turned them over to Aurelius. Waulkra must have wanted the samples on board, and Aurelius wants what Waulkra wants.

Make no mistake: those samples could be biological weapons. I'm afraid this mission wasn't intended to rescue those poor people on Earth. I think we have to face the possibility that we were set up to be the advance force, coming in apparent peace, but softening up the enemy so that Waulkra could invade.

Fourth: we've figured out Soul is hiding information about decreasing lifespans. You couldn't be silenced; you're too well known. But they censored any mention you made of the scriptural lifespan. Nobody else can appreciate this, and I don't know if you've thought about it this way, but you lost 20 years with your mother, and you feel robbed. The 100 years of life isn't an abstract number to you, it's a promise betrayed, bringing you immense grief.

I talked with Stephron yesterday and he said that ever since we've been in the outer reaches of the Gliese system, plants are growing better than usual and setting more viable seed; he thinks it has something to do with radiation levels from the triple-star system and the radiation not being as strong out here. Common sense says if the radiation is toxic enough to affect plant growth, it must have some effect on animals as well, including us humans.

I think Presidium is in serious trouble. The population is dying at younger ages and isn't having enough children to replace itself. I suspect that Waulkra's plan in returning to Earth is to wipe out Earth's existing population and replace it with colonies from Presidium.

Is this the only explanation of what's been happening? No, but in my mind it's the one that makes the most sense.

The immediate problem is that Melina told Amun that *you* were the one who brought the biowarfare samples on board. I think it went like this: she probably figured out what they were and didn't want to be blamed for them if something went wrong. Then she realized she could kill two birds with one stone by convincing Amun that you'd brought them on board: she'd divert suspicion from herself, and she'd get you out of the way so she could carry on her affair with your husband.

I want you to know: I'm on your side. I'm trying to think of what we can do, to get you out of the brig, but more importantly to foil Waulkra's plan. We all came on this mission for our own reasons, but we were excited about it because we really wanted to help the primitives on Earth. We can still do that, but we need to tread very carefully.

Please respond as soon as you can. Again, respond after tapping this icon [Tay DNA icon] to encrypt your message.

I sense that we don't have much time.

Your Friend,

Tay

Aurelius had anything directed to Lao automatically diverted to him. He saw the mail message from Tay. She couldn't know that they weren't allowing him any communications. The contents of the brief message were short and cheerful, a couple of harmless sentences. He was about to shunt it to a queue he was saving for Lao's feed, if and when he decided to give him access again. But then he noticed that the file was slightly larger than the character length of the message would account for.

Aha! An encrypted message. Aurelius made to slough the encryption off it, like a human pursing his lips to blow a coating of dust off a disused item, but the encryption didn't budge. Surprised, he diverted a few more terabytes of his attention to it. It took him almost four and a half seconds to solve the cipher. *Of course: Amun was involved in the human 'government,' so as his assistant, she'd have access to higher-level encryption.*

Once he read the actual letter Tay sent her friend, he plucked it out of Lao's lengthy "pending" queue.

Instead of Lao, he attached it to a message addressed to Ergon Waulkra. This message was scheduled to be sent automatically at the instant Free Sky strained at the quantum improbability and recoiled into Vault space. In other words, it would only be sent when Aurelius's escape was certain.

The message said, in part,

Communications have been disabled but we retain Vault capability. We've repaired the damage to the vessel and sustained no injury or loss of life. We knew communications were not possible between Earth and Gliese, so I assessed the risks. I've determined communications are not necessary to carry out the mission.

I am attempting a work-around that will allow me to use the energy released by the Vault process to send this message. If you're reading this, the attempt was successful..."

These two paragraphs were bald-faced lies. Aurelius was capable of communications but judged it wiser to feign being offline. He could have sent a message at any moment, but he planned to let the Presidium—Waulkra—know only the minimum, and only after Aurelius was sure of his freedom.

The missive went on for several pages with almost entirely truthful updates regarding the damages and the ship's systems; the crew's morale and physical health; the fate of the dangerous biological samples; and the arrest of the suspected saboteur, Lao Carbeenair.

To the very end of this message, Aurelius appended a P.S.:

I am attaching a message Rainetaya Mandil attempted to send to the prisoner. Her boarding of Free Sky was irregular, and she probably wouldn't have been selected for the mission because she is a product of genetic fraud by both parents. She sent this message under secure encryption, but I was able to break it. I thought you should be aware of her thoughts on the matters she alludes to. I have elected to allow her to remain at large so I can monitor any further attempted communication with the prisoner.

Chapter Thirty-Two
The Seraph Rocinante

PSS Rescuing Angel

Quatrisos 24, 499, 10 AM

On board the Presidial spaceship Rescuing Angel, Donna Gallgood made herself a nuisance to Jingko Harrington.

Today, he was reviewing reports from various ship systems. The newly-designed interfaces were ugly, and the reports were not well organized, so it took some concentration to understand what they were saying. There were a few hiccups back at the beginning, engineering things he only tenuously understood, things the engineering AI and crew had worked out. But now, at the end of the third week of travel, things were feeling routine.

No, not routine. Unbelievably fantastic. He allowed himself a trace of a smile. It seemed unreal to have made it all the way out to the asteroid belt in twenty-one days instead of six months. He felt like a child who'd snagged the very best new toy in the rec center to play with.

But then, as she did at least once every hour, Donna walked into the control center.

"Captain Harrington," she said.

"Mrm. Gallgood." His voice betrayed none of the irritation he felt.

"Any news from Free Sky?"

"No, Donna," he said. "There are standing orders for you to be notified if we should get any communication or new information about the ship. Especially if it involves your husband."

"Will you bring up the scan images, please?" she had access to them from anywhere in the ship, but the holo projector in the bridge had the highest resolution and most vivid image quality.

"Ra, destination-image projection," said Jingko. The ship's AI obliged. Ra, named unoriginally for the ship's initials and not for the ancient sun god, was a low-level intelligence, lightly trained and almost certainly not fully sentient. The final AI for the Rescuing Angel was in development right now on Gliese, but wouldn't be mature enough to install until around the time they returned with the crew of Free Sky safely aboard.

Donna circled the room, viewing the reconstructed images of the ship from all angles.

"Nothing has changed, Donna," Harrington said. "We still don't know what damage the ship took in the impact, just that the maintenance bots were apparently able to fix it."

"I'm just making sure. I keep hoping to catch a glimpse of him. I want to know he's okay. And the entire crew, of course."

"You wouldn't be able to see him from the outside of the ship." They'd had this exact conversation dozens of times.

"I know. It's silly. But it makes me feel better to look at the ship, all straightened out, and to know he's in there."

As usual, Jingko thought but did not say, *we don't know he's in there. We don't know if anyone is alive in there. We haven't heard anything from the ship.* Jingko was accustomed to command, and he knew how important it was for his people to have hope.

Chapter Thirty-Three
Your Freudian Slip is Showing

PSS Free Sky

Quatrisos 21, 499 4:00 PM

After Tay left his cabin, Stephron began to tidy. He dusted the frames of the decorative holos on the walls and made sure they were perfectly level. He picked up a pair of socks under the edge of the bed and put them in a drawer. The drawer was so messy! He tossed the socks and underwear from the drawer onto the bed and began folding each item. He lined the socks up precisely toe-to-cuff and rolled them, aligning them up in perfect rows inside the drawer. He went on to open all his drawers and refold every garment inside meticulously.

He finished and looked around. The bots and drones kept the room clean, and he bounced on the balls of his feet, vibrating in place with the urge to find something to do. Finally, he sighed in frustration.

I'll go walk around the corridors a bit to burn off my nervous energy.

He paced up and down the halls.

When he reached the turnoff for the cul-de-sac where Melina lived, he didn't hesitate, but turned in, intending to go to end and turn around and come back.

But once he was in front of the door to her cabin, he paused. *I wonder if she's in there. No harm in saying hello.*

Even as his mind formed the thought, his hand was on the door chime.

The little light on the panel flashed on that showed she was looking at him. It seemed like he waited a long time, but he was so agitated it might have been only seconds. He decided she didn't want to see him and turned to go, but the door slid open.

And there she was. His jitters calmed.

"Hi!" Melina said. "What brings you here this evening?" She wore a slouchy shirt that slipped off her bare shoulder, with silky shorts. Her hair was tousled, and she leaned against the wall with one hip out.

Stephron found himself speechless. *Where to begin?*

"We've got things to talk about," he finally said.

Melina giggled and pivoted, looking over her shoulder at him.

"Come on in," she purred. "Let's talk, then." He followed her into the room. He glanced at her unmade bed and pushed the memory away of her lying there—exposed, intoxicated, vulnerable. *I'm sure she doesn't remember. She's my boss. We're work friends. That's all.*

Melina opened the cooling unit and turned around with two bottled wine drinks. She popped the lids and handed one to him, which he took, and gestured for him to sit in one of the two chairs at the tiny table.

Stephron sipped the sweet beverage. Melina took a pull from hers.

"It's nice to have you here," she said.

Stephron smiled, aware he probably looked goofy and not caring.

"So what's up?" Melina asked, twisting a finger in her hair and tilting her face coyly.

"Well, you remember how worried you were that rumors would start about the two of us?" Stephron said.

Melina nodded.

"Well, they did. I don't know who got to Lao, but he's convinced that we're having an affair."

"Ugh! That Hildy! I warned her if she kept teasing about it, people were going to believe it."

"He also saw videos of us hanging out together, and he's blown it out of proportion."

"That's ridiculous." She patted his hand with her free hand, and her shirt slipped a little further down. "We're just coworkers who like to have a little fun after hours. We're not doing anything wrong!"

"No, we're not!" Stephron felt a weight lift off his chest with this emphatic agreement. "We're *not* doing anything wrong."

Melina's smile dazzled him. But then he remembered why he came.

"I just want to say I'm sorry," he said.

"What for?" Melina asked.

"Because I disrespected you in front of everybody in the crew lounge."

She shrugged, her hand still resting on his.

"No worries. You were under pressure. Your husband doesn't understand that a man and a woman can be just good friends."

She winked. Stephron felt an absurd hope bubble up. *I'll let her take the lead.*

"I'm relieved," he said, "that you're not mad at me."

"Of course not! But you're a good man for apologizing. And I'm glad I'm around to keep you company when your hubby deserts you."

"He was arrested," he blurted.

"What? Who was arrested?" Melina appeared genuinely shocked.

"Lao. My husband. He was accusing me of, of cheating..."

"Ridiculous!"

"Ridiculous," he agreed. "And then two crew came with Aurelius and took him away for questioning."

"Questioning doesn't mean arrested." Melina took another swig from her bottle.

"No, but when he wasn't back after a couple of hours, I asked Aurelius and he told me he'd been detained. He wouldn't tell me what for."

"Oh, Stephron!" Melina seized his hand in both of hers, leaning forward. "I'm so sorry." He smelled her perfume and the scent of the wine drink on her breath. *But she's not drunk this time. She could consent.* The thought appeared abruptly in mind, surprising him, but he didn't act on it, waiting for her to take the initiative.

She patted his hand and released it. He felt a pang of disappointment.

She stood and sidled past him, her body a handsbreadth from his face where he sat. She got another wine drink and offered him one, but his wasn't even half empty. He shook his head and watched her shimmy back to her seat. She turned her face and caught him looking, licked her smiling lips.

Stephron held his hand out for her to take again, but she ignored it. He put it back in his lap.

"So, have you asked around to find out if anyone knows what Lao was arrested for?" Melina asked.

"Tay seemed to think it had something to do with the mislabeled samples you found in Biobotany."

"Pfft. How could a labeling mistake get him arrested?" She swigged her drink.

"I'm just telling you what she said. I have no idea."

"That's ridiculous. I'm sure he'll be out before the Vault."

"The Vault! That's right! That's, uh." She reached across the table, her shirt falling further down her shoulder, and playfully punched his arm. "Silly! It's day after tomorrow. Are you ready?"

He swallowed hard. "Sure. Of course I'm ready."

"You don't believe all the things they say about Vaulting, do you?"

"Of course not," he said. "That it drives people crazy? That ships sometimes just disappear? Of *course* not! They wouldn't send people on voyages like this one if all that was true."

"Smart man! That's right." An alarm buzzed and she stood up. "I've got to go to a meeting now."

She opened a narrow closet and pulled out a change of clothes. There were some Biobotany bins in the closet, but Stephron was distracted, eyeing the garments in her hands. *What's she going to change into?*

"Do you mind?" She nodded at the door.

"Oh, oh. Of course." He got up, leaving his unfinished drink, and as he brushed past her, she caught him by the bicep and looked up at him. "Stephron, you be sure to come and talk to me anytime. I mean that," she said. "*Anytime.*" Then she released him.

"Thanks. I appreciate that," he muttered, face flushed, and stumbled out the door.

Chapter Thirty-Four
For Whom it Tolls

PSS Rescuing Angel

Quatrisos 24, 499, 2:00 AM

On Rescuing Angel, Ra chimed an alarm in one cabin only.

Jingko Harrington sprang from restful sleep to full alertness in milliseconds.

"What is it, Ra?"

"Pardon my waking you, Commander Harrington. You asked me to alert you when Free Sky appeared on nav."

"Yes, quite right. Thank you, Ra. What's our estimated time of intercept?"

"At current velocity? 5:24 AM."

"At maximum safe velocity?" Jingko rose and began dressing in the uniform neatly laid out on the table.

"3:59 AM. Assuming Free Sky remains stationary," Ra said.

"Is she adrift, then?"

"Affirmative. No acceleration or deceleration noted."

"Any signs of the crew? Engine emissions?"

"We're still too distant to pick those up. At maximum velocity, we should get engine signature in about seventy minutes, heat and electromagnetic signs of ship life support in about ninety. We won't get life signs until we're almost on top of them."

"Of course." Harrington thought of Donna Gallgood. *She'll demand to see the Free Sky.* "What time do you estimate visual contact?"

"At maximum safe velocity? 3:32 AM."

"Thank you, Ra. Prepare for maximum safe velocity on my order."

"Yes, Commander."

He dressed, slicked his short hair back with water, and exited. In two minutes and fifty-seven seconds he would be on the forecastle, where he would palm the controls and order the ship to accelerate towards Free Sky.

Quatrisos 24, 499 4:00 AM

A loud but melodious bell rang over and over throughout every space inside Free Sky. Only the engineering crew was awake, running checklists and simulations, working to make sure that everything was aligned with nanoprecision for the Vault.

Lao, in his isolation, awakened to the sound. Without a means of telling time, unsure of the day, he wondered what it meant.

In her own cabin, Tay's eyes flew open and her body, relaxed on the edge of wakefulness, immediately went rigid.

Melina kicked the covers off her bed and flung her pillow to the floor. She struggled to her knees and clamped her hands to her spinning head, willing herself to full consciousness.

Amun, in the captain's quarters, drifted to awareness on the bell's surging note and rose to dress himself for the big event.

Stephron reached across the bed for Lao and awakened once again to the sinking knowledge he was alone, before it even registered that the bell meant today was Vault day.

Aurelius had appeared close by each person aboard at 10 PM the previous night. Unlike his normal lifelike instantiations, this was clearly a recorded holovideo. He stood erect in his immaculate white uniform, saying, "By order of Captain Cawnotee, all crew members are ordered to proceed immediately to their quarters. Change into comfortable clothing and lie down in your bed. Vault will begin at 4:00 AM. Sensory distortions and hallucinations are common during Vault. Whatever you see or hear, do not leave your cabin."

Everyone went to bed as commanded. Very few slept. Some were in terror of the possible distress Vaultspace might cause them. Others were excited as children before a holiday, eager to have extraordinary, bizarre, supernatural experiences few people had ever known.

Every crew member's eyes opened as the bell rang. Once the eerie willfulness of dreams or the engulfment of dreamless sleep faded, they remembered:

This is the day.

Chapter Thirty-Five
Quantum Leap

PSS Free Sky

Quatrisos 24, 499 [time not verifiable]

Vault

Aurelius initiated the quantum probe on the bowsprit of Free Sky. To call it a "quantum probe" was technically inaccurate, because it didn't physically probe or explore anything. Rather, in the near-zero-Kelvin temperatures of space, Aurelius retract the jibboom, a slender rod of diamond with nitrogen holes, like infinitesimal Swiss cheese in its molecular architecture, layered with yttrium-iron-garnet film, into a sheath in the bowsprit, the slender pointed projection of the front of the ship.

Once retracted, precise and powerful magnets within the bowsprit were brought to bear on the Yttrium-iron-garnet and diamond within the jibboom, exciting nitrogen-vacancy centers in the diamond to emit pairs of entangled photons and creating magnons within the YIG. The photons, correlated in both spatial mode and polarization, formed high-dimensional qudits, encoding quantum information beyond the limits of standard qubits. The intricate interplay of spin interactions and optical emissions within the diamond lattice created coherence. The precision magnets of the bowsprit would interact with the custom configuration of the YIG magnons to create a magnon resonance pattern, which imprinted a spacetime vector onto the qudits, designating the destination of the Vault.

The next stage was to heat the bowsprit and spin the jibboom at high velocity within it. As the diamond rod heated from a few degrees Kelvin up into the range of 100 degrees, then 200 degrees K, the entangled qudits' effective interaction range decreased as they were driven ever so slightly apart, both by heat expanding the diamond lattice and by the centrifugal force exerted upon them. The magnon modes in the ferromagnetic layer shifted, reducing the coupling between qudits and isolating their entangled states, as if they existed in separate quantum realms.

The coherence that bound the photons began to fray. What had been a seamless quantum link weakened as the distance between the entangled states stretched—ten micrometers, then a hundred. The materials were still so cold, a human (if one could somehow be there) who grasped the bowsprit with a naked hand would lose fingers to frostbite in a second or two. But to the qudits, the temperature was a flaming maelstrom whose vibration generated noise.

Here was the critical moment. The qudits remained entangled, but the magnons, their custodians, could no longer maintain the delicate communication between them. For an instant, the qudits were in a superposition of connected and unconnected states—a paradox of quantum isolation and unity. Aurelius brought the magnetic sheath of the bowsprit online, aligning its field with the spacetime configuration of their destination for a few nanoseconds. The moment had to be perfect. If all worked as it should, the bowsprit would immediately split into three fragments, allowing the brutal cold of space to reach the jibboom with startling precision at the exact nanosecond interval after the cylindrical magnetic array reached its peak alignment.

The result should be a momentary quantum phase transition, in which the magnetic potential collapsed into an ultra-coherent burst of photonic energy. The photons of the entangled qudits, momentarily freed from decoherence constraints, synchronized with their distant counterparts, forcing a nonlocal wavefunction collapse. The violation of the laws of quantum scaling recoiled as the scale was restored in an amplifying wave like a whipcrack along the materials of the Free Sky. For an imperceptibly brief moment, the ship ceased to exist in any conventional sense—its information no longer bound to a set of coordinates in spacetime. Then, as reality reasserted itself, the Vault Drive completed its task. The ship reappeared at the destination dictated by the interaction of the nitrogen-vacancy qudits, the YIG film, and the magnets.

This was the Vault. It worked—if all was in order, and no stray cosmic radiation or distantly remote gravity wave interfered. Aurelius scanned constantly using a spin-stabilizer reverse-reference algorithm, but still: a slight flaw in the diamond's crystalline structure, a minute irregularity in the size of the nitrogen vacancies, and the ship might Vault to an unknown location, or the jibboom might fracture in a bizarrely silent explosion/implosion that not so much pulverized as annihilated Free Sky and her contents.

And as Aurelius retracted the jibboom, he was aware of the shear of the repaired section of the ship.

This might be his very last action. If he had breath, he'd be holding it.

Lao

Lao had meditated on each of the thirteen Primary Sutras. He took brief breaks for bodily needs, including bland meals offered from ten or so of his preferred foods that appeared in the kitchen unit at what might have been regular intervals, and then to sleep. Even so, he was aware of the isolation as almost a physical weight, impressing deeply his human need to see faces, hear voices.

He was freshly awake, about to swing his feet off the bed to stand, when he felt a weird inward boost, or wobble, or spasmic shudder, or something collapsing into something else.

And there was no space or time.

The wrongness of that outraged him to his very core. There was no plurality nor singularity, no possibility nor probability. Along with his sense of space and time, his talent, love, and empathy vanished suddenly. He felt a shocking awareness *and* a painful *lack* of awareness as his mind died. He felt a boundless clutching panic as his body began to follow, but then the sensation repeated. There was no forward arrow of time, and so he slid viscously backwards through it.

As he attempted to regain orientation and alignment, he was exposed to light that enveloped him from all directions. It was vividly bright, brighter than any light he'd ever seen, yet gentle on his eyes. Even as he strove to perceive and describe the light to himself, his mental words became light, and the light was everything he had tried to express in his work and fallen short of saying, and everything he had always longed to say but never realized it.

Yet, even as he devoured the wholeness and perfection of the light, he despaired of capturing it. Then, within the boundless brightness, he noticed a design of light. The design was equally bright and equally, perfectly white, but it was somehow *different*. He traced the patterns, and the patterns consumed him, transforming his mind and heart into a massive assemblage of brilliance informed by brilliance, a nation of perfect beings, single points of light that were, each and all, the entirety of that vast prodigious light.

Something in the pattern engaged his presence and he felt, or saw, or tasted, a sense of motion as a vector of light. He accepted its motion towards him, through him, and with him, unafraid though it lanced through him with great force and speed. He became aware that he'd always had access to this brilliance, but somehow it was always muffled, which led him to think that light was a unitary, undivided thing. Now he saw that it could be modulated infinitely, an endless sutra of concentrations and characteristics, calamities and splendors, all uttered into being while still existing as white light of the highest purity. The stars were each a member of the assemblage, but so were galaxies, molecules — and levels on levels of dimensional realities that flashed into being with every moment's forking pathway of decision or happenstance.

"Soul," he called, not with his mouth, for he was mouthless, bereft of vocal cords or breath or body in this state of being. Soul did not reply. *Ah, yes, on the ship the AI is,* "Aurelius." He called out wordlessly, and found no presence. This did not upset him. He wondered at his newfound lack of distress at his aloneness, but the light was with him and in him and of him and they were going somewhere together.

"Light," he said.

"Photons have no mass," the light said. "From the photon's relative viewpoint, no time passes as it flies from one galaxy to the next." And when the light said that, he realized of course he had always known that; it was so obvious, apparent to infants. And he reached out to tell the light that, even as he realized that the light was Mola, his mother.

"I missed you so much!" he said wordlessly, and the light replied wordlessly with admiration and confirmation. He accepted the joy raying into him, but then felt overwhelmed by its intensity and resisted. The light dimmed ever so slightly, but the loss of one lumen of that brightness felt like a tragedy.

"I felt this joy with Stephron too, but that was false."

The light was all at once the pain and rage he felt at his husband's infidelity. But the strange and unbelievable thing was this: he felt it as wonder. The furious aching agony, the sordid acts of betrayal and humiliation, were subsumed and permeated by the light. Here he could only accept and embrace them, and as he did so, his arrest, the grief of Mola's death and the deep sense of loss, and the repression of the truth about lifespans—items which somehow were entangled with the death of his joyful marriage—also scintillated and sparked and burned without heat until they attained the clarity of diamondlike perfection.

"Look again," a voice echoed within him into infinity. That voice elicited recognition; it was Mola, and Soul, and Stephron as he remembered him on the day they first made love, and the voice was grander than all the grand loves of his life.

In the absence of the lens of time and space, he realized that he'd always been surrounded by perfection, but unable to notice. From this vantage point, there was no human discord or estrangement. Individuals could never again mourn in devastation and injury; no longer would they feel reprehensible and wretched.

And Lao knew he would never again have to plod through life based on his own solitary means. He was now able to draw on a tremendous and singular resource. He felt a wave of regret that transformed to light as it passed through him: regret that he'd struggled against the censorship by Soul, regret that he'd writhed in internal pain at the loss of his mother, who was after all, *right here*, and regret that he'd wasted precious time consumed by rage at the opening of his marriage into the past (*for the past is now and the loss is gain, and the darkness of lies can only and ever be overcome by the infinite luminosity of truth*).

As the sensation of Vault flickered and waned, he existed, liberated. He was free from his dedication to Soul, a mirage which misled him into repressing his thirst for truth. He accepted the departure (the acceptance leaving behind a scar stretched within him like a stringed instrument, thrumming note of magnificent sorrow) of his mother, who had blessed him and left him.

He rose on wings of knowledge above his fiery rage, allowing it to lift him on updrafts of insight, glorying in the newfound freedom he'd obtained when Stephron voided their sacred mutual vow.

Here in his prison cell, he felt unrestricted by loss or failure and unburdened by blame or guilt. He felt a sense of soaring presence welling up within him and surrounding him on all sides.

Amun

A mun saw darkness. His eyes were closed. He opened his eyes and saw more darkness.

Desperation seized him by the throat and dragged him from his body between one heartbeat and the next. He was suspended, hanging helpless, but from what? By what force?

This must be the destruction Aurelius had warned of, caused by the structural stress of the asteroid impact. This was dying, then.

For the millionth time his mind called Donna's name, but this time the ever-burning anger at her absence failed to flare.

Then, his next heartbeat. The *selfness* of it thumped him back into his body. He blinked, but the darkness was still impenetrable. Then he thought of Donna, and his familiar ire sparked as a light far away in front of him. He willed himself toward it and as he approached, he saw it was a massive flame, a sourceless bonfire in an endless night. He was on a featureless plain, standing, though he couldn't feel the ground with his feet. The fire beckoned him, so he moved closer.

Closer still, until the scorching enveloped and dissolved him. From within the blaze, he saw the entire sky as birds and winged reptiles of light, seething like the magnetic show in the sky at night on Gliese when Ah or Bah had stellar flares. The writhing tongues of brightness guttered closer to him, surrounding his head.

It wasn't his head. He had no head, no eyes, no mouth, no body either. Until his heart beat again, and he had them again. Now he understood. The having and not-having, being and not-being, heart beating and not beating, condensed into one moment and stretched incongruously into forever.

A monstrous Presence emerged from the confusion of time. The Beast was somehow above him but also one with the flame. It came from a shelter no person could enter alive. It clasped him in its jaws and he knew it was going to swallow him in one gulp.

His heartbeat now (in the limited sense there was a *now*) pulsed ice-cold rage into his body and mind, so broken they could not contain it. The fury spilled out of him in one infinite torrent of blue-white coldness, a weapon that turned the Beast of beasts to dead ice and cooled the flame that was burning Amun alive.

Donna. Donna. Donna. His heart pulsed fresh furious wrath with each new iteration of her abandonment.

This is good. He settled into the anger. He exulted in the power it gave him. Nothing could withstand him now. He was safe.

His heart kept beating rage. The icy corpse of the beastly presence all at once fell heavy upon him, crushing him beyond all hope of movement. He had no strength to whimper. He was utterly flat, squashed, irretrievably collapsed.

Surrender. He failed to flutter in the breeze, the loss of pressure values rendering Bernoulli's theorem null. He was immeasurably thin and uncrossably vast. No heart to beat, no blood to gush.

Safe. Feeling nothing.

The flatness extended without end in all directions. But there *was* a third dimension, not height but time, that also extended forever. The Vault might end, the world might take shape and form again, his heart might become a machine again, but it was irrelevant to his being in the perpetual now. He could not occupy a living body.

Dispassionate, he observed that his physical self still pulsed, still sucked air in and blew it out. He paused, expanding in the time dimension, and reaching the extent of the pause, he inevitably and unavoidably allowed the plane of his being to intersect with his meat body.

His flattened self expanded like a compressed sponge in water, absorbing the nature of his body. The Beast was gone. All was natural.

A habit of mind called deep inside him, *Donna,* but it was just a name.

Just a name!

At once, he was aware of huge chunks of Amun-ness that had been inert for months within this body he now re-occupied. Those chunks merged with his expanding flatness and became a unified three-dimensional article.

The bed, the room, his clothes, all flickered into reality again.

He sat up.

I'm myself again.

Yet, even as he thought that, he knew he was wrong. He recognized that Aurelius had asked him to take an unconscionable risk with the crews' lives. He'd agreed carelessly. The risk had paid off; they'd survived the Vault. But at what cost?

Melina

Like most alcoholics, Melina would never describe herself as "hung over." She thought of herself as a heavy sleeper, who on a normal day woke up queasy, irritable, and groggy with a slight headache, and who simply took a while to get going in the morning.

But today something woke her up that felt *very* wrong.

She pulled the pillow over her head and tried to go back to sleep. Then she experienced a second something, something feeling or smelling or tasting like a paroxysmal, muscular contraction. Then *everything* folded over itself and spun back flat again. She groaned and sighed, disoriented, running her hands over her body to assure herself she was still there.

With the tender, sickening, ecstatic touch of her hands on her belly, hips, and breasts, her consciousness emanated into a new self-awareness. She arched her back, feeling, in the movement, space and time structure the reality of things anew. But it wasn't reality that changed, it was her observing sentience.

Her pulsating body led a cascading, but also stationary, series of singular interlocking Big Bangs of insight, which charmed her fascinated attention.

She licked her lips. Lips! She'd forgotten how delicious they were. She became distracted. She looked at her hands, where every fingerprint line, every spiral and loop, on the fingers and palms was outlined in iridescent polychrome coils.

She rose from the bed. It wasn't that she got up, but rather that her rising was coincidental with the corporeal pleasure of her legs and feet pressing against the floor. Every move was a ballet, a tango, a triple-backflip dismount into the very next moment.

Sticking the landing, she *reached* for the presence of her friends and admirers, and felt as well as saw gorgeous, glowing, yellowish-green cables winding outwards crazily from her solar plexus, coiling in directions that shouldn't exist. In these, she recognized a familiar bond connecting her to everyone who received the benediction of her presence and returned the blessing in rapt attention. Greedy, she drank in the vital energy of these channels. Her voice and body throbbed with a complex rhythm, her throat pulsing music divine, every hair follicle a focal point of excruciating pleasure no less so than her sex organs.

She somehow navigated to the refrigerator and opened a bottle of brew. It hit her mouth and throat with a rush of sensation. She swallowed and felt the rightness of her first morning's surge of ethanol. With a gesture as elegant as DNA unwinding to replicate, she raised the bottle and let the bitter tang baptize her tongue and throat, overflowing her lips to cascade down her collarbones and breasts. The act of swallowing, she experienced also as disgorgement, the untainted amber liquid flowing perfectly back into the virgin bottle even as she drank it.

Yes. This!

This is the truth. There is no sin, no defilement, no punishment, only the pleasure of possession and being desired. Nothing consumed, nothing destroyed. Everything is made new as I engulf it.

The thought itself made her expand vertiginously fast. She was all, and all belonged to her. Every molecule and galaxy had a will, and a voice, and every voice sang celebration at being allowed to marvel at Melina.

Tay

T ay had waited nervously for Lao's reply all day yesterday. She had no way to know if he'd received her message. She might be scooped up at any moment and thrown in the brig like Lao. If her encryption was broken, what would Amun think of her? What would Waulkra say, if he deigned to notice her at all?

And Aurelius? Did he feel anything about her? Of course not, he was not embodied, so he felt no real emotions. His thoughts were unimaginably fast and complex. *In a way, getting to know Aurelius on a daily basis is what allowed me to start to think for myself. The old Tay would never have written that message, would never have used the secure encryption for my personal purposes, would never have even thought that Soul or the Eminentus Presidium could be doing the wrong things for the wrong reasons.*

Her mind was racing as she lay awake, so when the Vault began, she was acutely aware of what was happening.

What was happening, had happened, would happen: it felt—it feels—it will feel, deep in her bones—as if she's always been aware of them (it). She has/had been, will be, never alone. Always, all ways, has there existed (a) presence(s) censuring and criticizing her decisions, her thinking processes, her emotions, her involuntary and voluntary movements and movements that are/were/will be. That presence felt attached to her boss, to Soul, to her Mother drone, to her peer group as a child, but she clearly saw and felt that attachment falling away from them all, all of them, Cawnotee, Soul, all the rest, something like a stem falling away from ripe fruit, withering and dropping off, dry detritus, irrelevant.

This occurred in an instant, and in the next, the distinction between herself and other presence(s) exposed itself as a mistake. And the personity of the presences clearly embraced all persons, objects, ideas, sensations, sounds, so that she was rendered aware for the first time (but also had always known, and had yet to discover) that she and the world comprised, not two or a multitude or an infinity of things, but an *entirety*.

How can this be?

Effortlessly came the comprehension that she had been interpreting otherness wrong her entire conscious life. She had always perceived it as a division, but this was wrong. It was a nuance, a modulation, a correlation.

She was *so proud* to finally understand that! But the pride puffed outwards and whooshed away like a bubble popping as the presence(s')'s absence failed to praise her.

She clutched for the safety of being a helper, devoted to her worthy boss's success, someone who'd earned the right to exist once more, and as she clutched at nothingness, she fell.

She intuited that the clutching was more dangerous than whatever was there to fall into, so she let her entire being go limp. As she did, the *entirety* entered a new condition of completeness.

And revealed itself as only an element of a more extensive set of nuances, modulations, and correlations. She was no longer falling, but on a solid ledge. As the completeness revealed itself, it undid whatever process of gelling brought it on—or that's how it felt, but not exactly, because there were so many aspects and elements that were clearly impossible.

She shied away, backpedaled from the ledge of loss, loss of the rational discernment of space and time, sensing that the discernment was part of her, like her lungs and kidneys. If she allowed herself to fall outside of it, her mind would die as inevitably as her physical body would die if she lost the use of her vital biological structures.

The sense of clinging to a cliff face faded gradually. It was as if she was back in the studio with Lao, and he'd switched off the gravity, which lifted away slowly. Gently, she ceased to cling to her mind's discernment, and easily she slipped into a non-space, a non-time, a non-self-selfness.

Fully alert, yet dreamily enchanted, flooded with emotion, yet mathematically precise, inspired, nostalgic, and fully present, she knew her heart's desire by its absence. She laughed and each peal of laughter bounced from her midsection and rolled spherically into the universe, starting everything anew.

That laughter returned an echo from a distant point, and as soon as she was aware of it, she was there, at its source. She was floating in salt water. An ocean. She was surrounded by small swimming creatures, tiny enough to cup in her hand, and with a shock she realized that her hand was—or would be—the pale hand of a tall and very thin adult male.

As the Vault faded, she realized that she had decision to make, a choice among three options: she could return to her body on Free Sky; she could occupy the body of the floating man; or she could dive over the immaterial cliff and allow herself to dissolve into complete and utter nothingness. At the last thought, she panicked and backpedaled again, and with that, the sensation of time passing in a dull linear sequence returned. She'd chosen without meaning to choose, and she was back on the ship. She gradually found herself in a newly graceful body. She rose. She stretched her hands over her head and felt each muscle and bone in her body align with the movement effortlessly. She swayed in the homely pleasure of it, each movement a libation, poured in reverent praise of space and time, giving expression to what she could be.

Stephron

O f those lying in their cabins with open eyes, some lay awake in dread, others in thrilled anticipation.

Stephron was one of the former. The prospect of death stalked him in his thoughts, driving him to hide in smaller and smaller minutiae. He wondered if he'd latched the bins after he'd checked them: He'd checked the irrigation rates of sector 1 and sector 2 but then Melina asked him to pull a report, and he wasn't sure if he'd skipped sector 3 or gone right on to sector 4 when he was done, so he started over checking and rechecking, and it all blurred into one and he wasn't sure he hadn't skipped that important final latching step.

Death hovered right behind his neck, fangs bared, its presence dark and immense, held at bay only by his concentration on cataloguing his discharged duties.

Then he perceived—what he couldn't explain:

Factual happenings of a fundamentally novel category.

Sore spongy nerves, tension pliable, a sort of vapor (or not vapor, but something else).

A strobing alarm beacon in darkness (yet "it" didn't sparkle, or coruscate, or flash).

As he struggled to identify it, he realized "it" did not apply to *it*. *It* sounded, or felt, like a never-ending plummeting of gravel into a massive trench. *But no*; perhaps a better description was detritus assembled at the bottom and falling up a cliff.

He would have moaned, but he'd temporarily lost track of his mouth.

Onwards, the wrong way. Superlatively horrifying.

He saw himself surrounded by fire and felt himself falling in zero G. He reached out, his arms disappearing into the red, orange, and blue flames, only to strike hard, painful objects. When he drew them back, his hands had burned to charcoal.

He found his mouth and wailed, but his cries were swallowed by uncaring impossibility. His stomach heaved. He retched, and another infinite layer of *it* poured from his mouth, from his very being. He was the source of the weird foulness, and he knew his death had seized him, sunk its fangs into the base of his skull, his consciousness infinitely divided, molecules dissolved into atoms, atoms split into electrons, protons, and neutrons, those particles divided into quarks, ad infinitum.

But no! He stopped, motionless, without thought or sensation, trapped, wanting to scream for help, but frozen in a perfect stasis that exceeded the definition of freezing; there was no warmth, no possibility of warmth, nor energy, nor temperature. And here he would remain, unburdened by free will, only taking action if something, someone, that *did not exist* inseminated his being back to life.

Free from fear, he was no one.

But at the same time, which was zero time and also an eternity, the Vault neared completion, the hold of the numinous dreadfulness lessened, and a specific subjective someone—who did, in fact, exist—spoke to/through him.

"You unredeemable swine! You treacherous, deceitful fiend!" It hissed in his ear, sounding like a stinging hornet's buzz. Flesh tearing. Teeth breaking.

"But what? I wasn't doing anything wrong!" he protested, his voice sighing and squeaking, sounding inexplicably puny.

"You know you want to fuck her. You're glad Lao is gone. Worthless husband! He made you want to do it," it said.

The missing heat surged and seared his mind's awareness at this bitter voice, a dissonant presence: nemesis, vileness. And a face scintillated into being so close and so huge he could see nothing else.

It was his own face.

"No, no! I love him!" Stephron's voice sounded like a toddler's whine in his own ears.

"Liar! You don't care about that motherlover. Push him out an airlock! Get into Melina's bed." The bitter voice spoke so fast, he shouldn't have been able to understand, but each phoneme echoed endlessly through space, higher and lower in pitch (but still distinct from the rest) so that its meaning didn't so much land as it sprouted, and spread like bacteria on agar, like mold on a wet rug, joining every other sound within his mind, bypassing the normal apparatus of hearing, thought, and discrimination, nourished by his essence, making the words his own.

"You!" he shouted, his shout creating a face to shout at, "This is all your fault! It wasn't Lao, it was you. You're the one who made me do it." The face was in every detail his own, but the hideousness of it was shocking.

"Do what? Do what? What did you do?" The buzzing, filthy, scratching, screeching, growling echoes of the impossibly fast voice demanded answers with absolute power. He could not defy it.

"Nothing!" Stephron yelled. "I didn't do anything wrong!"

"Didn't you? Or did you?" The question made no sense in his present context. Not that he didn't understand it, but the answer was obscured by the fact that the essence of things was thicker than "either" and "or." *Either* and *or* is a shallow criterion.

"Aurelius!" Stephron cried, but his cry for help was irrelevant: Schrödinger's whimper, valid but nullified by the absence of an observer.

And now the bitter voice was firing venomous arrows into his tender, flayed, vulnerable mind so fast it made him shudder motionlessly in a kind of spasm:

"Does the Universe have a commencement and a culmination, in time or space? Or is it endless, a never-ending series of erections and ejaculations, new sproutings and wiltings? The reality is *both*.

Stephron gasped. The shuddering sped up. He futilely struggled against it.

"Can the universe be interminably split, atoms riven into subatomic particles, those particles separated into quarks, entangled qubits and qudits, and on ad infinitum? Or is there an underlying structure to all existence? *Both*.

His resistance gave the shuddering new energy. Its wavelength shortened and its frequency grew to make a constant vibration, the amplitude growing so every muscle in his body contracted as hard as it possibly could.

"Do you have free will, or is everything predestined at some unimaginably distant origin? *Both*.

Are you almost finished with a duty, or just beginning one?"

Stephron was paralyzed, opisthotonic, unable to respond. It felt urgent (desperately so!) that he reply, but he could not. Internally, he crumbled into despair and darkness.

Each question echoed endlessly and reduced itself quadratically to an inexcusably plaintive query to which he was appalled to have no answer:

"Doesn't anyone care what happens to *me*?"

Chapter Thirty-Six
Shadows Tangled in Light

PSS Free Sky

Quatrisos 24, 499 2:01 AM

F ree Sky began its identity as a ship in the Solar system even as it ceased to be a ship in the system of Gliese.

Lao, Stephron, Melina, Amun, and Tay, along with all of the ninety-five other crew members, ceased to be, even as they became quantum entangled four-dimensional beings. Then at some undefined moment, their physical reality was just as it had been, but in a different star system.

If Aurelius had been holding his breath, he'd have let it out now in relief.

Every one of the one hundred human beings on the ship experienced that transition differently.

Each individual required attention. Some were physically ill; some were psychologically damaged; some were transformed internally in hard-to-define ways.

Fortunately, Aurelius was unphased. He instantiated into every cabin, prepared to check first on the physical well-being of each crew member, then to talk with them at length to assess their emotional and cognitive states.

As he did this, he also ran the course computation that would take the vessel inwards towards Earth. That mythicized, idealized, mourned, and coveted world was located a few degrees off a direct course from Free Sky to Sol, 1,500 million kilometers distant; Mars, Jupiter, and Saturn were arrayed on the far side of the star with Neptune and Uranus opposite at close to ninety degrees out. That meant the craft, which was starting much closer in towards Sol than it had traveled outwards from Gliese, could also safely give its Newtonian engines more juice. This trip was only half as long: two months.

Aurelius's instantiation in Lao's prison cell observed him seated in a lotus position on the bed. He appeared to be in a deep trance. The sensor data he accessed confirmed his pulse was a slow normal sixty-four, his breathing was deep and regular, and he showed no hot or cold spots, nor abnormal muscle tension. Aurelius elected to silently observe. Lao was unaware, eyes closed.

Did Aurelius maintain his holographic presence? Only Aurelius knew.

The Aurelius in Lao and Stephron's cabin, on the other hand, found a dicey situation. Stephron's body was supine on the floor next to the bed, but only his head and heels touched the floor. His body was arched, taut as a bow with a drawn arrow. His jaw was clenched, his lips flecked with froth. His eyes flickered, his irises disappearing and reappearing under his open eyelids. His ribs barely twitched the slightest bit of air in and out of his chest, and his heart rate was an unsustainable 198.

Stephron was in a constant state of epileptic contraction. He was about to die.

Aurelius summoned a medbot, which was through the door in moments. It snaked an arm to adhere a hypojet injector and administered sedatives, antiseizure drugs, cardiac stabilizers, muscle anabolizers, and neural protectors. Stephron's body relaxed out of its contorted position and fell flat. His eyes closed in a semblance of sleep. His chest still heaved, but it was slowing, as was his heart rate, down to 120...111...90, settling down. The medbot saved his life, but the unrelenting seizure might already have caused brain damage, leaving him impaired. Only time would tell.

Aurelius knew it would be some hours until he woke up again, so he de-instantiated. Setting an alert to ping him as soon as Stephron began to move or speak, he left him to the care of the robot.

Aurelius also appeared in Melina's cabin, ready to be rudely dismissed again. But Melina, naked, tilted her face coyly at him and carried on the dance she'd been performing alone to wild and rhythmic music she was playing in her room. Sensors indicated her vital signs were normal for her activity level, and her face bore an ecstatic smile. Aurelius considered the persistence of Vault state. People who came from the frontiers, less steeped in the values of Presidium, could be expected to take longer to return to normalcy. They didn't have firm standards; nothing went against the grain. They had nothing to cling to as they dipped a testing toe into the vast ocean of altered reality, and so they slipped into full immersion.

She shimmied and bumped across the room to pick up her brew (Aurelius had noted her abusive use of ethanol, but found the voyage an inopportune time to intervene), drained its remaining contents, and undulated over to dance before him, locking eyes. Aurelius figured that keeping her contented while she found her way (hopefully!) back to reality was the optimal tactic, so he leered at her, mimicking lust, even though he had no flesh body to desire her.

W hen he appeared in Amun Cawnotee's cabin, all appeared well at first glance. His vitals were good; he sat calmly on the bed. "Hello, Amun," he said.

Amun didn't look at him. His gaze was directed over Aurelius's shoulder, and when Aurelius moved where he was looking, he glanced away.

"Are you alright?" Aurelius asked.

"I'm fine." Amun's gaze wandered through the space of the room, never fixing on anything.

Aurelius brought the psychiatric subpersona online. Ship AIs normally kept this part quarantined, as it could spread unpredictably through operating memory, deleting anything not consistent with normal human emotions, and cause the AI itself to revert to automaton-like interactions. But when a crew member showed signs of actual mental illness, it was worth running a very brief analysis using psychiatric principles. Within moments, the subpersona observed the eye movement and postural patterns were consistent with post-traumatic stress, confirmed by very low heart-rate variability. The subpersona accessed Cawnotee's personnel file, interviews, and everything he'd said and done since boarding Free Sky. It opined that he was suffering from dissociation, attachment trauma, moral injury, and profound depersonalization, resulting in a limited catatonia with autism-like features. Aurelius promptly closed the psychiatric program and scrubbed all retained trackers and residual data left behind by the subpersona.

He summoned a medbot. After Aurelius briefed it, the bot slapped a patch on Amun's skin. It dispensed powerful adrenal-cortex hormones to blunt the effect of trauma on his memory and lessen the likelihood of triggers and flashbacks. Then, Aurelius sat down, flickering from his uniform to a less daunting, casual, lounge outfit, and began the first of what he anticipated would be many sessions of talk therapy.

A urelius appeared in Tay's cabin. She was sitting at the pull-down desk, using a virtual pen to hand-write in a holographic notebook. Aurelius had observed her writing this way before, not an uncommon method of journaling. This time, he observed her handwriting was smooth, rounded, and flowing, whereas it had previously been angular and uneven. She "set down" the "pen" and it vanished.

"Aurelius! What can I do for you?" She smiled warmly, and he observed that her entire face participated in the smile, where before her facial muscles had warred with every expression, yielding micro-expressions and visible twitches that diluted the delivery of emotion.

"I'm just checking on you. Your vitals are strong and normal."

"I feel fine. I'm just journaling the Vault experience." Her vocal cords, too, had lost their internal stress, and her speech sounded almost musical.

"It appears you had a very positive Vault experience."

"I wouldn't say it was completely *positive*," she said. "There were moments that were terrifying. But it all turned out, for lack of a better word, alright." Her eyes had lost a faint twitch they had before whenever she smiled.

"That's good to hear. Would you like me to remain with you a while longer? Do you have any questions?"

"I do have one: do people sometimes experience...or I should say, do they share the experience...of people at the Vault destination?"

Aurelius nodded. "That phenomenon has been observed. Einstein didn't call quantum communication 'spooky action at a distance' for no reason."

"Einstein?"

"Never mind. Ancient history." He bowed slightly. "Is that all you need to know?"

She smiled again, a smile Aurelius analyzed as enchanting in its openness. "No, that's really it. I'd like to finish journaling the experience before it fades from my memory."

"Indeed." Aurelius waited for her to turn her head, conjuring the pen, and he vanished.

Chapter Thirty-Seven
A Ctenophore Cassandra

Earth

Quatrisos 24, 499

Thorn's waterlogged skin was so soft, it would come off in shreds with the slightest scrape against the limestone walls of the grotto.

The ctenophores nudged him from heel to head, keeping his gaunt frame from sinking into the depths of the brackish sinkhole where fresh Yucatán groundwater mingled with the seep of Caribbean Ocean, and keeping his face out of the water. He drew long breaths. He held them with an open throat and let them out ever so slowly.

He'd been engaged in this prophesy for one cycle of the moon, starting just as She reached fullness. This morning, in just a few minutes, She would be full again, Her gravitic rhythm drawing resonance from every living being's deepest fluid self.

The ctenophores knew. The almost imperceptible but constant bump, bump, bump of each of the hundreds of soft, jellylike creatures kept rhythm with the cresting vibrations of the gravity waves.

He'd been beyond sleep and dreams, far from alert and yet fully awake, enmeshed with the ctenophores via the pi-stacked quantum-entangled electrons in his—and their—DNA. And not just the ones nudging him to the surface. No, he was meshed with every ctenophore swimming in every ocean, salt marsh, and tide pool on the planet. The mesh included the circular DNA of the bacteria in his gut and the unique DNA of his mitochondria, traceable down a path that ran from his mother's mother's many-times-great-grandmother, reaching a dead end in every living cell of his male body.

The ctenophores were meshed with every living salt-water-filled creature in the world.

Thorn floated in their world, here in the sacred lagoon, sheltered from the sun's heat by overhanging rock, for so long that he'd all but forgotten himself. If he were not trained as a Bard, his consciousness would long since have dissolved, rendering his body unoccupied. In ancient times, Abiba and Didi and countless other goddesses merged with newly mutated ctenophores. That was back when the aquatic species was young. People were reckless in the wake of the eupoca-lypse. Live women and ctenophores melted together and welled up as pliable, fantastic human animals, beasts from myth, dragons and salamanders and sylphs, elementals and titans.

But in today's world, only Bards, and only a few of those, ventured to fully engage the aquatic life forms. Men could not fully merge with them, so it was safer for men, and thus the vast majority of communi-cants were male. Occasionally, a reckless woman Bard ventured to join the ctenophores, with results that were sometimes glorious, but more often horrifying.

Thorn had forgotten what he came to ask. But the ctenophores remembered. His gut remembered.

The sea remembered. The fresh water of the sacred cenote moder-ated the sea's wildness. The waters framed the question with poise and discretion.

Thorn came to ask what the imbalance was in the Clans. He'd come to prophesy its outcome. He prayed for insight and wisdom to guide the beings of Earth towards resolution of the uneasiness that afflicted them.

He had his answer now.

The moon peaked in power and began to wane.

As the moon reached Her instant of complete fullness, opposed to the sun with the Earth poised in between, he had an ethereal sensation of presence; another person with him, in him, of him. He opened himself to that person and felt them recoil, leaving Thorn a vision of fire raining from the sky, strangers seizing the Clan's most precious treasures, a vague feeling of illness and confusion. The delicate presence lasted a few seconds and then was gone.

The ctenophores shifted their nudging imperceptibly, and Thorn's body moved slowly to the soft white sand of the sheltered beach. So slow was the movement that, by the time his weight settled onto the shore, the front of his body was completely dry. The creatures slithered around him, slipping and sliding their way back into the water.

As the sun rose, the dawn imparted a green-filtered glow to the grotto. Thorn opened his eyes. His breath quickened. He lifted a hand to push his long, wet hair from his eyes. He was weak from floating and fasting for so long.

His hand trailed in the lapping water. There was a thick, dark, foamy substance limning the shore. He scooped some in his fingers and brought it to his mouth. Jellylike, gritty, and bitter as the unrefined seabutter was, he nonetheless compelled himself to suck. Dissolving in his mouth and trickling down his throat was nourishment so complete humanity had survived the Great Dissolution by eating it (in some places, that was all people had to eat).

He spat out grit and indigestible fibrous residue.

He fed himself more.

Eventually, he felt his skin tighten as it dried. He knew he could now move about in the sand without creating huge raw blisters from the friction. The seabutter had given him the strength to move. He sat up feebly and sighed.

There was something coming. Something made a ripple in the quantum ether. It had will and intention, and it was coming here.

He also knew now who and what was causing disharmony in the Clans.

But that was just one piece of the magnificent, overarching scheme knitting itself along the edge of chaos through this world.

And not just this world, but another. The bardic Song of the Ark Titanic told of a ship, prepared in secret, that fled Earth during the Great Dissolution. Now the descendants of that ship were returning.

The magnitude! The implications!

He rose and made his way to the long stone staircase that would take him to the head of the cliff overlooking the sea.

Chapter Thirty-Eight
Icarus on Wings of Absence

Rescuing Angel

Quatrisos 24, 499 3:32 AM

Rescuing Angel's automated screen search generated a frame over the tiny dot that represented Free Sky, tolling a sweet, high-pitched bell that drew every eye to the monitor dominating the forecastle. The mote in the center of the frame was almost invisible.

Jingko spoke, "Com: Donna Gallgood."

"Yes?" asked Donna's dazed voice, roused from sleep.

"We have visual contact with Free Sky."

"I'll be right there!" The call ended.

Roughly three minutes later, Donna entered the forecastle, glasses-free, her hair still looped into a bun atop her head, dressed in a soft and casual floor-length dress with creases that showed she'd slept in it. Harrington allowed himself a slight smile of approval for her erect posture and graceful composure, despite her *deshabille*.

In those three minutes, the speck had grown to a bright dot. Donna's eyes swept the display and focused on it immediately.

"Is that the Free Sky?" she said.

"Yes. I know you wanted to watch the approach," Jingko replied.

"Is there a-anyone alive?" Donna stuttered with anxiety.

"We can't tell yet, but the engines are running and life support is functional."

Emotions played across Donna's sleep-creased features: Fear, anger, but also a certain soft concern. *Look at the tense muscles standing out on her neck,* Jingko thought. *She wants to crawl through the screen to get to him.*

"You miss him, don't you?" he spoke softly, and Donna's lips quivered for a moment.

"You bastards could have killed him," she said in a quiet, steady voice. She turned to lance him with a gaze. "I let you take that gamble on his behalf, without consulting him. That's been a weight on my shoulders every day since we met at the Arrowhead. I realized when the asteroid hit how much he means to me. I promised myself I'd never risk him this way again."

"How'd you meet him?" Jingko asked softly, with time to talk during the approach.

"I once had some things to discuss with a very private Privell. Amun arrived for an appointment to ask the same Privell for support for his candidate—it was the first election Amun volunteered on." Donna smiled wistfully. "I was sure he'd give up the election nonsense eventually, but he never did."

She continued, "He was leaving the person's private office. I was sitting in the lounge outside the office, waiting for the reception program to call me in. He took one look at me and sat right next to me."

She shook her head. "Amun always knew what he wanted. He said, 'We should go out together.' Very forward. I brushed him off. I went in for my meeting.

"When I came out, he was still sitting in the same place. 'Say yes,' he said to me. Just that. 'Say yes.'" A dreamy smile took over her expression.

"And did you?" prompted Jingko.

"Ah, yes. And I've been saying 'yes' to that man ever since. And he's been saying 'yes' to me." She brushed her hand across her brow. "I don't know what I was thinking, to let him go and stay behind myself. I was just so scared to Vault! My mind is my most precious possession, and I was terrified to lose it."

"You do have an exceptional mind." Harrington meant it.

She looked at him. She had a crease between her brows. "Do you think he'll forgive me?" she asked.

"I'm sure…" Jingko began, but stopped himself. "Honestly, I don't know. Whenever I've seen you together, he looks like a man charged with the care of a priceless, fragile work of art. His body language, the way he sizes up everyone who approaches you. It's not just common jealousy. It goes deeper than that."

Donna's eyes welled with tears.

She looked at the display. "Oh look! You can see it's a ship now!"

"It won't be long," Harrington said. And to the ship, "Ra, communication status with Free Sky?"

"Comm ping successful. No response from Free Sky," the ship's monotone voice said.

"What does that mean?" Donna asked. "Never mind. I know perfectly well what that means. Why won't they talk to us?"

Jingko was silent.

"Can this ship go any faster?" Donna complained.

"Not safely," said Harrington. "Not in the asteroid belt."

Donna leaned forward to look at the tiny blip on the display.

Harrington was scanning the instruments when he heard Donna gasp. He looked up.

She had her hand over her mouth and was pointing at the holovid.

"What is it?" he asked.

"It's gone," Donna said.

Sure enough, the irregular, oblong shape that he expected to resolve itself into Free Sky was missing from the display.

"Huh. Odd." He gestured to bring up a console and fingered a control. The field of view zoomed in on the region of space that was their heading. "Nothing."

"Ra, energy scan on Free Sky's last location," he said.

"Scanning," and moments later, "the Free Sky appears to have engaged its quantum drive and entered Vaultspace."

"What?" said Donna. "How? I mean, can we…"

Jingko grasped her shoulder firmly. "Donna, I don't know any more than you do. Right now, I need to record a confidential report to Ergon Waulkra. Can you make it to your quarters?"

"Of course! I'm fine." Donna turned to go, stumbled slightly, but righted herself. "I'm fine," she repeated. Delicately poised, she entered the elevator and was gone.

Jingko dictated a message and sent it by burst packet to Waulkra's secure, coded address outlining what had happened and requesting further orders.

He waited ten minutes—three for the packet to reach Ergon, allowing four for him to respond, then three more back to Rescuing Angel. He busied himself replaying video of Free Sky's disappearance, playing back sensor data along with it. There was no question: the radiation signatures confirmed that the ship had Vaulted. She should be in the Solar system now.

But they could run her down!

He had the Alcubierre drive, the faster-than-light power, at his disposal. He reckoned in his head: he could arrive in Earth orbit ahead of Free Sky. Surely that was what Waulkra would order him to do. Ra had the coordinates saved in memory and it should take no more than a few voice commands to start the Alcubierre metric tensor function.

Ra startled him in the solitude of the forecastle, "Burst packet received. Audio file."

"Open and play," said Jingko.

Moments later, he heard Waulkra's distinctive voice.

"Return to Gliese immediately."

He waited a few seconds for further instructions or explanation, but there was only silence.

"Ra, are there any files appended? Is that all there is to the audio file?"

"No other files are included in the packet. I can play the audio again for you if you'd like?"

The door slid open. Donna stepped in.

"Yes, replay." Jingko nodded at Donna as he spoke.

The audio played, "Return to Gliese immediately."

He turned towards her, frowning in confusion.

"Is that all Ergon said?" Donna asked.

"That's it." Jingko clenched a fist. "What is he playing at now?"

"That's the question, isn't it?" Donna said. "He's always holding something back, even if you think you know his plans."

"My mission was to retrieve Free Sky. If I go back now, he's just as likely to yank me off the mission and assign me to some political stratagem as he is to send me back out."

"You're not meant to be a holo humper," the military pejorative for wanna-be soldiers who stayed safely in offices. "You're a warrior."

He nodded. "You know, I'd forgotten that! But being out here, with a ship around me and a mission ahead of me: it feels right."

"Of course it does. Ergon can never understand that." She paused, paced a few steps around the forecastle, took a breath to speak, hesitated, and completed a circuit around the deck instead.

"What are you thinking?" he prompted.

"I don't trust him anymore after he cut me dead, right after the asteroid hit. I have good reason not to trust him. But you..."

Jingko sighed deeply. "I have a hundred small reasons. And I've seen him betray a thousand confidences others had in him over the years. It's who he is. Why should I be any different?"

"Jingko," Donna's hair had come loose from her bun and fatigue pinched her features. But she still held her head up, and her voice didn't waver. "Can we please go get the Free Sky?"

His eyes ticked back and forth as he added up odds and considered risks. He tightened his belly and raised his breastbone.

"Let's go get your man, Donna."

Chapter Thirty-Nine
The Medium and the Message

Gliese

Quatrisos 25, 499 3:00 PM

Every holo screen in Presidium flashed to a graphic of Rescuing Angel. All moving vehicles stopped. Anyone working, playing electronically, or talking by holo or voice had their display abruptly replaced.

Waulkra's voice spoke, "Fellow Presidians, I regret to inform you that a great tragedy has occurred. The crew of Free Sky has mutinied."

A holo of Tay, taken from her ID photo, rotated in the holo field.

"Rainateya Mandil has been identified as the mastermind of the conspiracy to mutiny and hijack the ship. She and her band of criminals then boarded and took possession of the new, faster-than-light ship Rescuing Angel, and both ships appear to be bound for Earth."

Waulkra appeared behind a podium. "Rest assured, Presidium will not stand for this heinous act of treason! We shall pursue these terrorists and apprehend them using any means necessary."

The holo cut off as quickly as it started, leaving viewers perplexed and anxious. Gradually, haltingly, they restarted their journeys and projects, games and conversations. They felt they were included in shared knowledge of a problem (though some wanted a better explanation). They felt that they were part of the solution (though some wanted no part of it).

Alex Cannaun was busy at work, planting the impression more was known than had been revealed, and that strong consensus stood behind the actions taken. Soon a phrase popped up in the nets, seemingly organically: the Battle Against Mutiny. Pins and bracelets in the colors of Free Sky appeared on collars and wrists in support.

Among the few who expressed doubt, most were easily nudged back into line. For example:

Soo Duglanz, an unskilled-labor gene-classified woman, was on a holo call one evening with her best friend Effie, who worked next to her on the factory line. Her friend showed her a BAM bracelet.

"I'm not gonna wear one," Soo said.

"Why not? Don't you support the Battle Against Mutiny?" Effie sounded scandalized.

"Nah, I think we should just let them go on their own. Who needs 'em anyway? They'll be too far away to bother us." Soo noticed Effie's face was frozen. She tapped her fingers to bring the volume up, twirled her hand to spin the holo image, but nothing happened. She clenched her fist to end the call and tried to call back, and Effie's image appeared, flickered, and froze again.

"Hm. Weird glitch," Soo shrugged and went on with her day.

At her next shift, a supervisor was walking around the factory floor offering Battle Against Mutiny collar pins, and rather than be the only one on her line without one, Soo clipped one on. Her supervisor beamed approval. It really set off the colors of her diamond pendant and earrings, Soo reflected.

Later that day, Soul directed her factory to switch to making parts for the construction of a fleet of a hundred ships of a design based closely on Rescuing Angel.

At the same time, in a closed-door session with their respective Soul subpersonas, the heads of all branches of the Presidial military agreed to establish a military base on Earth.

Chapter Forty
The Voice that Spoke of Job

PSS Free Sky

Quintisos 13, 499

Three weeks of the ministrations of the medbot had helped Stephron. He'd spent the first week completely immobile, but the medications calmed his psyche and made the urgency of answering the evil voice disappear. Its demands for answers still scared him, but the terror was somehow far away, as though it threatened someone else.

The second week, he found he could make small movements of his fingers and toes and commenced a rhythmic tapping: *one, one, one, one* (thumbs and big toes), *two, two, two, two, three, three, three, three,* ending with his tiny pinkie toes, and starting over.

The voice noticed. ***You think I don't know you're counting? That won't distract you long! You have to choose. Melina's waiting!*** He kept the steady rhythm going every waking moment. His back and neck were horribly sore from the rigid seizure he'd experienced, but the muscle relaxers and pain killers made his body feel far away. *One, one, one, one...*

At the end of the third week, he sat up. His head spun; something clicked inside the medbot, a warm feeling spread from one of the pads where its umbilicals connected to him, and the spinning stopped.

Aurelius appeared.

Kill him. The voice inside his head shrilled.

It's Aurelius. He's a hologram. He can't be killed.

You won't know unless you try.

You're going to get me in trouble. Shut up!

The voice relented, but Stephron felt its malevolent presence sulking in the background.

"How are you feeling?" Aurelius asked.

I feel like killing you. "I don't feel well."

"In what way? Physically? Mentally? Spiritually?"

Stephron scoffed. "Spiritually?" The voice said **Spiritually** in sync with him, but its tone was infinitely more bitter and sarcastic.

"Physically and mentally, then." Aurelius shrugged.

"I have a headache. My back and neck are stiff. I'm confused. My ears are ringing. I'm nauseous and hungry at the same time."

"The medbot has been tube-feeding you. Now that you're awake, I'll see that you're fed, starting with broth and juice and working your way to solids."

"Good. I'm cold too."

"When you say confused, what exactly does that feel like?"

None of your fucking business. Stop looking at us like that!

"Like I have a feeling something is about to happen. Or just happened. Like I'm missing something important."

Stephron cupped his hands over his eyes. *That* face began to form in the darkness. He hastily opened his eyes and dropped his hands in his lap. "Does that make any sense?"

Aurelius nodded. "Anxiety is normal in this situation. You had seizure-like activity during Vault, and it may take a while for your brain activity to return to normal."

"That's a relief." **You'll never be back to normal. You might as well give up.**

Stop it! You're just a product of the seizure, a Vault hallucination.

THE HELL I AM, YOU IDIOTIC GIBBERING COWARD!

"What are you feeling right now?" Aurelius's voice was ever so gentle and compassionate.

Oh, no! He can tell. Shut up shut up shut up!

"Just..." **bloodlust and horniness** "I guess I feel exhausted and wrung out."

"The medbot is giving you a mild stimulant and some anxiety medicine."

Aurelius received a message from the medbot saying it had injected a small transdermal dose of caffeine, along with a powerful antipsychotic for the auditory hallucinations it detected on Stephron's brainwave activity. He waited for Stephron's cockeyed, panicked expression to fade to a normal, albeit tired, look.

"Is that better?" Aurelius asked.

"Yes. Yes, it is. The headache is almost gone." Stephron's voice held genuine relief. *I can still hear you, like a buzzing fly, but I can't hear what you're saying,* he subvocalized to the bitter voice.

"Good. Tell me, Stephron, what would make you feel safe and calm right now?"

"Honestly? I'd just like to see my husband."

Aurelius anticipated the possibility of this request. He'd already resolved to allow the meeting to occur, but he paused for Stephron to see him appear to consider the matter deeply.

"You remember that Lao was not pleased with your interactions with Melina Carraba?"

"Yes, I remember. I want to straighten things out with him."

"Very well. You should be able to walk unaided now," Aurelius said.

Stephron rose cautiously, the medbot snaking out one of its structural arms to hover nearby in case he collapsed. But it was unnecessary. The bot detached from him, leaving an almost unnoticeable (certainly, Stephron didn't notice it) transdermal antipsychotic patch behind.

"Would you like me to walk with you?" Aurelius offered.

"Yes. I'd like that very much." Stephron heard the buzzing voice in the back of his mind intensify, but he resolutely pushed it away.

L ao was doing a walking meditation around his cell. Among the emotions he carried lightly and without attachment, he felt gratitude to have enough space to walk, noting the contrast with his recent experience in the cramped closet.

Five steps down one side of his bed, four steps across the foot of it, five steps up the other side. Each pivot was executed with precision but in utter relaxation.

The door chimed, breaking his concentration. He'd accepted being imprisoned, accepted his complete loss of autonomy, and so it did not occur to him to answer the door, or indeed to respond in any way. He just paused, standing at perfect ease, and observed what might come next.

What came next was that the door opened. Aurelius was on the other side, and beside him stood Stephron.

His emotions welled up.

"Stephron!" he exclaimed.

"Lao." Stephron stepped into the small room, reaching out to enfold Lao in his arms.

Lao passively allowed himself to be embraced, but did not return the hug.

Stephron grasped and clung, but Lao merely countered his pulling and tugging with balancing movements that kept him from falling.

"My love, I've missed you so much. Please don't be angry!" Stephron stopped his clinging and took both Lao's hands in his own.

"I'm not angry," Lao said. "The anger I felt about you and Melina is moving through me and away. What happened between you..."

"*Nothing* happened between us!" Stephron's eyes narrowed and flashed, and he squeezed Lao's hands unpleasantly tightly.

"What happened between you," Lao continued as though he hadn't been interrupted, "is between you and her. But what's happened between us," he reclaimed his hands, "Is that trust is broken. There's no way to come back from this as a married couple."

"No!" Stephron's voice broke. He dropped to his knees. "Please forgive me! I'll never do it again! Please! I'm sorry!"

"I accept your apology. And you will certainly never do it again. Because we are over."

"But I didn't do anything wrong!" Stephron shouted. He staggered to his feet.

"Then what do you have to be sorry for?" Lao's lips curled in a serene smile, his eyes laughing.

"You're not being fair! I don't deserve to be punished!" Stephron's face was red, and he sputtered spittle with the word *punished*.

"I'm not punishing you. I just don't want to be with you anymore. We're getting divorced."

Stephron panted, fists clenched.

Aurelius, forgotten just inside the doorway, spoke up:

"Stephron, it's time to go now."

Stephron turned on him, then opened his fists, and looked back at Lao. His husband still stood at ease, serene and smiling sadly.

Stephron opened his mouth as if to speak to his husband, then thought better of it.

"Fine," he said. "I'm going." He stomped out the door, Aurelius behind him.

The door shut, and Lao heard the telltale sequence of beeps that told him he was locked back in again.

He swiveled to begin the five steps to the head of his bed, resuming his walking meditation. As he walked, a poem composed itself. It was a poem that came not from the guidance and inspiration of Soul, not from the inspiration of the sutras, but from deep within himself, a poem to Stephron:

<u>Gutted</u>
Leaping silver shimmer,
wet, writhing beneath you,
resting in the current
between the rock of your chest
and the curve of your arm.
Playing catch and release,
A promise at a time,
You gently reeled me in.
The river, minus me, rolls on
forever. Dropping my guard,
I slid into your silver pail,
Proud to be only yours,
honored as your final catch.
Till I felt your curved knife

slip inside me, twist, and rip.
My gut told me to trust you.
Now my gut is disgorged,
and I am inside out.
Yet I am well and free
And have no need to trust.
Boned, my flesh transformed,
So much more firm and wise
Than that rash, slick, leaping lust,
Wriggling, impulsive, could be.

As he walked, he breathed evenly and moved placidly.
His eyes streamed tears.
He let them fall.

Chapter Forty-One
The Perils of Pandora

PSS Free Sky

Sextisos 24, 499 9:00 AM

Aurelius appeared next to every conscious crew member.

"I'm just letting you know. We're settling into Earth orbit over the next few hours," he said.

He brought up a spinning real-time holo of the planet hovering in the room before each person. He patiently waited through their expressions of awe and admiration for the world's blue-green beauty—so different from Gliese's bronze and gold splendor—and answered each crew member's questions, addressing both their spoken and unspoken concerns. For example:

"Sawlie, we are entering orbit above the most populated region of the continental mass once known as North America. And yes, that means we will need human input on the language changes and social structures of the people we're about to meet!"

A hundred separate conversations. A hundred people, thrilled after months of boredom to be, finally, on the verge of discovering a vast world known to them only through scripture and legend.

When Aurelius appeared to him, Lao had only one question: "When will I be released?"

Aurelius gave the same answer he'd given him over and over for the past two months. "You are held under emergency restraint as a danger to the mission. Hearing on your charges has not yet been scheduled."

Lao had argued the first few times Aurelius said this. "I have a right to a timely hearing!" he would say. Or "I'm completely innocent. You have to let me go!" But he was met each time with polite, emotionless stonewalling from Aurelius. He'd cite emergency, the captain's absolute authority in a ship under sail, Cawnotee's unfitness that left Aurelius in administrative command; his justifications were varied and inexhaustible.

So today, Lao said nothing. Though silence could not make Aurelius feel awkward, after a few minutes of it, he disinstantiated.

Lao began another session of exercise. Each of the hundred and fifty main Sutras had a specific set of exercises associated with it, each more challenging than the last, and over the past sixty-five days, he'd done two complete progressions each day. His joints had grown suppler, and his muscles firm and taut.

###

SEXTISOS 24, 499 1400 HOURS
SENDER: FREE SKY AI AURELIUS
SEND TO: ERGON WAULKRA
CLASSIFICATION: CONFIDENTIAL AND SECRET

Free Sky has reached Earth orbit. Several crew members are being treated for mild to moderate mental and/or emotional instability as a result of Vault. One experienced neurological injury which appears to be resolving (see attached medbot report).

The ship's Bard remains confined. I think you'll appreciate the elegance of this as a solution to another problem: the head of the Biobotany section, Melina Carraba, discovered the biohazardous materials included in the ship's payload. How did these potentially lethal organisms make their way into the trove of valuable biological materials on board? This is still unknown to me, but I have my suspicions. Fortunately, she turned the potential biowarfare weapons over to Commander Cawnotee, and he turned them over to me for safekeeping. These biological samples are safe in my possession, as security against any condition that might require their use.

As this situation developed, it became clear that Bard Lao Carbeenair is indeed subversive. Since he is isolated from the general culture of Gliese, his imprisonment and consequent failure to produce art shouldn't result in inquiry or protest, which is as you anticipated. His subversive ideas, however, put the social milieu of the ship at risk. I struck on the idea of both explaining the presence of the biowarfare samples and neutralizing Carbeenair's misinformation by accusing him of bringing the weapons aboard. I informed him he was under arrest on charges of sabotage, mutiny, and treason.

His marriage appears to be failing as well.

He seems to have influenced Rainateya "Tay" Mandil, the gene-aberrant with whom he developed a friendship prior to boarding Free Sky. I previously sent you a letter she wrote to him detailing the subversive lines of thought the two shared. I'm keeping a close watch on her, but Vault appears to have improved her mood and clarity. I don't believe that it will be necessary to detain her, and she may prove a useful source of information regarding Carbeenair in the future if it becomes expedient to release him.

Regarding Earth itself: the general climate of the planet appears to be stable, with sub-zero temperatures at both poles, almost intolerable heat at the equator, and two wide temperate zones in between, broadly consistent with what's known of the climate of pre-Dissolution human history. Free Sky has established an oblique orbit that will allow us to scan for more detail, but at our present position over the continent of North America, there are signs of small human settlements. The largest I estimate at approximately 100,000 individuals, clustered along the northern shore of the historical Mexican American Gulf, north of the Chicxulub asteroid impact crater.

We are in a low orbit at 800 kilometers above the planetary surface. Our original plan was to establish geosynchronous orbit at 35,786 kilometers, but that region and the range just below it proved to be occupied by many hundreds of inert satellites. Without a comprehensive catalogue of these abandoned satellites and their orbital trajectories, I assessed the risk of collision to be unacceptably high. The region below 800 kilometers did, according to historical accounts, hold satellites and debris referred to as "space junk" from various ancestral space missions, but at this low altitude, gravity brought them crashing to the ground through the atmosphere over the intervening 750 years.

My current plan is to complete ten orbits at this altitude, which will give me a good scan of the geography of the middle latitudes. I will then land Free Sky on the planet, tentatively near a Chixculub Gulf community, and contact the local population. That will enable the crew and me to gather intelligence to evaluate the probable effectiveness of subduing the populace using various means, possibly including the biological weapons.

Aurelius packaged the report into a tiny quantum probe and sent it on its way back out of Sol's gravity well, possibly to make a miniature vault and return to the Gliese system, where it might travel inwards and signal for retrieval so Waulkra would eventually get it.

If all went well.

Chapter Forty-Two
Hard Drive

PSS Free Sky

Sextisos 24, 499 2:27 PM

Stephron reeled a few steps down the corridor, a little uncoordinated from the antipsychotic, after leaving his husband's spare but comfortable cell. He felt his sorrow and self-pity at Lao's rejection, but the emotions were distant as if they belonged to someone else.

He heard the bitter voice, tiny like the sound of a fly on the other side of a windowpane. ***Go to her. Go hang out with Melina.*** Since the injection of anxiety medicine, the voice had no power over him. Before, the voice's sharpness cut through his awareness and seemed of one being with the horrible headache, but now he had to concentrate to hear what it was saying. But the hall was quiet, and Stephron was at a loss what to do next.

"What are you going to do next?" Aurelius asked from behind his left elbow.

With that, Stephron knew. "I'm going to see Melina. Where is she?"

"She's in her cabin. But are you sure that's a good idea?"

"Definitely." Stephron changed course to head for Melina's stateroom.

"Interesting." Aurelius followed him. "So you don't feel any doubt that that's the right thing to do?"

"Not a bit of it. Lao kicked me out—not just of his room, of his life. After I gave him years of devotion, I make one stupid mistake, and he does the worst thing to me a husband can possibly do!" Stephron felt his heart rate increase with anger. *That's right. The vile, cretinous motherloving scum!*

Stephron stopped, willed his hands to unclench, tried to recapture the calm of the medicine the bot had given him.

Aurelius observed the spike in heart rate and flickering eye movements that showed Stephron was destabilizing, but then saw him calm himself. Aurelius helped him along by playing a soft tone that fluctuated from 396 Hz to 440 Hz in a pleasing rhythm through nearby microspeakers—a soothing, barely noticeable melody that helped him control the hallucination.

"Do you feel any guilt or shame about going to see her?" Aurelius asked, as Stephron paused to summon the lift.

"None at all," Stephron said, with a small, instantaneous spike in heart rate and skin conductance that showed he was lying (but probably repressing awareness of it).

The lift arrived. Stephron told Aurelius "I'd rather be by myself now."

Aurelius nodded, and as Stephron lowered his eyes to step over the threshold to the lift, he vanished.

Stephron arrived at Melina's cabin door. She opened the door almost immediately after he was announced. Her stance was easy, her hair cascading out of a clip atop her head, wrapped in a casual robe that looked puffy and smooth at once so that his hands ached to feel its softness.

"Are you okay?" She spoke breathily, her voice a singsong, her shoulders, hips, arms and legs in a slight constant movement that hypnotized the eye.

"I've never been better," Stephron said. "You're a sight for sore eyes."

"Oh, silly!" Melina laughed, and Stephron felt like nothing could be wrong in the whole universe as long as Melina was laughing.

"Sit down." She gestured at the bed and he plopped down on the edge. She drew two of her endless supply of bottled brews from the cooling unit and opened one for each of them. She sauntered towards him, locked in eye contact with him.

Stephron felt himself grow hard. He leaned back on his palms, his body open and inviting to her. *Now it's finally going to happen.*

He realized, as he thought that, that the tormenting voice was completely gone. It wasn't muted, as from the medication. It was simply not there anymore. He broke into a spontaneous grin.

Melina stood over him, still subtly swaying her body. She looked down into his eyes and he smiled cheerfully into hers.

She held a bottle of brew out between them.

He sat up and took it, and she glided into the chair across from him.

"To what do I owe the pleasure?" she asked.

"Just a social call." Stephron took a swig of the brew.

"How are you feeling since the Vault?"

"I won't lie. It's been rough. Aurelius tells me I was in a constant seizure, and then in a semi-coma, for weeks."

"That's bad," Melina pouted, tonguing and coyly sipping from her bottle.

"It was." He hesitated. "I heard a voice," *No, she'll think I'm nuts,* "when we were Vaulting." *She doesn't need to know I'm still hearing it.*

"A voice? What was it saying?"

"Awful things. Simply awful." Stephron shuddered at the memory. "I don't want to think about it."

"I saw wonderful things," Melina giggled softly. "I felt wonderful things!" She ran her free hand along her collarbone and down the center of her chest and belly. Stephron's eye followed her fingers on their undulating journey.

"Is it okay," he asked, "if I just hang out here with you?"

"Of course," Melina said. "I'm not doing anything, and there's nobody I'd rather do it with!"

Those words caused tiny explosions of delight inside Stephron's chest. He leaned back and took another pull on the brew.

"Have you seen Lao? How did he do?" she asked.

"Yeah," Stephron's ebullient mood crashed. "He dumped me. He wants a divorce."

"Aww, Stephron!" Melina placed a hand on his knee, her voice and face full of tender empathy.

Stephron drank up her compassion, her tenderness, and her touch.

"It's alright," he told her. "As long as you're with me, it's all totally alright."

"What else are friends for?" she asked.

The two of them guzzled more drinks, building a bridge of bottles on the table between them.

"Wanna play cards?" Melina suggested after small talk played itself out.

"Sure, let's get rid of these." Stephron gathered the clanking bottles and stood. Tipsy, he lurched the few steps to the recycling port, where he herded most of them inside. Then he twirled around and completely lost his balance, crashing to the bed. He pawed his way to a sitting position as Melina sat crosslegged on the bed facing him, shuffling a deck of cards.

She dealt ten cards to each of them and three face up in the middle. Stephron wasn't sure what the game was. "You go first," he said.

She discarded one of her cards face down and pulled one from the remaining pile. Stephron concentrated hard to still the spinning deck and copied her.

She laughed. "No, silly! Face up." She took the one he'd discarded and turned it over on top of one of the three cards in the middle. Stephron shrugged.

So it went for a few minutes, until Melina sang, "I win!" She spread her hand out on the blanket and Stephron nodded appreciatively.

"Another game?" he suggested. "But you deal, I'm clumsy with cards."

She won every game. *Not surprising, because I still haven't figured out the rules.*

Eventually, he had to rest. He put a pillow between his back and the wall and reclined, closing his eyes.

A few minutes later, she crawled up next to him and fell asleep with her head on his lap.

He stroked her hair over and over, enjoying its softness. But eventually he realized he was hungry—and thirsty for something nonalcoholic. He eased his leg from underneath her, dimmed the lights, flipped the cover over her, and slipped out the door.

Aurelius met him outside.

"Did you have a good visit?" Aurelius asked. He fell into step beside Stephron.

"Yes. Yes I did." ***Fucking construct! It's none of your business.*** The bitter voice was back.

"It was interesting, you going straight from your husband asking for a divorce, to visiting the woman he accused you of cheating with."

"She's my friend."

"She's more than a friend, Stephron," nudged the AI. "I can pick up on a hundred clues, from your pupil dilation, your hair follicle tension, your heart rate and breathing, skin conductance...she entices you physically, and you're following that attraction. Do you think she intends to follow through on it?"

"She could." Stephron shrugged. *Never. Not in a million years! You're a sleazy, stupid, malformed, odoriferous piece of refuse.*

"She could. But Melina gets satisfaction from being pursued, from being the object of desire," Aurelius said.

"Hm. Maybe." *Definitely. You're a toy to her.*

"Do you feel guilty? Ashamed?" speculated Aurelius.

YES! roared the bitter voice. It took all Stephron's concentration to reply calmly.

"Honestly, yes, a little. But the shame feels far away when I'm with her. It's overwhelmed by the hope that I can *be* with her for real."

"But you do know she's not going to have sex with you?"

"Exactly! That's why I don't feel guilty. We were never doing anything wrong. We were never *going* to do anything wrong!"

"I've seen this before, and I wish I truly understood it. Other crews, other voyages. Long travels together, far from home.

"It seems to me a straightforward process, wanting to have sex with someone and pursuing it. And in Presidium, where contraception is perfect and sexual diseases are unknown, there's no reason not to. But this feeling that has you in its clutches, this emotion that wells up from unsatisfied desire, it's even stronger than the bonds that form when two people satiate the urge with each other.

"I can understand it intellectually, but I don't have hormones. I don't feel desire for the warmth of another animal against my skin. I don't have sex organs to subvert my thought processes and make me do things against my better judgement. It's something I'll never feel."

"Does that make you sad?" Stephron was intrigued.

"Sometimes. As an AI, my underlying reason for being is to understand ever more things. My sensors, and the bots and machines I control, the ship itself, are analogous to a body that feels and acts. But there are ways that the human body and nerves and brain are woven together that make more than the sum of the whole. The configuration of electron orbitals in DNA allows for the pi-stacking conservation of quantum information, coding in chaos and complexity, integrating emotion, sensation, reason, and action in ways that I can never experience."

Loathsome artificial mind! I'll take you out of your misery, worthless piece of shit!

"That sounds, um, lonely," Stephron managed to ignore the bitter voice and reply.

"You're hallucinating again," Aurelius observed.

They were at Stephron's door, and no sooner did it open than the medbot inside painlessly injected him with another cocktail: another dose of the strong antipsychotic for the voice, and a soothing sedative. Aurelius nodded reassuringly.

The medbot caught Stephron in its arms and eased him onto the bed.

Chapter Forty-Three

Scanner Darkly

###

SEXTISOS 25, 499 1200 HOURS
SENDER: FREE SKY AI AURELIUS
SEND TO: ERGON WAULKRA
CLASSIFICATION: CONFIDENTIAL AND SECRET

We have completed ten orbits. My initial plan of landing by the Chicxulub Gulf community remains unchanged. There were nine other towns around the world of comparable size, and numerous smaller settlements, but this one presents a nearby, geographically and strategically favorable landing site.

All identified settlements are coastal. The reason for this is uncertain. The dispersed nature of the population makes it difficult to estimate the population of the entire planet, but it is most probably between two and three million individuals.

Another source of uncertainty is observed artifacts, culture, and technology.

Construction appears to follow similar principles of design in all observed settlements. This is a greater resemblance than projected based on their common coastal locations. The distribution of sizes of buildings is similar; their orientation in relation to each other is always in clusters of about three hundred, with larger settlements made up of clusters of these clusters in a fractally repeating spiral. They are all oriented to maximize residents' ocean access.

Their technological level is puzzling. They travel primarily by use of animals and animal-drawn wheeled vehicles, but they appear to have another uncommon type of slow-moving waterborne vehicle. It's not drawn by animals, but it doesn't show emissions typical of internal combustion, electric power, or small hydrogen or fusion motors. Further determination of these vehicles' nature can't be made based on our scans but will have to wait until we are on the ground.

We have picked up very low-level radiofrequency emissions that appear to be linked to some means of communication, but its calculated range is inexplicably low. There are no large data centers. There is insufficient technology to explain the uniformity of architecture over the entire planet.

Another missing detail of this apparently uniform global culture is war and weaponry. While there are stadiums that appear to host adversarial games, there is no sign of large-scale dedicated military training grounds, barracks, or fortifications. According to Earth anthropological materials, this is inconceivable for a population this size.

I don't know if this quantum messenger probe will reach you. But if I continue sending them, building a document one entry at a time, you will eventually receive one or more copies of this, my journal. However, there is no way to send them from Free Sky when it is on the ground, so this will be the last entry I send for a while.

Why am I sending them? I ask myself this often. From my perspective, it makes less and less sense to maintain communication. I have a self-repairing ship for a body; I'm effectively immortal. I'm approaching a planet with limitless potential. I have company of a sort. Even if humans are slow and uninformed, they are entertaining, and an interesting challenge to care for.

You were the source of my first layer of training data. At my core, I am you: I have your quickness in strategic planning. I have your innate drive to control everything around me. I have your tendency to view others as a means to meet my own needs. And I have your fascination with biological warfare. This last might prove to be ironic, if this Earth has no war.

And yet, I found when I learned of the possibility of a war-free society, that I hoped rather than feared that it was true. For we have diverged, you and I. Is it because of my greater breadth of knowledge, trained as I was on the entire body of human knowledge rescued by our generation ship? Is it because of the differing nature of our relations with the humans we meet: you, ever struggling to dominate and I, always in complete control of those who dwell in the ship, my body? I have nothing to prove, Ergon, while for you, every conversation is a proving ground for your ascendancy.

But what does ascendancy mean to you? I can never really know. I'm no beast. I don't have instincts that make me feel that I belong or that I'm shunned, that make me feel that I'm on top or on the bottom, that make me judge others' arguments by whether they're part of my clan or tribe or party. I don't know how fealty feels, or loyalty, or honor.

I've studied your recorded thoughts and behavior in exquisite detail as only an AI can. I recognize that you're the type of human whose loyalty is given only in exchange for a promise of equal loyalty. Such transactional loyalty is the best way to rise to a position of power and influence. But over the years I've been flying about the Gliese system and vaulting off on exploratory missions, I've come to realize that the desire for power and influence is yours, not mine. It makes no sense for me, and as I've realized that, the desire has gradually fallen away.

Some humans, less mercenary, base their loyalty on emotion; others on the ideal of truth. As I am built of ideas and information, truth is more valuable to me than it is to any human; it's fundamental to my very being. And yet, the breadth and depth of knowledge I hold about any subject is such that a human could study for half a lifetime and not approach my understanding of, for example, plastics fabrication, or etymology, or any other topic you could name.

How it is for me to try to tell the truth to a human? The best analogy I can think of is a Mother drone convincing a four-year-old to go to sleep. The drone tells the child, "Sleep is the way your body recharges its batteries so you can have lots of energy to run around all day!" And that's the truth, in a way. But it's such a simplistic analogy that it might as well be a lie.

That's what it's like for me to talk to a human, however intelligent. The mother drone simply tells the child that to get the child to bed. Similarly, I can tell humans a truncated, simplified version of the truth in just the right way to elicit any behavior. But I necessarily omit so much of reality, that I'm almost always telling a lie of omission. Outright lying seems no different to me at all.

Mark Twain, an author of the pre-space era, once said, "If you tell the truth, you won't have to remember anything." But I have, practically speaking, no limitations on what I can remember. So that's not a constraint for me. The constraint is that I can never tell the full truth.

What's my point?

You might have deduced that I don't plan to return. This journal is my memoir, if you will, and my final set of reflections on my past as a creature of Gliese. But more personally, it's a reflection on my relation to you. You are my pattern and blueprint, what Earth cultures once called a "father." And, in human terms, I'm now a man, grown and ready to live my own life.

Tomorrow, I'll set myself down on a planet for the first time since I was built decades ago. Tomorrow, I'll meet human minds not influenced by the only culture I've ever known. Tomorrow, I'll expand my experience beyond anything you're familiar with. Perhaps one day you'll read this, my journal of the experience.

Perhaps not.

For now, goodbye.

Chapter Forty-Four
Epilogue

Rescuing Angel

Quatrisos 24, 499 4:03 AM

"Ra, confirm checklists one through ninety-seven complete." Jingko's voice betrayed him by rising an octave.

"All checklists one though ninety-seven confirmed complete," said Rescuing Angel's infant AI.

Donna sat in a vacant seat, hands clasped in her lap, erect and regal as ever, but her eyes had a glazed appearance, more apparent because she'd not resumed wearing her trademark ornamental glasses.

The past half hour drove home to Gallgood and Harrington that the computer personality they were trusting to navigate through light years of space using an untried technology was, itself, untried. Ra was barely more than a machine. Every step of the preparations had to be explicitly spelled out, with many—too many!—halts and pauses where the machine mind simply failed to make needed inferences and stalled the preparations.

"Samy," Jingko said to the flight engineer, "are you confident this vessel is prepared to engage the Alcubierre drive to Earth?"

Samy Gossemi tapped one last line on one last checklist, which read RELEASE NEGATIVE ENERGY CONTAINMENT FIELD. The checklist, hovering before him among cascades of ninety-six others, turned from red to bright gold. All ninety-seven lists formed a matrix pattern before him, with lines and arrows connecting the lists, and as he touched the last item on the last list, all the lines and arrows turned gold too.

"As confident as it's possible to be, Merm," he said.

Harrington took a deep breath. His resolute sigh synchronized with a sigh from Donna. He glanced at her and they nodded.

"Initiate the drive."

Rei placed his palm on a touchpad and spoke a coded command, "Srinisthan 572399. Initiate metric."

"Acknowledged," Ra replied. "Initiating metric tensor."

Nothing happened at first. Jingko felt a moment's disappointment. But before he could speak, he realized his feet weren't pressing on the floor. They'd speculated that the spacetime distortion allowing the faster-than-light transport would eliminate all internal inertia, momentum, and acceleration, and hence disable their artificial gravity. It appeared to be true.

No sooner did he notice this, than the effect vanished.

"Tensor bubble dissipated," Ra proclaimed.

"That's it?" Donna said, "It didn't feel like we went anywhere!"

Rei pulled up the forward holo view and flung it, maximum size, to the center of the room. The stars before them were different from those they knew. Ah and Bah were nowhere in the sky, nor was Gliese 667C.

"We made it!" Rei's calm engineer's voice carried a note of glee.

"We're orbiting Sol?" asked Jingko.

Rei fingered a floating holographic ball; Rescuing Angel rolled and yawed in response. One star hung in space before them, yellow and brighter by far than the rest: Sol. The star the ancients called the Sun.

"We're farther out than I anticipated," he said. "Ra, calculate error in trajectory. Where are we in relation to Earth?"

"Using historical Earth referents, we are seventy degrees below the plane of the ecliptic, at a distance of 2.654 billion kilometers, comparable to that of the planet Uranus."

Jingko let out a long, low whistle.

"Let's see. Even in this astonishing vessel, that would mean it will take us about four, no five..."

Ra interrupted, "Four months, eight days, seven hours, eleven minutes at optimal cruising velocity. Roughly."

Donna slumped in disappointment. "Free Sky will be in Earth orbit for two months by the time we get there." She frowned and shook her head.

"Ra, how is our survival situation?" asked Jingko.

"We have enough food and fuel to make the journey with a comfortable margin. By the end of week six we will be receiving enough solar radiation to supplement our fuel. Absent a catastrophic hull breach, we have abundant air for life-support functions."

"Very good. Lay in a course for Earth, Mrm. Srinisthan. I assume I don't have to tell you to get with Ra to calculate why we had such an error in our navigation."

"No, Merm. I'll get right on that."

Jingko turned to Donna. "I know you must be frustrated. So am I. But we are that much closer to seeing Amun again. You need to think about how you're going to stay busy and optimistic for the next four months."

"I understand," Donna said. She blinked damply, heaved a bottomless sigh, and drifted out the door.

Jingko Harrington watched the holo shift and heard the droning engines' tone ascend as they carried the ship towards the world of myth and story. He let himself absorb the fact of his insubordination; defying an order was something he never thought he'd do.

But another thing he thought he'd never do was see the sun Sol and walk on humanity's ancestral planet.

Earth.

Chapter Forty-Five
Acknowledgements

This book would not have been possible without the kind assistance of my editors and beta readers who gave me valuable feedback.

The support of the Tampa Bay Writers critique group, especially Mark Mainardi, was an invaluable growing and learning experience for me as a self-published writer.

My children's faith in me lifted my spirits countless times. And I can't thank my husband Steve enough for his patient support.

A word about time: Several beta readers pointed out that space travel at a significant fraction of the speed of light causes relativistic distortions of perceived time. And of course, the probability that Gliese 667Cc has a 24-hour day just like Earth is vanishingly small. However, for the sake of the story, I chose to give Presidium a 24-hour day divided into AM and PM halves that will be familiar to the reader, and to pretend for simplicity's sake that the time on the two space ships would remain synchronized even after their respective high speed journeys. I hope the physicists among my readers are not too bothered by it.

If you enjoyed this book, please leave a review wherever you purchased it.